You Think You Know

By Melinda Harris

Copyright © 2015 by Melinda Harris

Cover Design by Kara's Kreative and Necessary Design

Cover Image by Michael Meadows Studios

You Think You Know

Published by Triple "S" Publishing

ISBN: 978-0-9893306-7-1

All rights reserved. No part of this book may be reproduced or transmitted in any form or by any means, electronic or mechanical, including photocopying, recording, or by any information storage and retrieval system without the written permission of the author, except where permitted by law.

This book is a work of fiction. Any similarities to real people, living or dead, are purely coincidental. All characters and events in this work are figments of the author's imagination.

This ebook is licensed for your personal enjoyment only. This ebook may not be re-sold or given away to other people. If you would like to share this book with another person, please purchase an additional copy for each recipient. If you're reading this book and did not purchase it, or it was not purchased for your use only, then please return to author or publisher and purchase your own copy. Thank you for respecting the hard work of this author.

*To The Muses...Rose and I were in the dark.
Thank you for lighting the way.*

CHAPTER ONE

Divorce is such an ugly word.

Even saying it out loud...*Deee–VORCE*. Such an innocent, happy sound at the beginning with a hard end. Just like the real thing.

I entered my marriage with forever in mind–in sickness and in health, 'til death do us part.

Rose and Danny. Always and Forever.

Maybe I would have changed my mind somewhere down the road. Maybe I would have realized my mistake. Now I'll never know.

Danny and I were only married for a few years. We lived relatively separate lives as far as finances were concerned. We even rented the home where we lived, so in the end, there were no ugly court battles–no children, no pets, no arguments over who gets what. We simply went our separate ways.

That doesn't mean it didn't hurt.

When your husband comes home one night and tells you he doesn't love you anymore? That hurts. And even more painful is when you find out a few months later that he's engaged to his old high school sweetheart.

But the odd thing is it's been over two years since everything was final, and I barely miss him at all. Shouldn't my heart still be breaking? Shouldn't I still be pining over him, making myself crazy trying to figure out what I did wrong? Instead, I'm happy for him and that's how I know I was wrong about my forever. I was wrong about us, and I'm glad Danny had the courage to speak up because I'm not sure if I ever would have.

And still, I'm left with scars.

Whether it's based on experience, growing older, or both, I feel I've matured a ton over the past couple of years. Forced independence has a way of making you stronger, more confident, more comfortable in your own skin. On the other side of that I feel jaded, calloused by the loss of something I believed in with all of my heart, and that can be a very lonely place.

These days, love feels more like make-believe, not something that actually happens—at least not to me. And what frightens me most is how okay I've become with that reality. The old me was an eternal optimist, a hopeless romantic, but I can feel her slowly slipping through my fingers no matter how hard I try to hold on.

It doesn't help that I'm living at home again nursing my depressed mother back to health, as she tries to survive her own *dee-VORCE*. It's hard to look on the bright side when you're reminded every day of how much love can hurt. How much it's hurt me. How it's killing my mom.

I walk through the streets of my old hometown now and it may as well be another planet. My marriage is over. My friends have all moved away. My childhood as I knew it was some great façade.

My only saving grace these days is my job. It barely pays my bills, but the man who runs the place is like my very own guardian angel.

I knew it the night I met him. He came to my rescue one night when my car broke down on my way home from Atlanta, and he's been rescuing me over and over again ever since.

David has become a surrogate father, now that my own is no longer in the picture, and he's the only reason there are still pieces of the old, optimistic, sunshiny parts of me still floating around. David *is* the old me, but the difference is he's been through harder times than I could ever imagine and he's come out on the other side even better than before. He's so much stronger than I am. He's a fighter. He's my idol, and I've been trying for months to think of some way to repay him. I thought maybe I could help turn his restaurant around, so he can finally have the kind of retirement he deserves–anything to try and return the kindness he's shown to me.

"Good day to you, my angel."

This is how David greets me every afternoon when I walk through the door of *Geoffrey's*, my second home–the home I prefer these days.

"Hi David."

He winks at me before going back to his prep work in the kitchen, and I drop my purse in the drawer of the tiny desk in David's even tinier office. It's basically the cupboard under the small staircase in the kitchen, barely big enough for a built-in desk and a chair. I've suggested David take one of the dining rooms or convert part of one of the rooms into an office, but he insists his tiny cupboard is more than he needs.

"So, what's on the menu for tonight?" I ask as I tie on an apron over my standard uniform of black pants and a white, button-down shirt.

"Meatloaf and pork chops," he smiles. "But naturally I'll have my chicken and dumplins' ready for Mr. Malloy."

"And I assume we'll have blueberry cobbler on the menu as well?"

David nods. "You assume right."

Everyone loves David's blueberry cobbler, especially Mr. Malloy.

David and his brother, Geoffrey, dreamed of opening a restaurant from the time they were young boys. Unfortunately, Geoffrey passed away before he could see it through, but David spent every last dime he had converting this old antebellum home into his and Geoffrey's dream come true.

When the restaurant opened in the nineties, it was the talk of the town. I don't remember it, but from what I hear, David had more business than he knew what to do with. He had to close down for a while to tend to yet another ailing family member, and when he was finally able to re-open, the momentum was lost. A few other restaurants had opened around town, and times were changing. People were starting to eat healthier, preferring steamed vegetables and salads over David's heart-attack-worthy Southern fare.

Geoffrey's now caters to only a few regulars and the occasional out-of-towner looking for a "true Southern experience". I've tried to get David to make a few changes to the menu and give the place some much needed TLC, but he seems happy with his handful of customers. He always tells me he's too old and stuck in his ways to change now. If only he would take a break.

Thankfully, we're only open for dinner and closed on Sundays, but David is still here every night on his feet in the kitchen, pouring his heart and soul into this place. And even though I know he does it because he loves it–because it's all he has–I would still love to see him get a little something in return.

"David, you work too hard," I tell him, as I grab a bowl of fresh green beans that need to be snapped. "Why don't you think of hiring another cook, maybe just part time?"

"You know I can't afford that," David says with his ever-present smile. "I can barely afford you, my angel."

I nod in understanding. David pays me, but only when he can. I work mostly on tips, and seeing that the customers are few and far between, some nights I leave empty-handed. When I do get tips, I usually give the majority to David. As I said before, David may call me his angel, but in reality he's mine. I have money saved that is there when I need it. Of course it would be nice to save more, but that's not a priority in my life right now. I would go home empty-handed every night so long as I have a chance to be around David every day, a chance to surround myself with his light. It's worth every penny I give him and more.

"Don't you want to take some time off?" I ask him. "Everyone needs a vacation from time to time."

"I'm perfectly fine," he assures me. "You know I love what I do. I wouldn't be here if I didn't. And you got too much else to worry about. No need to spend your time worrying over an old man like me."

"Well, if I don't worry over you, who will?"

"No one, and I like it that way."

David leans over and kisses my cheek before putting his finished meatloaves in the refrigerator until they're ready to go in the oven. I finish snapping beans then start peeling potatoes, thinking the entire time about what I can do to help David bring this restaurant back to life. It's a beautiful place—two stories, tons of room and still full of a lot of the original décor and furnishings, including antiques to die for and the most exquisite cherry wood flooring I've ever seen. With a little work, *Geoffrey's* could be a five-star restaurant in no time. And the fact that it sits on a small lake, just outside of town and a little off the beaten path, gives it even more charm and appeal. I know David says he likes things the way they are, but I doubt he'd complain if we started making enough money that working every day would be a choice for David instead of a necessity.

By the time five o-clock rolls around, the meats and vegetables are prepared, the corn chowder is simmering and two batches of David's famous blueberry cobbler are cooling on the countertop, making the kitchen smell like heaven on earth.

"I'd better get out there." I remove my apron and replace it with a clean one. "Mr. Malloy will be here any minute."

David looks up from the pile of bills in front of him on his desk. "Thank you, my angel. I'll be here."

I study him a moment, noticing how impossibly small and frail he seems in the cramped space of his office. But even though he's covered in bills and paperwork, he still manages to smile—a genuine smile that brightens his soft, mocha-colored face and makes the skin around his light brown eyes crinkle in the corners.

I smile back and give him a small wave, which he returns before I leave the kitchen to head to the front door. I quickly get it unlocked and as expected, Mr. Malloy is standing on the front porch when I open the door. He greets me the same way he greets me every Wednesday by grabbing my hand, kissing the top and giving me a bow. It's because of moments like these, no matter my pay, I know my job is a blessing. In more ways than one.

CHAPTER TWO

"So, have you seen the new guy David hired?"

I take a break from filling salt shakers and turn to my friend. "What new guy?"

"Have you been living under a rock?" Lila hardly looks surprised that I'm out of the loop. "He started a couple of days ago."

Lila is David's only other employee. She comes once a month to clean the restaurant, but she's here more often than that doing little things to help David. I know that, from time to time, she cleans the upstairs where David lives. She also helps him with his laundry, even when he doesn't ask. She does it because she loves him like I do, like everyone that's ever met him.

I'll admit that, with only three employees, it is odd that I didn't notice anyone new starting. Even stranger is that no one told me about it until now. Or did they? Maybe I missed something. It wouldn't shock me these days.

"I think he's doing some contracting work." Lila shrugs and goes back to folding napkins. "I forgot my purse here Saturday night, but I was too tired by the time I got home to come back for it. I got up early the next morning and came over, and some guy was working on the dock."

I look out the back window at the dock she's referring to. The small lake is lovely, and I do enjoy sitting on the grass and staring out over the water. But that rickety old dock has been a hazard the entire time I've worked here, so I usually avoid it.

"He's fixing the dock?" I ask as I continue to stare at it, trying to make out any improvements. Even in the bright summer sun, it's still too far away to notice any differences.

"Yep," Lila nods. "And watching him sweat it out in a skin tight tank-top and shorts made me late for church."

I roll my eyes with a laugh. "Well, I'm glad he's fixing it up. Maybe David can start offering outside dining like he's talked about in the past. We could even extend it a bit, build a deck off to the side. That would be a perfect place for a private party."

"A deck would be great for a party," Lila agrees. "I'm sure Mr. Handyman can get the job done."

"*Mr. Handyman?*"

"Exactly. He's fixing the dock," Lila starts ticking things off on her fingers. "He finally stopped that leaky faucet in the kitchen. He trimmed David's rose bushes and patched up the hole Mrs. Summers put in the wall when she fell that time."

I shake my head at Lila and her puzzled expression.

"What?" She shrugs. "I'm still thanking the good Lord that woman didn't break a hip."

"I'm not worried about Mrs. Summers." I cross my arms with a knowing smile. "I was wondering how long you've been stalking this poor man while he works."

"Not nearly as often as I'd like." Lila wags her painted on eyebrows at me. "And unlike you, I happen to notice changes around this place."

She's got me there. "So do we know the new guy's name?" I ask, not wanting to discuss the fog I've been in lately.

"Nope, but I'll find out."

"Well, if David only hired him to do some work around here, he's probably temporary and not really any concern of ours."

"Oh, he's a concern of mine." Lila turns and gives me a wink. "You haven't seen him yet. Just wait."

"Yes, I get it. He's a looker." I smile as I toss a napkin at her. "And you're ridiculous."

Lila may be in her fifties, but the woman is still as boy crazy as they come. It's just another thing to love about her.

"He's not someone you'd want to bring home to Mama," she admits. "You know the type—gorgeous in that dirty, bad boy kind of way. But what am I talking about?" She dismisses me with a wave of her hand. "You date celebrities, so our new handyman will be small potatoes in your world."

"*Dated* celebrities," I correct her. "If you can even call it that. Vick and I went out a few times then he never called back. It seems I'm *not* celebrity dating material."

Vick Delacroix starred in one of my favorite television shows that happened to film right here in Delia. The show was cancelled a while back, but Vick and I had become friends by then and always kept in touch. We officially started dating about a month ago after reconnecting at my best friend's wedding. I thought everything was going well, but after only a few dates, I never heard from Vick again.

It broke my heart, but I think I miss his friendship more than anything.

"You are most definitely celebrity dating material," Lila argues. "I'd kill for that figure of yours, and don't even get my started on that pretty red hair. And just for the record, I'd be embarrassed to tell you what I would do for a date with Vick Delacroix. I wouldn't want you to think less of me."

"Vick Delacroix doesn't deserve you," I assure her with a smile. "And it sounds like there's some potential for you in the form of a sexy new handy man."

"Child, please. He looks too young for this old gal."

"Age is just a number," I remind her. "And maybe he's into cougars."

"Well in that case, I'm all over that like white on rice."

I swat at her arm and we both giggle.

"Either way, it doesn't matter," she continues. "The first time I saw him, I was going to do the polite thing and go introduce myself, but when I waved at him he just put his head down and got back to work. No smile, no wave, no hello, nothing. Little does he know, all of that brooding only makes him more desirable in my book."

Lila gives me another wink, but I know she's not really into this guy. Personally, I've always thought something may be going on between her and David, although that's probably just wishful thinking on my part. I'd love for David to find someone. I hate the thoughts of him being alone all of the time, and he and Lila would make a fabulous couple.

Lila finally drops the subject of the new guy, and moves on to other town gossip for the next half hour as she helps me go through the typical routine before we open. As we're finishing up, David walks in the front door in his usual, but very non-traditional chef's attire—slacks, a dress shirt and a bowtie—an ensemble he wears in a variation of colors every day. David says your clothing should reflect who you are, but also how you want people to perceive you. Lila and I have both told him if he's going for devastatingly handsome, he's got it covered.

"Good afternoon, ladies." David's bright smile is like an easily addictive happy pill.

"And hello to you, good sir," I say, matching his smile. "How was your day today?"

I take two of the four bags David is carrying and follow him to the kitchen, while Lila heads to his car to fetch the rest.

"Gretta had some amazing herbs at the market," David reports. "I cleaned her out of rosemary."

"So, fried chicken's on the menu tonight then?"

The menu at *Geoffrey's* changes daily and David typically offers only two or three options each night. Rosemary is one of the "secret ingredients" in David's fried chicken. The cholesterol level may be high enough to kill a small cow, but it's absolutely delicious.

"Actually, the fried chicken is for Nix. It's his favorite." David places the bags on the counter in the kitchen and starts emptying the contents. "I thought I'd surprise him with some for lunch tomorrow."

"Who's Nix?" I ask, as I grab a few items and head to the pantry.

"Didn't I tell you? He's my godson, come here for a visit."

"That's wonderful!" I stop what I'm doing and turn to David with a huge grin on my face. "Is he staying with you?"

"He refused. Insisted on staying in a hotel in town, but he's been having lunch with me every day, then spends the rest of his afternoons doing God knows what. I'm not sure how long he'll stay, but he says he's looking for a small cabin to rent out in the woods somewhere. He likes to keep to himself."

David smiles over at me, but something's not right. I don't question it though because it's none of my business. I'm just happy he has some company. He's never remarried after his wife passed away several years ago and he doesn't have any children of his own or any family nearby. It will be nice for him to have someone here that he's close to.

"Well, if he's looking for a little R and R, he came to the right place," I say. "He won't find much excitement in Delia."

"Too true, too true," David agrees with a sigh. "But I'm afraid Nix isn't very good at taking it easy."

"Well, I'm glad he's here and he's lucky to have you."

"Thank you, angel."

"Will we get to meet him?"

"I'm sure you'll run into him eventually." David shrugs. "He lasted less than a day before he was begging me to put him to work. Boy was driving me batty. I told him I had plenty of odds and ends to tend to here. He likes doing that kind of work."

I stop in front of the freezer, wide-eyed and as frozen solid as the meats inside. The new handyman is David's godson?

"Does Lila know who he is?"

"He's only been here a few days," David informs me. If he noticed the slight panic in my voice, he doesn't show it. "I haven't really had a chance to tell anyone yet."

I quickly make a mental note to alert Lila as soon as possible.

"Well, I think he sounds like a blessing, David," I say with sincerity. "And I'm sure he wouldn't insist if he didn't want to help."

"I agree, but he said he was coming here for some peace and quiet." David shakes his head in disapproval. "He deserves a break, but I guess the work will do him some good, keep his mind in the right place. I can understand that."

Yeah. I can understand that too.

David gets busy with his duties, and I get busy helping him. He starts working on the food prep for the evening, and I reach over to switch on the music. David turns to me with a wink that says "good idea". The fact that David forgot to turn it on when he entered the kitchen is a testament to how much must be on his mind with regard to his new visitor. I've started to think David can't do anything in the kitchen without Louis Armstrong or Ella Fitzgerald singing in his ear.

Oddly enough, my mind drifts to Nix as we work. I don't know if it's the excitement of having a new guy in town, the mystery behind him or all of the above, but I'm strangely curious and kind of eager to meet him. I've never met anyone close to David, so it will be interesting to meet someone he considers family. I just need to make sure to warn Lila before she does something to embarrass us all.

"Sorry, you two." Lila comes bustling into the kitchen with a couple of brown bags in her arms. "My mom called while I was out getting the rest of the groceries from David's car. She has a cell phone now. God bless her."

David and I both smile at her as she puts the bags on the counter then immediately starts singing the Billie Holiday tune that's playing. She grabs one of David's hands and forces him to dance with her, and after putting up a pathetic excuse for a fight, he starts leading her around the kitchen floor. I catch them sharing a look as they dance—one of those looks that make me believe there may be something more between them than just friendship, but what do I know. Either way, they make me smile.

After they finish their little dance break, Lila waves goodbye then turns to leave. I wipe my hands on my apron and remove it before following her out.

"Lila, wait up."

She stops in the doorway of the green dining room and waits for me to catch up. "What's going on?"

"I wanted to let you know that the new guy? His name is Nix and he's David's godson, here to visit for a while. I'm not really sure of anymore details than that."

"Godson, huh?" Lila pouts. "Oh well. I can still ogle him, right? No harm in that."

"No harm in that," I smile. "I just thought I'd give you a heads up on who he was, and let you know that this guy seems really important to David. I think we should do our best to try and make him feel welcome." Lila opens her mouth to say something, but I hold my hand up to stop her. "And you should try and keep your mind out of the gutter, if that's even possible."

Lila laughs then gives me that same dreamy look she had when she was talking about Nix earlier. "Just wait until you see him," she warns me again. "We'll revisit this conversation afterward, and I'm going to bet this talk about keeping minds out of gutters won't only be applying to me."

She pats my cheek before walking away, and I shake my head as I stare after her. Lila and I have been working together for almost a year now, so I thought she knew me better than that. It takes more than a pretty face to draw me in.

Vick Delacroix has a pretty face.

You Think You Know

My ex-husband has a pretty face.
Need I say more?

CHAPTER THREE

Today is Thursday. I've come to hate Thursdays over the last few months because it's the day I have to drag my mother, kicking and screaming, to her therapy session. I wish with all of my heart she would take this seriously, but I think she only goes because I threatened to leave her on her own if she didn't.

You would think after a year, she'd at least be a tiny bit better. I know the circumstances were much different, but I made it through my divorce, and I've always felt my mother was a much stronger woman than me. Surely she can figure this out. But when she walks into the kitchen and sits at the table, her appearance alone is a harsh reminder that she's not as strong as she used to be.

All the make-up in the world couldn't cover the dark circles that shadow her bloodshot eyes. Her hair is pulled up into a neat twist, and she's wearing a perfectly respectable outfit—black slacks and a favorite pink blouse. But these days, most of her clothing is at least two sizes too big for her. Her burnt auburn hair is streaked with gray, and her shoulders stay slouched, reflecting her weariness.

"I assume you heard the good news," she mutters and I cringe. The hate and loathing in her voice lets me know she's referring to my dad. And yes, I did hear the unfortunate news.

"How did you hear?" I question.

She barely leaves the house, except to go to church on Sunday mornings. And she insists we attend the early service, since less people are there.

"It doesn't matter how I heard. What matters is that you obviously knew and you didn't tell me."

Now the bitterness is directed at me, but I've learned not to take it personally. "I just found out last night," I confess. "I planned to discuss it with you after therapy, which we're going to be late for if we don't get a move on."

My mom doesn't move from her seat at the kitchen table. She turns to stare out the window, avoiding my eyes. "He called me last night." Her sad, quiet voice breaks my heart. "It was the first time I've heard his voice since he left, and he called to tell me he's marrying that...that...*girl*. He said he didn't want me to hear it from someone else. Can you believe he's marrying her, Rosie? She's not much older than you. She's a child. He's marrying a *child*!"

I sit down in the chair next to my mom and rub her arm, trying to soothe her, although I know it won't work. Nothing works.

"He called me too," I admit. "He wants me to come to the wedding."

My mom's tired eyes snap to mine. "Are you going?"

"No." I shake my head. "I told him he was obviously free to do as he wishes, but if he was looking for my blessing, he doesn't have it."

My mom smiles for the first time in months. It's small and weak, but I'll take it.

"Thanks, Rosie. I don't know what I'd do without you."

I put my arms around her, trying not to cry. She's so frail these days. She's aged ten years since the divorce was final, and as much as I want to be here to help her through this, it's torture watching her waste away.

"Come on, Mom." I stand and take her hand to help her up. "We need to get going."

My mom nods and I'm surprised at how easily she was persuaded. I try not to look too shocked as she grabs her purse and makes her way to the door. All without me begging, pleading or doing everything short of dragging her to the car.

I follow her out and hop into the driver's seat of her new Buick—something she bought shortly after the divorce, trying to make herself feel better, but she's never even driven it. Mom's never been much into cars, so it's no surprise the extravagant purchase didn't work to lift her spirits.

It takes close to an hour to get to therapy, since Mom insisted I find one outside of Delia. She said she would be horrified if one of her friends found out she was going. My mom thinks things like therapy are useless and embarrassing. I try and tell her that it's only useless because she won't give it a chance, but that seems to go in one ear and out the other.

When we arrive, I sit in the waiting room like I do every Thursday. But when she comes out this morning after her hour is up, something has changed. She's smiling. That's twice in one day, which is unprecedented.

I don't want to get my hopes up, but maybe she finally had a break through. I try talking to her about the session on our long ride home, see if I can pull a few highlights out of her, but as always, she refuses to tell me anything. She remains silent for most of the ride, but every now and then I catch a small smile on her face as she looks out the passenger window. And instead of wringing her hands the entire ride like she normally does, they sit linked together and perfectly still in her lap. These are all small changes that only I would notice, but at this point, any change is good.

It's lunchtime by the time we make it back home. I offer to make my mom something to eat, which she politely refuses. She claims she didn't sleep well the night before and heads to her room for a nap, leaving me alone in the kitchen. I make myself a sandwich although I'm not really hungry, but I know I should eat something before I go on my run today. I'll need the energy to work off all of this stress, so I quickly eat my peanut butter and jelly then go to my room to change.

My room at my parents' house hasn't changed since I left at eighteen, but I have no desire to redecorate. That would mean I'm settling in, and it's just too depressing to think that this situation may be permanent. Granted, my current living arrangement isn't necessarily by choice, but that doesn't make it any less depressing. Honestly, just being in this house is depressing. It feels like every happy childhood memory I have has been tainted by my father and his philandering ways. A decade of affairs, and now he's marrying the most recent, who happens to be over twenty years his junior. Part of me is dying to understand what would make him do what he did, but I haven't been able to talk to him about it, despite his many attempts to contact me. I know I should be the bigger person and hear him out, but living with mom this past year, seeing everything she's gone through, has been hard. It's going to take a while before I can look at my father the same way, if I even can.

Pushing all of the things I can't change out of my mind for a while, I head outside. At least I can be thankful it's a sunny day, and the temperatures have been relatively mild, considering it's June in the South.

I hop into my mom's old minivan that she gave me when she got her Buick. My trusty Honda finally died about a year ago, the night I met David, and although my mom's minivan may not be ideal, it was free and it's reliable...well, *fairly* reliable. I've been having trouble getting it started lately, but I'm not sure I should put any money into it. It would probably be best to look into getting a new car of my own, but I hate to crack into my savings. I guess that's another reason I should focus on helping David get more business. A few extra tips would be nice.

Since it's a beautiful day, the park is crowded and I have to drive through the parking lot a couple of times before I find a spot. I end up parking across the way from the entrance to the trails. Oh well. I guess a little extra cardio can't hurt.

I go ahead and put my earbuds in before I get out of the van. I start my music, strap my phone around my arm then stretch before making my way toward the trails. The sun is bright, warming my skin as I walk, and I immediately start to feel better. I've always been an active person, but running was never my choice, until one day about nine months ago. Bored and frustrated, I had to get out of my mom's house, so I came to the park and started on one of the trails. I walked until walking wasn't enough, then I started to run. In a sweater, jeans and dress flats, I wasn't really dressed for the occasion, but I ran until I could no longer take the blisters on my feet or the lack of oxygen in my lungs. I remember all but crawling back to my car afterward, but even with my ruined feet, I felt amazing. I've been coming here three or four times a week ever since.

By the time I reach the start of the trail, I'm nice and warmed up, so I break into a jog as soon as my feet hit the dirt. When I passed the playground, it was crowded with kids, enjoying their summer vacations. The trail, however, is empty. Just the way I like it.

I listen to the pounding rhythm of Missy Elliott pouring into my ears and lose myself to the woods around me. I've done this trail so many times now I don't even have to look at the markers to know how far I've come. I've learned to recognize landmarks instead—fallen branches or missing bark forming a unique pattern on a tree trunk. There's a sharp turn up ahead, and when I reach it, I'll be two miles into the five I usually run. And since the trail has been void of anyone outside of myself this entire time, I increase my speed, racing to the bend before I have to slow down to make the sharp left. Unfortunately, I don't slow down soon enough, and the trees are so overgrown this time of year that I don't see the person coming at me until it's too late. The last thing I remember is a pair of huge, black eyes. Then it's lights out.

CHAPTER FOUR

When I come to, I reach up to rub at the spot near my left temple that's throbbing so severely I can barely breathe. But before my hand can reach its destination, something rough and warm pushes it back down. I slowly open my eyes, thinking I should probably find out who or what is here with me, where I am and why, but the minute the sunlight touches my irises, I slam my lids back down. *Ouch, ouch, ouch.*

"How do you feel?"

The voice is low, deep and really pleasant, but as I gather my senses, the alarms start going off. I force my eyes back open then turn my squint toward the direction of the voice. After a couple of painful blinks, I'm able to make out the outline of a man sitting a couple of feet away from me, leaning against a tree with his arms resting on his knees. His posture seems harmless enough, and he's wearing a dark t-shirt, shorts and running shoes, so I can presume he's here for the same reason I am. If he was going to kidnap me, he would have done so while I was unconscious, right?

I'm beginning to think my head may hurt too much to care, but self-preservation eventually wins out, and I continue to try and assess the stranger. As soon as my eyes are fully focused, I recognize the same pair of black eyes from before I was knocked out cold, and it all comes back to me in a rush. *Oh no.* I close my eyes again, not sure which is worse at this point—the pain or the embarrassment.

"I feel like I got hit by a Mack truck," I confess with a groan. I try rubbing at the spot on my head again, but the same warm hand is there to stop me.

"You have a nasty goose egg, but you'll live."

When I open my eyes this time, he's standing over me, a smile teasing his lips. *Wow.* I get a good look at him for the first time now that he's upright, and as Lila would say, *I wouldn't kick him out of my bed for eating crackers.*

I take his extended hand and he gently helps me up, but I sway a bit on my feet once I'm upright. Thankfully my savior is there.

"Feeling dizzy?"

"Just a little," I admit, as he grabs on to my shoulders to steady me.

Oh God, this is so embarrassing.

"I'm going to walk you back to your car," he states—a command, not a request. "I don't think you have a concussion, but we may want to get you checked out, just in case."

My head feels so foggy I can barely nod my agreement. He takes one of my arms and pulls it around his waist, then puts his arm around my shoulders. I wish I were more coherent so I could enjoy this. He's incredibly good looking, but mostly it feels good to be held, to be cared for. I've missed that. It's been a long time.

I lean into him as we walk, and he doesn't appear to mind. He goes slowly, but only a few minutes in I stumble, feeling dizzy again.

"Are you okay?" He stops and I try and lift my eyes to his, but it hurts to open them too widely against the afternoon sun.

"I'm not sure," I answer truthfully. "I'm feeling really dizzy."

That's when the nausea hits.

"Come on," the stranger says to me, and I cringe, thinking he's going to make me walk some more. Instead, he bends down and lifts me into his arms as if I weigh no more than a feather.

"You can't carry me to my car."

"Why not?" he counters. "You can't weigh much more than a hundred pounds. I've carried men twice your size over much tougher terrain. I think I'm good."

Carried men? Huh?

"And I'm a little concerned about your head," he continues. "I thought it was nothing, but based on your color and how dizzy you feel, I think you definitely have a concussion."

I've forgotten what I was going to ask him by the time he stops talking. Now all I care about is my queasy stomach and the fact that he's about to carry me over two miles to my car. "It's too far," I mumble, trying to push back the foul taste in the back of my throat.

Dear God, please don't make me lose my lunch in front of this beautiful stranger. Amen.

"It's not that far," he disagrees. "Trust me."

For some reason, I get the feeling I won't win this one, and I'm not sure I want to. So I do my best to relax, closing my eyes and resting my head on his shoulder. *Mmmmmm.* His scent is surprisingly calming. He smells like the woods around us, mixed with sweat and spice and something altogether *man*. I breathe him in, taking deep, slow breaths, and pretty soon the nausea starts to subside.

Grateful for the relief, I nuzzle in closer, feeling safer and more secure than I've felt in ages. I hold him close, lost in his heady scent, lost in the feeling of protection he's providing, and without thinking, I press my lips against his neck and kiss him right below his ear. In my barely coherent state, it was a perfectly acceptable thank you. But then I feel his arms go rigid beneath me, and when I open my eyes, I see his neck muscles are strained, his jaw is clinched, and heat pours into my face as I realize what I've done. *Oh no, oh no, oh no!*

"I'm so sorry. I was just...it was only meant as a thank you." I try to pull away but he keeps walking, his movements robotic and his eyes straight ahead, every muscle in his body pulled tight with tension. "You can put me down. I'm starting to feel a little better."

My head is still hurting, but the dizziness and nausea seem to have passed. The embarrassment, however, is back in full force.

"Honestly, I think I'm okay now," I try again. "You don't have to carry me."

He finally stops walking and slowly puts me back on my feet. His face is a cool mask, but his eyes...God, they're as black as night and absolutely mesmerizing, but there's fear there. So he's not angry, but afraid? Afraid of what? *Me?*

I wrap my arms around my waist, suddenly self-conscious. "Thanks for the help, but I'm sure I can make it on my own."

"Look...I just..." He runs a hand over his short, brown hair, as his eyes avoid mine. "Make sure to get that bump looked at," he reminds me, then without another word, he turns and takes off in the opposite direction.

I watch his back until he takes the sharp turn where we collided earlier, then I lose him in the trees. I pull my hand up to the bump on my head and touch it lightly with my fingers. *Ouch.* It's on the left side of my forehead, near my hairline. I didn't notice a bump on his head, so I must have hit some other part of him. His shoulder maybe? With that body there are plenty of hard angles to choose from.

Either way, the bump is tender, but I'm starting to feel better by the second. I doubt I have a concussion, but maybe I'll run by the Delia Urgent Care Clinic on the way home, just in case.

I walk slowly back toward the start of the trail, trying not to think of my bizarre encounter with the tempting stranger. But as embarrassing as it was, it was probably the most exciting thing that's happened to me in months.

I know he's not from around here. Someone like that would be hard to miss in this town, especially with all of those colorful tattoos covering both arms, and the piercing I noticed beneath his bottom lip. He must be visiting a relative, or with my luck, a girlfriend. That's probably why he looked like he was ready to toss me into the trees when I snuggled into him.

Way to go, Rose!

Blocking out the embarrassment, I enjoy the memory of his handsome face and his chivalry until I reach the van. I'm feeling much better now, and I'm not sure if it was the long walk or the thoughts of Mr. Tattooed and Tantalizing that have me overheated, but the lukewarm water in the cup holder of the van is very welcome. I down half of it before jumping into the driver's seat and starting the engine.

As I go to back out of my spot, something—or some*one*, I should say—in my rearview mirror makes me do a double take. I slam on the brakes and turn to focus on the figure standing at the edge of the trees near the parking lot. Even with the distance between us, I can feel it when his dark eyes find mine, but he disappears so quickly back into the woods that I have to wonder if I imagined the whole thing.

I exhale a breath I hadn't realized I was holding and pull back into the spot. I know I should probably be terrified, because either I'm hallucinating or some strange man is stalking me, neither of which would be anything to smile about. But somehow I know he was real. And somehow I know he was checking up on me.

And for some strange reason, that makes me really, really happy.

CHAPTER FIVE

I didn't have a concussion.

I stopped by the clinic on my way home, and as ridiculous as it sounds, I did it for him. I don't even know his name, but I thought if he cared enough to make sure I got to the van okay, then I owed him a check-up. In the end, the doctor suggested some pain killers and rest. I took two Advil when I got home, but there won't be any rest until my shift is over tonight. Thankfully, it's been a really slow night, so I've managed to take it easy for the most part. The only customers we have currently are the Wilson's, and I've spent the last twenty minutes sitting in a chair, chatting with them.

The Wilson's come every Thursday for dinner at six-thirty sharp. David makes them the same meal every week, even if it's not on his menu, which they enjoy with huge smiles on their faces. They're an enchanting couple, about to celebrate their fiftieth wedding anniversary next year. And the lost-but-not-quite-forgotten hopeless romantic in me never tires of the stories they love to tell—the way they met, stories about their first date, their wedding day or the days their children were born. They make it a point to celebrate every anniversary by doing something special, and they've told me the story of every one, more than once. It makes me want to find someone I can eat the same meal with every Thursday for the rest of our days. I think I would love that life.

I move to the kitchen to go get Mr. and Mrs. Wilson a refill on their sweet teas, but David stops me.

"Why don't you go home for the night," he suggests. "I can handle James and Roberta."

"But who's gonna help you clean up?"

I don't know why he would want to send me home. David never offers that, no matter how slow we are. Then I notice he's already started breaking down the kitchen. Technically, we're open until ten, but I think he knows as well as I do that no one else is coming in tonight.

"I decided to close up a little early, and I thought you could probably use the rest." David wipes his brow before looking over at me. "Especially after what happened today."

"What do you mean?"

I didn't tell anyone about my embarrassing collision with the beautiful stranger, so I'm a little surprised when David eyes the bump on my forehead and gives me a small smile.

"I heard about your accident today at the park."

"You did?" I cross my arms, feeling confused. David smiles a little wider. "How did you know about that? Did you see me?"

"No, I wasn't there."

"Well then, how...?"

"Nix told me."

My arms fall slowly back down to my sides, as the dread settles in. "N-Nix? That...that was *Nix*?"

Dear God, no.

"Heard it was a hell of a meeting." David, seemingly enjoying my shock and awe, goes back to his evening routine and I continue to panic.

There are so many bad things about this situation that I don't know where to start, but me kissing Nix's neck is the one that immediately comes to mind. *Dammit, Rose!*

"We literally bumped into each other at the park today." I shake my head at the humiliating memory. "But I had no idea it was him."

"Did you go get checked out like he asked you to?"

"I did."

"Good. He'll be happy to know you stopped by the doctor. He called earlier to check on you."

"God, I'm so embarrassed."

I lean against the counter-top and close my eyes. *This can't be happening*, I think to myself, but then what David said finally registers.

"Wait..." I open my eyes to find David looking at me as if he's surprised I'm just now clueing in. "Did you say he called to check on me? But how did he...?"

"Nix knew who you were today at the park."

"How is that possible?"

"Who knows." David shrugs a little too innocently. "Got some photos of you around, and of course I talk about you like you're my own."

"But why didn't he tell me?"

David shrugs again. "He said you didn't ask."

"I was a little out of it."

"So I hear."

Oh no. Did Nix tell him everything that happened? I look down at my shoes as my cheeks flush.

"I was worried I had upset him," I confess. "But then I saw him watching me when I got to my car. I didn't know who he was at the time, but I was happy to see maybe he wasn't as upset with me as I had thought."

David mumbles something under his breath then looks over at me. "Nix is good people, but he's a complicated man, angel. Been through some rough times."

"I'm so sorry to hear that." My genuine concern for this stranger surprises even me. "Will he be okay?"

I immediately feel bad for prying, but David gives me a kind smile.

"I think he will be."

"Is there anything I can do? I mean, I'd at least like to thank him for helping me today."

David nods. "Just keep it simple, and I'm sure he'll love it."

I smile, happy I'll have the chance to thank him properly. And if I'm being honest with myself, I'm kind of excited about seeing him again.

Let's not get ahead of ourselves, Rose.

Much to his disapproval, I refuse David's request to leave early and head back out to the dining room with tea refills for The Wilson's. After the happy couple leaves, we have another couple come in, but they only have dessert and coffee. I help David close up shop, and as usual, he insists on walking me out.

"See you tomorrow, my angel." David gives me a hug then watches me walk to the van from the front porch.

Once I'm in the driver's seat, I turn and wave to David as he walks inside, then I roll down the window to let in the sultry summer air as

I drive. I pull out of the driveway and look to my left and right, then to my right again when I notice a car sitting on the side of the road. As I'm staring, the headlights come on and my nerves kick up. I pull out of the driveway, praying whoever it is won't follow me, but the car pulls out behind me, bringing my worst fears to life.

I pull my phone from my purse, prepared to call nine-one-one if necessary, but when I look at the screen, I have a text from an unknown number. I wouldn't normally condone texting and driving, but something tells me I should check it before I make a panicked call to the police.

I don't trust doctors. Wanted to make sure you got home safely. Hope you don't mind.

I stare at my rearview mirror with wide eyes. *Nix?* Nix is following me home?

My heart is beating like crazy as we drive through town. I have no idea if I should be frightened or flattered. I assume David gave him my number, but why? Did Nix ask for it?

Let's NOT get ahead of ourselves, Rose!

I hope I'll get some answers when I get to my mom's house, but when I finally pull into the driveway, Nix pulls his black Jeep in behind me then immediately backs out. He starts driving away slowly, and I assume he's waiting for me to get inside. I hurry to unlock the door, and as soon as it closes behind me, I hear the roar of his engine as it picks up speed.

I lean back against the front door, as the feeling resurfaces from the park earlier today. Once again, I'm reminded of how it feels to be cared for, and by a complete stranger, no less. The man must be a saint.

Eventually, I make it back to my room. I toss my purse on my bed, and when my phone falls out, I remember I now have his number and should probably thank him. Sitting on my bed, I type out a quick text.

Thanks for today and for seeing me home, but I promise I'm fine. No need to stalk me.

I lay my phone on the nightstand, hoping my teasing comes across as innocently as it was intended, then head to the bathroom for a quick shower. While in the shower, I start to regret my playful remark. What if he thinks I was flirting with him? *Was* I flirting with him? *Oh no.*

By the time I get out of the shower, I'm kicking myself for putting entirely too much thought into one simple little text message. I dry off and try to convince myself I don't care if he's responded, but the minute I enter my room, I nearly trip over my own feet trying to get to my phone. There are two texts from him, and I anxiously swipe my finger across the screen to read the first one.

Just trying to do the right thing.

It's hard to tell after that text how he interpreted my remark, but then I read the next one and start to smile.

Glad you're okay, even if you do think I'm a psycho.

I put my phone down, thinking he could be upset with me, since I don't really know him and I can't decipher his tone from a text message. However, he did say he was glad I was okay. *Hmmmm.* There's only one way to find out.

I was only teasing you. Your chivalry is much appreciated, sir.

His response is quick and makes me smile even wider than before.

You're very welcome, ma'am. Now get some sleep. Night, Rose.

So bossy, but I like it.

Goodnight, Nix.

I lie back on my bed, holding my phone close to my chest. I have no idea what's happening, but today has been filled with one surprise after another. And for the first time in what seems like forever, I go to sleep with a smile on my face, looking forward to what tomorrow may bring.

CHAPTER SIX

I didn't see or hear from Nix all weekend, and it wasn't until the following Tuesday that I got up the courage to ask David if he had left town for good.

"He had to go back home for a few days," David tells me, as we prep the menu items for the night. "His grandfather is ill, and he's taken a turn for the worse. Such a shame. He's a good man."

"You know his grandfather?" I'm all ears now, eager to learn anything and everything about Nix.

"I used to work for him," David nods. "I grew up in Oakland but moved to Sacramento for a job right after college. The job didn't work out, and I was about to move back home when I met Mr. Taylor in a farmer's market. We talked for a while, found out he owned a farm in Pollock Pines and somehow we ended up talking about my dream of opening a restaurant one day. He was kind enough to offer me a job selling his produce to local markets and restaurants. Said it would be good experience for me, and he was right. I learned everything I needed to know and more, and he paid me very well. He's the reason I had the money to open *Geoffrey's*. He's an admirable man."

"So that's how you know Nix? Through his grandfather?"

David gives me a proud smile. "Known that boy since he was a baby. His father and I are best friends. I was honored when they asked me to be his godfather."

"They made a good choice."

David takes the compliment grudgingly, but with a smile. "Nix should be back tonight. Found him a cabin right before he left, so I told him I'd help find some furnishings tomorrow." He turns to me then with a thoughtful expression. "You should come along. Surely you're much better at decorating than us boys, and every home needs a woman's touch, in my opinion."

"Oh, that's okay." I immediately start shaking my head, even though I'd secretly love to go. "I wouldn't want to impose."

"You wouldn't be imposing," David argues. "Nix is supposed to call when he gets in tonight. I'll let him know you'll be joining us tomorrow."

"Are you sure Nix won't mind?" I bite at my bottom lip, worrying this may be a bad idea. "I barely know him. I'm not sure he'll be comfortable with me tagging along."

"He'll be fine," David assures me. "And it'll be good for the two of you to get to know each other better. He could use another friend around here besides me, someone more his age."

Friends? I can be friends with Nix, right? Of course I can.

"If you're sure he won't mind," I finally concede, "then I'd be happy to come along."

"He won't mind, and I'm thrilled." David's smile is bright and sincere. "We'll get an early start tomorrow, since we'll have to drive into Bristol. I doubt we can find him much of anything worth buying here in Delia."

I nod my head in agreement. "Just let me know what time, and I'll be ready."

David and I agree on nine in the morning, then spend the rest of the time before we open jamming to Pops Staples while we prepare the fried catfish David has on the menu for this evening.

By the time we close, I've practically chewed my nails to bits, thinking about shopping with Nix tomorrow. I try and keep telling myself David will be there too. There's no need to be nervous. We're all adults, just doing a little shopping for a new friend in town. No problem.

But it is a problem.

It's not about getting to know someone new. I'm not that shy. As a matter of fact, I love meeting new people, but Nix? He's different. You'd have to be blind not to be attracted to that man, which wouldn't normally be an issue, but he's David's godson so I feel I should tread lightly there. And that's what makes me nervous. What if treading lightly isn't a possibility?

"You heading out?"

"Yes, sorry," I mumble before removing a tattered fingernail from my mouth. "Let me grab my purse from the kitchen."

David seems suspicious of my flustered state, but thankfully, he doesn't ask any questions. "I'll wait for you in the foyer."

I move quickly to the kitchen, grab my purse, then head back out to meet David. "Goodnight, sir." I lean in and kiss his cheek before heading to the van.

"Meet here at nine tomorrow," he reminds me. "Don't forget."

"I won't," I call back over my shoulder. "See you in the morning."

For shopping.

All day.

With Nix.

Oh, the butterflies. Make it stop.

I jump into the van and roll down the windows, before making my way down the long drive. Even though Hickory Grove isn't a well-travelled road, I still look left and right before pulling out. As soon as I take a left, a familiar set of headlights come on behind me.

I immediately pull my phone from my purse and check my messages, but there are no new texts. All I can do now is put my phone down on the seat and use the ride home to try and figure out why he's following me again. It's been almost a week since our "run-in" at the park. The bump on my head is long gone. I'm perfectly fine. Surely he knows that.

I pull into the driveway at my mom's house, hoping Nix will pull in behind me and stay this time. I'd love to see him. But to my disappointment, he turns around just like before and sits, idling at the end of my driveway.

I step out of the van and wave to him, but he doesn't wave back. He just stares at me a minute then tilts his chin in the direction of my front door, telling me to get inside.

Ohhh-kay.

I unlock the door and open it, then look behind me. Nix gives me another long, lingering once over before driving away and I enter the house feeling all sorts of confused.

I head to my room and question whether or not I should text him. I guess I should thank him for seeing me home safely again. Instead, I go with my first thought.

Glad you're back and safe.

I sit my phone on the nightstand and head for the shower. I take a long one because I need some time to think about Nix's behavior this evening. I haven't seen or heard from him in days. Then he decides to follow me home and doesn't even speak to me. All I get is a nod urging me inside and a couple of prolonged stares that...well, I honestly have no idea what those were all about. I have no idea what any of this is about.

When I get back to my room, I slip on my pajamas before checking my phone. There's only one text from him waiting for me this time.

Thank you. Goodnight, Rose.

I stare at my phone, knowing I shouldn't push, but I can't resist.

My head is fine, you know. You can stop stalking me now, psycho.

There's a long pause before he responds. So long in fact, I start to worry that maybe I've crossed a line again. But when he finally texts me back, I'm happy to see he's taking my teasing in stride.

Thought you appreciated my chivalry, ma'am.

I do. But it's not that far of a drive for me. No need to go out of your way.

I don't mind.

I have to smile at that brand of kindness, but I really don't want him going through all of that trouble for me.

I'm perfectly capable of getting myself home safely, but if it would make you feel better, I could text you when I get home. Save you some gas money.

I add a smiley face to make double sure he understands I'm teasing again. But then there's another long pause, so I sit and wait, assuming he's typing back a lengthy reply.

No.

Or maybe not.

You're against saving gas money?

I said I don't mind.

I narrow my eyes at my phone. Why do I feel like there's something he's not saying?

Nix, why did you follow me home tonight?

Yet another long pause.

Truth?

I wait for him to continue, but it doesn't seem that's going to happen, so I text back a simple **Please.**

I wait through the pause this time feeling a little nervous about what this "truth" may be.

I like knowing you're safe.

I take a moment to appreciate his thoughtfulness, but I still don't want him going through all of this trouble for me. I start to type my reply, suggesting once again that I simply text when I get home, but another text comes in from him before I can finish.

Plus, these past few days have been ugly.

Oh, Nix. I erase my previous reply, as my heart breaks over what he must be going through with his grandfather. This time, I go to type my apologies instead, but I'm interrupted yet again.

And I wanted to look at something beautiful.

My fingers stop mid-stroke as I read and re-read his last text multiple times. The next thing I know, several minutes have passed, my eyes are watery and I still haven't responded.

I continue staring at my phone, trying to decide how in the world I'm supposed to reply. I'm shocked when a drop of water hits the screen and I realize it's a tear. Why am I crying? *Oh for heaven's sake.* I wipe at my eyes and take a deep breath. I can do this.

Thank you, Nix. For everything. And I'm so sorry about your grandfather.

Thank you, Rose. Sleep well.

Sleep? Is he joking?

Goodnight, Nix.

I toss my phone back on my nightstand and fall back into my bed. So much for treading lightly. I can't speak for Nix, but my heart just pounded through the "friend zone" like a T-Rex on a mission. He's gorgeous, thoughtful and that's probably the sweetest thing any man has ever said to me.
　Trouble.
　God, I'm in so much trouble.

CHAPTER SEVEN

When I pull into the driveway of *Geoffrey's* the next morning, I'm surprised to see Lila coming out the front door.

"You didn't come to ogle, did you?" I tease, before giving her a quick hug. "He should be here in a few minutes."

"Not this time," Lila giggles. "I'm here because David called. One of the refrigerators went out last night and the kitchen is a mess."

"Oh no!" I gasp. "Well let's go in and see what we can do to help."

I try and push past Lila, but she stops me. "He asked that the two of you go on ahead to Bristol today. He and I can take care of the mess."

I look at Lila in confusion. "I'm sure Nix will be fine leaving a little later," I suggest, just as his Jeep pulls into the drive. "I bet he'll want to help David try to fix the refrigerator."

"David can handle it, and if he can't, we'll just get a new one."

"How could he afford that?"

"Would you stop worrying and go on," Lila scolds, then turns her attention to Nix as he comes to stand next to me. "Please tell her to stop worrying."

I look over at Nix, waiting for him to ask what's going on, but instead he says, "Stop worrying, Rose," and gives me a small smile. "Ready to go?"

I shake my head and look from him to Lila and back again. "Did you know that one of the refrigerators went out last night?"

"Yeah," he confirms with a shrug. "David called me this morning. Said he's got it covered."

Oh well. I guess I am being a worry wart. If Lila says they can handle it, and Nix seems to be okay with everything—including me hanging out with him today—then I should probably just drop it.

"Okay then." I hitch my purse up a little higher on my shoulder. "I guess it's just you and me."

"Guess so." The cheery grin on Nix's face has me feeling a little lightheaded. "Are you ready?"

"Sure." I try and shake off the dizzy spell before I turn to Lila. "You're certain the two of you will be okay?"

Lila rolls her eyes at me. "Please get out of here before I beat you senseless."

"Fine," I smile and give her a goodbye hug.

"Call us if you need anything," Nix tells her, and I stifle my giggle as Lila swoons.

"Thank you, Nix, but we'll be perfectly fine. You two have fun."

Lila heads back inside, leaving me alone with Nix who looks like heaven, wrapped in cargo shorts and a faded San Francisco Pirates t-shirt.

"I'll drive, if you want," I offer. "There's plenty of room in the back of the van, if you find some things you like."

Nix seems to ponder the thought a moment, but eventually agrees. "I'll buy you a tank of gas then. It's the least I can do."

"You don't have to do that."

"I know." He opens the driver's side door for me. "But I want to."

Knowing there's probably no sense in arguing any further—and frankly that smile of his is frying my brain—I simply smile back and say "Thank you."

I start the van as Nix hops into the passenger side. Habit has me rolling down my window, but then I think I should probably be a little more hospitable. Plus, I'm nervous and sweating more than normal in the summer heat, so the air conditioner may do me some good as well. But just as I reach for it, Nix starts rolling down his own window then hangs his arm out the side.

"I don't mind the fresh air," he tells me. "But you better have some good music."

I smile at his teasing, and since he doesn't seem nervous, I decide I shouldn't be either. It's just shopping for furniture. With a friend. Not a big deal.

But I really do wish he would stop smiling at me like that.

"This van is old, so there's no auxiliary input." I pull out of the driveway, feeling no less nervous than before, but doing my best to hide it. "I have a few CD's in the console, if you want to take a peek. Or we can always just listen to the radio."

Nix heads immediately for my CD's. "Not bad." He nods his head in approval. "I wouldn't have pegged you for an AC/DC fan, but I guess you never know."

I smile to myself. "I'm a Southern girl. We wear our classic rock like a badge of honor."

"Consider me educated."

Nix smiles as he continues to thumb through my collection, opening and closing boxes until he finally chooses one and goes to insert it into the player. I know from just a glance at the artwork on the top what he's chosen.

"You like Ed Sheeran?"

"Never heard of him," he shrugs. "But the CD case is broken, and the CD itself is faded and worn, so I assume it's a favorite."

"Well, yes," I admit, "but I have plenty to choose from in there and I like them all. You could have chosen something you like as well."

"But I wanted to hear *your* favorite."

Thankfully, we're sitting at a traffic light in town or I probably would have wrecked the van.

"Green light," he smiles, as he points a finger toward the windshield and it's like I've forgotten how to drive, all of a sudden.

Right side, accelerator. Left side, brake.

I reluctantly pull my eyes from his to concentrate on the road as the task of driving a car starts slowly coming back to me.

"How could you have never heard of Ed Sheeran?" I ask, trying to remind myself that no matter how I feel about him, it's probably best we remain friends and nothing more.

Friends, Rose. Friends.

"I haven't listened to the radio in a while," he divulges, as he stares out the passenger-side window. "I was overseas. In the Army. Got out about a year ago."

"Really? Well, thank you for your service."

I smile over at him, but he doesn't move his eyes from whatever he's staring at out the window. He doesn't reply either. I shake my head at myself and my big mouth.

Thank you for your service? Seriously, Rose?

Obviously, he doesn't want to talk about it, so I don't press. "Well let's continue your education, shall we? First lesson...Ed Sheeran is fabulous."

Nix looks over at me then with a smile. "Tell me why you like him."

"Let's see...he's extremely talented to be so young, and I love his lyrics. He writes the most amazing love songs. Plus, he's a ginger, and we gingers have to stick together."

Nix eyes my red hair with an approving grin. "So what else have I missed?" he asks, and we spend the remaining ride to Bristol with me quizzing him on everything from music to movies and Nix wasn't kidding. If it came out any time within the last five to ten years, he's completely oblivious. But the conversation did lead to him asking me to join him at his place for a Netflix session sometime. I can't say I'm complaining about that invite.

"So, what does your new place look like?" I ask as we browse the living room furniture at American Signature.

"It's small, surrounded by trees with a creek in the back and a couple of rocking chairs on the front porch. It's perfect."

"Sounds like it." I smile, knowing I'd probably love the place. "So you have room for maybe just a sofa? A sofa and a chair?"

"Just a sofa." He leans down to check the price on the leather sofa in front of us. "I like this one."

I know without looking that sofa costs a pretty penny, but it doesn't seem Nix has much of a budget in mind. Without a second thought, he's calling a sales person over and asking about delivery for the sofa and a nearby coffee table.

"I'm not sure we can get it out today," the sales guy tells Nix. "But Friday is probably doable."

"That's too bad," Nix shakes his head. "I'm in the market for a bedroom set and a desk as well, but I really need everything today or tomorrow."

Nix turns to give me a wink, and I look at my feet so the salesman doesn't catch my smile.

"I'll tell you what." The salesman puts a finger to his lips. "I'll go see what I can do about the sofa and table, while the two of you look around."

"Sounds good." Nix smiles over at me as the man scurries toward the back and we head over to the office furniture.

Nix finds a desk even faster than he found the sofa, and since the salesman hasn't returned, I offer a notepad and pen from my purse so Nix can write down the information.

"That was easy." I smile at him. "At this rate, we'll have your entire place furnished in no time."

"Yep. Now I just need a bed."

"A bed?" *Just friends, Rose. Just friends.* "I mean, are you sure you want to look here or would you like to go someplace else? There are a couple of other stores we could try. It depends on what you have in mind."

Nix looks around the store then back at me. "I'm sure I can find something here. As you've probably noticed, I'm not really picky when it comes to furniture."

He leads the way toward the bedroom furniture and I follow closely behind, pondering the fact that the man may not be picky, but he sure has expensive tastes. That sofa wasn't cheap. And even though the desk was small and fairly simple, the name brand alone would make it one of the more expensive pieces in the store, but Nix barely considered the price. Maybe he has money. Not that I care one way or the other. It's just another unanswered question, which will most likely remain unanswered since there's this air about Nix that screams *DON'T PUSH ME.*

I guess I'll have to follow my gut and let him come to me. Anything I find out about him will be on his own terms. Something tells me that's important to him.

Nix spends a little more time looking at beds than he did the rest of the furniture. Or maybe it's just that I'm anxious to move past this particular process since Nix stretching out his tall, lean body on various different mattresses has me sweating like a thief at church. His t-shirt has ridden up a couple of times, and of course he has a tattoo on his stomach, ensuring my eyes are drawn there every single time.

"I like this one," Nix says as he hops off the last bed and I sigh in relief. "I wish I could do a king-sized, but I don't think the room will hold it. This queen will have to do."

The salesman walks up as if on cue. "Have we made any decisions?"

Nix discusses the desk, along with the bed and a chest of drawers he's chosen with the salesman. Miraculously, all can be delivered tomorrow morning, and Nix even manages to get him to wave the delivery charge–probably because he's buying some of the most expensive furniture in the store.

Nix fills out all of the necessary paperwork, and we leave the store a half an hour later. "What's next?" I ask as we make our way back to the van. "Do you need anything like lamps or dishes for the kitchen?"

"All of the above." Nix opens the driver's side door for me again, and I try not to dwell on it too much. He's obviously a gentleman—a beautiful, thoughtful, incredibly sexy gentleman.

Friends, Rose!

"There's a Bed, Bath and Beyond not far from here," I offer, as we pull out of the parking lot. "Or if you like stuff a little off the wall, there's a string of antique stores about fifteen miles south, just off the highway."

"What do you prefer?"

"It's not my house."

"And I'm not really good at the decorating part," he admits. "So I thought maybe you could help me."

"Oh, well I like antiques, but..." I think about the simplicity of the furniture he just bought and try to imagine his small cabin in the woods. "I think I have the perfect place for you."

He fiddles with my CD collection again, settling on Journey's Greatest Hits, while I drive us to Hathaway's. It's this town's version of Pottery Barn—not really my taste, plus it's a little on the pricey side. But since money doesn't seem to be an issue for Nix, I think the store's muted colors and clean lines will suit him just fine.

Nix is as easy to please with the décor as he was with furniture. He tells me the walls of his new house are all mostly a light beige color, except for his kitchen. Apparently, it's a horribly loud shade of blue, but Nix admits he kind of likes it. So, together we choose a few lamps, some dishes that he claims will go perfectly in his blue kitchen, a set of pots and pans, some silverware and a few other kitchen necessities, including a University of Georgia bottle opener that Nix just had to have. It plays the fight song every time you open a bottle. "When in Rome..." he says, and all I can do is smile.

I choose a few things for his bathroom and a quilt and sheets for his new bed, but he refuses any other décor, such as wall art, candles or this fabulous clock I found that would look great in his bedroom.

"I don't need all of the extras," he tells me. "I'm not sure how long I'll be staying."

I try to pretend that statement has zero effect on me, as we push the overflowing cart up to the register. Nix doesn't even ruffle when she tells him the total, while I have to bite my bottom lip to keep my mouth from hanging open. I wasn't paying attention to prices while we were shopping, assuming he would refuse anything he couldn't afford. Now I'm starting to wonder if there's anything he *can't* afford.

By the time we load the back of the van with all of our finds, I feel like I'm melting in the summer sun, even though I'm wearing only a light sundress and sandals.

"Are you hungry?"

I wipe my brow then look up at Nix with a smile. "I could eat. Do you like seafood?"

"Love it."

"There's a great restaurant on the way back to Delia that serves these amazing fish tacos. Sound good?"

Nix nods as he moves over to once again open my door for me. "Fish tacos sound perfect."

By the time we back out of the parking lot, Nix has already switched CD's. This time it's Johnny Cash, and I start humming along as soon as the music starts. Nix looks over at me with a thoughtful smile.

"You have interesting tastes in music."

"I grew up listening to people like Johnny Cash, Willie Nelson, The Judds and Patsy Cline. I still like listening to them from time to time. Makes me think of my grandmom, especially Patsy."

I immediately feel bad for bringing up a grandparent, but Nix doesn't seem to mind.

"My parents raised us on classic rock mostly, with a little Captain and Tennille thrown in for good measure. My mom is your typical California hippie," he muses. "I can also appreciate a little jazz, thanks to David, but that's about as far as my musical reach goes."

"Well that's a shame. We'll have to change that."

Nix has such an easy smile, it makes me curious about why he came to stay in Delia. David gave me the impression Nix was going through some tough times, and those pretty brown eyes do seem a little heavy today, complete with dark circles underneath. But I'm sure sleeping has been tough lately with all the worry over his grandfather. Other than that, Nix certainly doesn't seem very troubled at all. Then I remember our brief and extremely awkward conversation about him being recently out of the Army, and I decide that must be it. Maybe he had some bad experiences overseas and he's having a hard time adjusting to being back home. I can't even imagine some of the horrors he's probably seen.

"You have a great voice," Nix says, and I laugh.

"Did someone pay you to be nice to me or something? I think I may have to limit time spent with you, or else my head will be too big to fit through my front door."

"No one paid me," Nix chuckles. "You're voice is so unique, deep and rich, really soothing. And I love your accent."

"I don't have an accent," I try, but Nix gives me a protesting stare and I cave. "Okay, fine. It's bad. I know."

"It's beautiful. I can even hear it when you hum." He leans his head back on the headrest and closes his eyes. "With a voice like that, I'd bet you could turn any song into a lullaby."

My hands start shaking on the steering wheel, and I can barely breathe with the way my heart is skipping around in my chest. Who says things like that? No one. No one says stuff like that, and certainly never to me.

"Did I upset you?"

I look back at Nix again and there's legitimate concern in his eyes. "No, no," I quickly reassure him. "It's just that..." Do I question this? Will I ruin this? *Please God, don't let me ruin this.* "May I ask you something?"

"Sure."

"I know this is going to come out all wrong, which is why I probably shouldn't even say it, but I have to know." I pause to check his face. He's staring at me intently, his face uneasy. *Just spit it out, Rose!* "Why *are* you being so nice to me? Don't get me wrong, I appreciate it, and I'm extremely flattered. But you barely know me and you're following me home at night to make sure I get there safely. You're saying all of these nice things to me and opening car doors. Are you sure I'm worth all of this?"

Nix gives me a curious look. "Do *you* think you're worth it?"

I jerk my head back, surprised by him turning things around on me like that. "I guess?"

"You guess?" he scoffs. "Are you worth it Rose? It's a simple question."

I lower my brow, trying to figure out where he's going with this, but he doesn't give me a chance.

"Don't think about it," he all but barks at me. "Just answer the question. Are. You. Worth it?"

"Yes."

"Rose, are you worth it?"

"Yes," I say a little louder this time, but apparently it's still not good enough.

"Seriously? You can do better than that. Are you worth it?"

"Yes."

"What?"

"Yes."

"I can't hear you."

"YES!"

"Good." Nix smiles over at me. "And I totally agree."

I laugh, but only so I can hide the adrenaline rush I'm currently experiencing. Good heavens. This man is an emotional roller coaster ride.

"I'm glad you agree," I say when I start breathing semi-normally again. "I'm not sure, however, if *you're* worth it."

"Oh, I'm definitely not worth it," he says with a smile. "I'm just enjoying every second I can until you finally figure that out."

No chance, I think to myself. *No chance in hell.*

"Well, I love *Murphy's* fish tacos," I tell him. "So you have through lunch."

"I'll take it."

Even with the lunch crowd, we're seated quickly at the rustic but quaint *Murphy's Bar and Grill*, and the entire time we're eating, Nix somehow manages to keep the conversation focused on me. He asks me a million questions about myself, my family, my childhood and growing up in Delia. I answer each one and even tell him a little about my mom's current situation, hoping it'll be my turn to ask the questions sometime in the near future, but then he hits me with a tough one.

"So tell me, Rose. Are you seeing anyone?"

"Currently, no," I answer candidly. "The last guy I dated....well, it just didn't work out. We stopped seeing each other about a month ago."

"Was it serious?"

"No." I shake my head. "He was a good friend. We tried to make it more, but it didn't work."

Nix nods thoughtfully. "Are you still friends?"

"No." I give him a rueful smile. "Unfortunately, that part didn't work out either."

"I'm sorry." Nix pushes his plate away and stares at me from across the booth. "I'm sure you'll find someone one day that will treat you right, and you better promise me you won't settle. You're worth it, remember?"

"I promise," I smile at him. "And thank you, Nix. This has been fun today. I'm glad you didn't mind me tagging along."

"Day's not over," he points out with a sweet grin. "But lunch is about to be."

He signals the waitress for the check and refuses to let me pay.

"Maybe I should have considered the Army," I remark as he signs the bill.

"Why's that?"

"Well, it seems that you haven't worried much over spending money at any point today."

He raises his head and looks at me. His face is soft, but his eyes are serious. "Is money important to you, Rose?"

"It pays my bills," I answer with a shrug. "But I wouldn't say it's *important* to me. I've lived most of my life middle class and that's worked perfectly fine so far."

Nix smiles at me, so I smile back. "Ready?"

I grab my purse before standing to join him. "So, I guess we're heading back to *Geoffrey's*?"

"Actually, I thought I'd show you my place," he says as we walk to the van. "Is that okay?"

"Sure."

I'm trying not to show how excited I am that I get to spend a little more time with him, but it's like my body is physically craving information about this man, as if I'll wither away to nothing if I don't know every single detail, big and small.

"Let's stop by *Geoffrey's* first." Nix opens the car door for me. *Again.* "That way I can pick up my Jeep, and you can follow me out to the cabin."

"No problem." I glance at my watch. "But I have to be at work around four, so if it's okay, let's swing by my mom's house first so I can go ahead and pick up my uniform. Is your place far from *Geoffrey's*?"

"About twenty minutes or so. Not too bad."

It's not until Nix takes a slow step backward that I realize how much I was crowding him. Perhaps my body is craving more than just information. Oh God, how embarrassing. It's like the first day we met all over again, and the memory has heat sliding quickly up my neck and into my cheeks. I wish I could stop it, but it's too late.

"I'm sorry." I stare down at my feet, feeling horribly awkward.

"Don't worry about it." Nix and his remorseful tone have me raising my head in curiosity. "We should get going."

He doesn't even give me a chance to respond before he's walking around the front of the van to the passenger's side. I try to shake it off before I get in, but I barely know him and it's hard not knowing what he's thinking. I've had a great time with him today. I don't want to ruin this friendship before it even starts.

As I pull out of the parking lot, I expect Nix to choose a new CD for the ride home, but instead he stays still and silent—one arm across his waist, his head leaned back against the headrest as he stares out the passenger window. Yes. I definitely wish I had some clue what was going on in that lovely head of his, but he's quite possibly the most enigmatic person I've ever met. A few hours with him today and he knows my entire life story. I don't even know his last name.

Thankfully, it only takes a few miles before Nix snaps out of whatever emotion was holding him hostage. He reaches into the console and starts thumbing through CDs, and I smile as I wait for him to choose.

"Great choice," I note, as Freddie Mercury starts crooning about a "Killer Queen".

"My sister loves Queen," Nix says, and I'm excited to have another bit of personal information about him. "My dad's a huge fan as well. I think Lennon picked it up from him."

"Lennon," I muse. "What a pretty name."

"Told you my mom was a hippie." I look over at Nix and I'm glad to see he's smiling again. "My dad is about as conservative as they come, so they're an odd pair but it works. Unfortunately, he let her have the final decision when it came to baby names, so my sister's name is Lennon, as in John, and my name is Phoenix."

"As in River?"

"No." Nix chuckles. "As in the bird that goes up in flames, then reemerges from the ashes."

"It's a beautiful symbol, the phoenix. I love the idea of renewal, of second chances, of hope, even though sometimes it's all easier said than done."

"Indeed," Nix sighs, his face thoughtful as he stares out the front windshield. "So where does your mom live?"

I pause, thrown off by the rapid shift in conversation. "What do you mean?"

"Didn't you say we were stopping there first?"

"Right. Sorry." I shake my head. "When I told you about her earlier, I neglected to mention I was living with her now, so you actually know where she lives."

I wait for the judgment, but I get an understanding smile instead. "Is that the house you grew up in?"

"Yes," I laugh. "And it hasn't changed much over the years. My mom's not big on change, just another reason this divorce is practically killing her. Although I'm sure separating would be hard for anyone after being together thirty-two years."

"I'm really sorry to hear about your parents," Nix frowns. "But it must be hard for you too, putting your life on hold to be with your mom."

I blink back my surprise, not used to anyone showing me sympathy or asking how I'm doing with all of this. Don't get me wrong, I'm not the type of person that needs that kind of attention, but I'd be lying if I said it didn't feel nice to think someone cares.

"The worst part for me is dealing with all of this anger I feel toward my dad," I confess. "Well, toward my dad *and* my mom, really. I don't think either of them are handling things the right way. I mean how can my dad disrespect my mom like that? Over thirty years with someone who took care of you, loved you without question and that's how you repay her? By cheating on her with a dozen women, then marrying one who's only a few years older than your own daughter? And my mom..." I shake my head in disbelief. "I secretly keep hoping she'll get angry too, or happy or vengefully murderous for all I care. Anything would be better than the zombie she's become over the past year. She's stronger than that. I know she is. I just--"

"Breathe."

Startled by the interruption, I do as I'm told and take a deep breath.

"I'm sorry." I glance over at Nix. "Forgive my rant. I shouldn't have said those things."

"Are they true?"

"Yes."

"Then you don't have to apologize. You have a right to your feelings, Rose."

"Thanks," I whisper, as I try to push down the tears now clouding my eyes. "I really do appreciate you being so nice to me."

"We've been over this. You're worth it."

"Or maybe you're just a nice guy."

"Trust me. I'm not all that nice," Nix laughs and I have to disagree.

"I think you are...at least from what I can tell so far."

"Just give me time. I'll prove you wrong."

I look over at him, wondering why he keeps thinking he's going to get rid of me, when I've only known him a few days and it already feels like the strength of a thousand men couldn't pull me away.

"We'll see about that," I haughtily reply. "I'm a fantastic judge of character."

"Doubtful. You can go sell that nonsense somewhere else."

I turn to him with wide, teasing eyes and he laughs, light and easy, genuinely happy.

And absolutely beautiful.

We continue our light banter back and forth until we pull into my mom's driveway. I'm kind of sorry to see she's home, not that I expected her to be anywhere else. I've just had such a nice day, and selfishly, I don't want her mood bringing me down.

"Do you want to come in?" I offer, thinking my mom will probably be offended if I don't invite Nix in to meet her. "Hopefully Mom's decent. Maybe I should have called first."

"*Decent?*"

"Don't worry. I'm certain she's not running around naked," I reassure him with a smile. "She just doesn't like to meet new people unless she's showered with some make-up on."

"Okay then." Nix seems kind of confused by this, but he doesn't know my mother. Appearances are important.

"Mom?" I call out when I open the door, but there's no answer. "She may be taking a nap," I tell Nix. "Stay here and I'll go see if I can find her."

I leave Nix in the living room and head toward the back of the house. Just as I'm about to open Mom's door, I hear a scream. I whip my head in the direction of the sound and start walking that way. Suddenly, my mom crashes into me in the hallway, eyes wide with fear.

"There's a strange man in my house!" she screams. "Some hoodlum, probably here to rob us blind! We have to call the police!"

She starts frantically pushing me toward her bedroom, as if she's pushing me to safety, but all I can do is laugh.

"Mom! Mom!" I have to call her name a couple more times before I have her attention. "That's a friend of mine," I explain in a slow, soft voice so I can get her calmed down. "He's not here to rob us. He's with me."

My mom finally stops trying to shove me down the hallway, then she blinks a few times, her face slowly changing from panic to disapproval. "*That* man is a friend of yours?" she asks and I nod. "The one with the black eyes and all of those...*things* on his arms?"

"Tattoos," I correct her, feeling defensive. "And please don't judge him. He's a very nice man."

I look over my mom's shoulder, wondering if Nix is still where I left him or if Mom scared him back to California.

Mom lets go of me and brushes at her blouse. She's showered and dressed, which is a surprise, but a good surprise. And the red in her cheeks lets me know she's now more embarrassed than anything.

"Well, a phone call wouldn't have killed you."

"I thought you may have been napping," I admit. "I'm glad to you see you up and moving around."

Mom rolls her eyes at me, and I have to smile at her sass. That's new too. And I like it. "Let's go meet your friend, then."

In case her initial reaction to him wasn't enough, it's obvious in the way she just said the word "friend" that she doesn't approve of Nix. But hopefully he'll change her mind and remind her you should never judge a book by its cover. Although, I find Nix's "cover" to be pretty spectacular myself.

When Mom and I walk into the living room, I have to bite my bottom lip to keep from laughing. Nix is standing next to the front door, his arms crossed over his chest, looking just as shaken as my mom was moments ago.

"She thought you were a burglar," I explain to him, trying not to smile so I don't offend either of them.

Nix slowly uncrosses his arms and approaches us. He wipes one of his hands on his shorts before extending it to my mom. "I'm Nix. Sorry if I frightened you, ma'am."

My mom takes his hand and gives it a brief shake. "Yes, well, perhaps I shouldn't have jumped to conclusions. I'm not used to Rose having men over, except for Vick, of course."

I give my mom a look that she doesn't catch because she's too busy sizing Nix up. No way. She can't be doing this to me.

Nix's eyes flash briefly to mine, then back to my mom. "Yes ma'am, well I'm new in town and your daughter was kind enough to show me around today."

"He's a friend of David's," I mention, hoping this helps Nix's case. Mom loves David. "I helped him find some furniture for the house he'll be staying in while he's here."

There are a few beats of uncomfortable silence as Mom stares back and forth between me and Nix, apparently trying to figure out if something is going on between us. I wouldn't mind having the answer to that one myself.

"So how long will you be in town?" Mom asks Nix and he shrugs.

"I'm not really sure," he tells her. "I plan to help David do some repair work on the restaurant over the next couple of months, and I haven't thought much past that."

Mom glares at me, then turns her condescending smile on Nix. "Well, it was nice to meet you. And I do apologize for my mistake earlier."

"It's no problem." Nix offers her a genuine smile, which she has no use for, and I'm fuming at this point, furious over the way she's treating him. I'll definitely be having a talk with her later.

"Come on, Nix. You'd better stay with me." I give my mom a pointed look. "Seems some of us have forgotten our manners."

With a loud "harumph", Mom turns on her heel and heads to the kitchen. Nix must notice the tension between Mom and me, but he doesn't say anything as he follows me back to my room. I honestly surprised myself with that snide remark to my mom, but even more surprising is that I don't feel guilty about it. I don't make it a practice to disrespect her like that, but I couldn't stand there one second longer with the way she was treating Nix. He deserves better.

"Wow." Nix looks around with a huge smile on his face. "You weren't kidding when you said things haven't changed much over the years."

I laugh as I walk toward my closet. "Yeah, the last time I lived here I was eighteen."

"Who's this?"

I turn from my closet to see him checking out the poster on the back of my bathroom door. "That's Ryan Atwood," I tell him. "From *The O.C.*? I had a thing."

"I see." Nix gives me a mocking smile, so I make sure to roll my eyes at him before turning back to my closet. "Wow. You look really happy here."

I toss my work pants and shirt over my arm before moving to his side in front of my dresser. I smile down at the picture he's referring to. "Those are the friends I was telling you about at lunch. The blond is Sydney, the taller one with the dark hair is Liz, and the one that looks like she's trying to squeeze the life out of me, that's my best friend, Sam."

"You and Sam grew up together, right?"

"Yep." I smile to myself, happy that he was actually listening to all of my ramblings earlier. "Sam and I've known each other since we were kids. We didn't meet Sydney and Liz until a few years ago when we were all working together at the courthouse downtown."

Nix looks at the picture again and then back up at me. "And they've all moved away?"

"Unfortunately," I give him a sad smile. "Sydney's recently engaged, and her fiancé is a musician, so she's been touring around with him all summer. Liz took a new job in Washington D.C. several months ago, and as I mentioned at lunch, Sam moved to California a couple of years ago to live with her now husband in L.A. They're the ones who got married this past spring."

"You must miss them."

"So much," I admit. "It's hard being back here without them, especially Sam."

Nix returns the picture to my dresser and grabs the one next to it. "And who's this?"

"That's Vick," I tell him. "He's a friend," I tack on at the end, feeling very uncomfortable all of a sudden. "Or used to be a friend, I guess. We don't really talk anymore."

"Right. Your friend, Vick. Is he the one you were talking about earlier?" I nod and Nix quickly puts the picture back in its place and doesn't ask anything further.

Memories of the day that picture was taken flash through my mind, as I grab a duffle bag from my closet and continue packing my things. Vick loves selfies, and he insisted we take one in front of this bizarre turtle sculpture that he had fallen in love with on one of our lunch dates in Atlanta. Right before he snapped the picture, he turned to kiss my cheek. My eyes are wide from the surprise attack, but I'm smiling like crazy. It's my favorite picture of the two of us, but that day was also the beginning of the end. We went on our first official date a few days after that, and it was all downhill from there.

"Ready?" I step out of my bathroom and Nix is standing in the doorway of my bedroom, leaning against the frame. He's staring in my direction, but not at me. "Are you ready to go?" I ask again, getting his attention this time.

"Yeah. Sorry." He comes toward me and takes the bag from my hand. Such a gentleman.

Mom is piddling around the kitchen when we enter the living room. She steps out, wiping her hands on a dish cloth, but she's not fooling me. She looks suspicious, and even though I'm nearing thirty years old, I wouldn't be surprised if she was eavesdropping on our entire conversation.

"We're heading out," I tell her. "I'll be back later."

"It was nice to meet you." Nix offers another sweet smile, but the one my mom gives him in return is forced and tight.

"Nice to meet you, Nix."

I gesture for Nix to walk out before me then turn to glare at my mom. She shrugs innocently, which angers me even further. I shake my head and walk out the door before I say anything I'll regret.

CHAPTER EIGHT

"I don't think your mom likes me very much," Nix says after we get in the van. He's smiling, but for some reason, I get the feeling it bothers him.

"Believe it or not, she used to be a nice person," I tell him. "I wish I could say she used to be less judgmental, but unfortunately, that seems to be engrained in her DNA. You should hear her and her friends when they get together. No one is safe."

"Well, gossiping is like a religion in the South, right?"

"Most definitely," I agree. "And it's all fun and games until you're the subject of that gossip. Of course my mom used it all to her advantage, turned it into sympathy to help her cause. Some of us aren't so lucky."

"And why would someone gossip about you, sweet Rose?"

I force a smile, not really interested in talking about my own divorce. "People in this town will gossip about anything and everything. Like you said, we take that pastime seriously down here."

"Good to know."

I can tell Nix knows there's something I'm not telling him, but I'm glad he doesn't push. As a matter of fact, he changes the topic to *Geoffrey's* and all of the things David has him working on. I get excited listening to all of the new improvements.

"David's lucky to have you around," I tell Nix, after he goes through his "honey-do" list. "You're quite the handy man."

"I don't know about that." Humility is downright adorable on him. "But I'd do anything for David. He's like a second father to me, and it's about time *Geoffrey's* gets a face lift. It's such a beautiful place."

"I completely agree. I feel like I owe David a ton as well. He's kind of my happy place these days."

"Lucky guy."

"What did you say?"

"Nothing." Nix shakes his head, and before I can decide if what I heard was a figment of my imagination or not, we're arriving at *Geoffrey's*.

"So where is your place exactly?" I ask, before he hops out of the van.

"It's in Evanswood, if I'm remembering the name correctly."

"Yes, Evanswood is about twenty miles from here, and if you were aiming for secluded and remote, you nailed it."

Evanswood is one of those "blink and you might miss it" kind of towns. I didn't even know people lived there.

"Secluded and remote were top priorities on my list," Nix smiles. "The cabin is a couple of miles off Highway fifty-two, on Shiloh Road."

"I think I know where we're going, but I'll follow you, just in case."

"Stay close."

Nix gives me a wink, then shuts the door of the van and hops into his Jeep. I pull out behind him, silently praying for my heart's sake that he never winks at me like that again. Then I obey his orders and follow him for what feels like an eternity, due to the narrow two lane roads that lead to Evanswood. But at least it's a beautiful drive—like a winding path cut straight through the woods, nothing but trees and lush greenery on either side.

Eventually, Nix takes a right at an old wooden mailbox and as soon as his place comes into view, I stare at the cabin in wonder. It's definitely small, but very well kept—the picture-perfect cottage in the woods.

I park the van and join Nix on the porch. "It's amazing. How did you find this place?"

"One of David's regulars owns it." Nix moves to pick a few weeds from one of the flower boxes. "Apparently, it's been vacant for a while. The man seemed happy to have someone using it again."

"This used to be a favorite getaway for Mr. Lowell and his wife," I muse, realizing immediately whose cabin this is because I remember him talking about it. "He mentions their trips to the cabin often, but I didn't know he still owned it. She's been gone for a long time."

"Apparently, they used to like to fish together." Nix unlocks the door and we step inside. "There's a Jon Boat and some nice equipment in the garage that he says I'm welcome to use. He said it's the only thing he couldn't bring himself to get rid of."

"You like to fish?" I ask, as I look around the small space.

"I do." When I look back at Nix, he's still near the door, watching me. "So, what do you think?"

"I love it." I give him an honest smile. "I'm surprised by how many windows there are. All of the natural light is wonderful. And the backyard..." I stare out the sliding doors toward the dark, running waters of the creek in the distance. "No wonder Mr. Lowell and his wife loved this place."

I'm so lost in the scenery, I barely notice Nix come to stand beside me. "I think I'm going to like it here," he says quietly, and when I look over at him this time, a moment passes between us that I know I won't forget for as long as I live.

Suddenly, Nix clears his throat and I blink away the bewilderment. "Why don't we go get the things from the van?" he suggests. "If you don't mind, I'd love your help getting everything organized and put away."

"Sure," is all I can manage, then I follow him to the front door so we can grab his many purchases from today.

I have no idea what's going on between us, but it feels big–bigger than friends, bigger than...everything, but I can't be sure. I can't trust myself to know if this is real because I've been proven wrong too many times. I only know that Nix has come into my life for a reason. Whether it's for me to help him or him to help me, I'm not really sure. But I'm certainly looking forward to finding out.

****

It took Nix and me a couple of hours to get everything unpacked and put away, then I changed into my work uniform and made my way to *Geoffrey's*.

"So how did it go today?" David asks as soon as I enter the kitchen.

"It was great." I put my purse in the desk drawer then grab an apron from the hook outside the office door. "Nix was easy to please.

We only went to two stores, then I helped him get everything put away. The cabin is lovely."

"Well, I hate that I missed it but hopefully, you two had a nice time."

I look up at him just in time to catch the guilty look on his face. I glance over at the good-as-new refrigerator and realize that Nix and I were definitely set up.

With my hands on my hips, I cock an eyebrow at David. "Get the refrigerator fixed?"

"Sure did." He's focusing awfully hard on snapping those green beans. "It was just a fuse. No problem."

"Mmmm hmmm."

David won't look at me, but the smile trying to break through on his guilty face proves he knows I'm on to him. I decide to drop it, however, because I'm secretly grateful for the favor.

I move next to him and grab a handful of green beans. "Let me do this, so you can get to work on the main courses....Mr. Matchmaker."

David's smile finally bursts into a laugh. "I have no idea what you're talking about, so you just get to preparing my vegetables while I take care of the rest."

I shake my head with a smile and do as I'm told. The regulars start showing up about thirty minutes after opening, and by the end of the night, we've seen several customers, including a few walk-ins, which was a pleasant surprise. I did my best to help make their visit a memorable one and each of them loved the food and agreed to be back again soon.

"It was a good night," David remarks as I grab my purse from his office. "You always manage to charm the devil out of everyone that comes in. You're such a blessing, my angel."

"You're the blessing." I lean over and give David a kiss on the cheek. "Have a good night."

"Let me walk you to the door," David insists, but I shake my head.

"I'll be fine. You finish up in here. I'll see you tomorrow."

David reluctantly agrees, so I slip out quickly before he changes his mind and doesn't get his paperwork done for the evening. He's terrible about doing his paperwork.

The temperature today was record-breaking, and the second I step outside, the left-over humidity covers me like a wet blanket. I immediately go for the buttons on my long-sleeved shirt and yank it off, thankful I have on a tank-top underneath.

"Hey there."

After I jump a good three feet into the air, I place a hand over my chest, hoping that's enough to keep my heart in its rightful place. "Are you trying to give me a heart attack?"

I turn around to find Nix lounging in one of the rocking chairs on the porch, struggling not to laugh.

"I didn't mean to scare you."

"Of course you did." I correct him with a smile. "What are you doing here?"

"Are you ready to go?"

"You're going to follow me home again?" I pause, questioning his sanity. "You know that's not necessary, right?"

"Yes, I know." Nix stands and takes a few steps closer to me. "It's just that…I have this messed up…"

He shakes his head and runs a hand over his hair. Why's he so flustered? God, I wish it wasn't so endearing. And sexy. *Really* sexy.

"You don't think I can make it home without your supervision?" I'm pleased I'm able to tease a smile out of him.

"Oh, I think you'll be just fine."

"Well then why do you insist on doing this?"

Nix crosses his arms and glances around nervously. What did I say this time?

"It's not that I don't appreciate it," I quickly add, afraid I may have insulted him. "I don't think I've ever experienced this level of gallantry in my life."

"That's a shame."

His smile is back. I'm always happy to see his smile.

"You know what? If you have nothing better to do with your time than follow me home, so be it," I tease him again. "I guess I should take advantage while I can, since I'm sure you'll find something better to occupy your time soon enough."

I have no idea what made me say that, or why I felt this rough squeeze on my heart as soon as the words came out, but I smile to cover it all up. I can't expect him to follow me home every night. Even though I want him to. Every day. For the rest of my life.

Stop it, Rose!

Right in the middle of me working out my internal debate, a warm hand lands on my forearm, but it's gone before I can fully appreciate the energy that just zinged between us.

"I'm sorry." My eyes fly to Nix's and his are just as wide as mine.

I look down at my tingling forearm then back up at him. "It's okay."

I decide I need to say something else before things get even more awkward, but awkward doesn't begin to describe what happens as I instinctively reach out to touch his arm in consolation.

Nix yanks his arm back with such force that he nearly trips and falls back into the rocking chair behind him. It's amazing how quickly tears flood my eyes, but I'm not sure if it's from the rejection or because I'm scared for him.

I put a hand over my mouth and take a few steps backward. I feel like I should leave. He obviously needs his space, but the look on his face has me rooted to my spot on the porch. It's clear his reaction was just as instinctive as mine.

"Dammit." He rubs at the back of his neck, his eyes focused on his shoes. "You just...startled me. I'm so sorry, Rose."

I don't say anything for a moment because even though I believe he's sorry, it doesn't make me feel any better about what happened.

"Nix?"

I want him to look at me, but it takes me calling his name once more for him to look up. Still, his eyes barely glance across mine before he's staring off into the distance.

"Nix, I know we just met, so I have no right to ask anything from you..." I trail off, questioning my motives, but I have to know. "I'm not going to ask you anything about what just happened, but what I need to hear is whether or not that was about me or something else entirely."

Nix's eyes are back on mine in a flash. "Truth?"

"Always."

"Well, then the truth is..." Nix takes a step closer, too close. "You scare the shit out of me, Rose."

My mouth pops open in shock. "I scare you? Why would I...How could I...?" My words are barely sputtering out, so I decide I should stop while I'm ahead.

"I'm not sure I can explain it." Nix exhales his frustration. "I'm not even sure I even understand it myself. I just know that from the moment we met you became...*necessary*."

Nix takes a step back and I'm grateful. I can't think clearly with him so close to me.

"*Necessary*?" I repeat, attempting to make sense of what he's telling me.

"Yes. Necessary," Nix confirms. "And that's about all I know at this point. I hope it's enough."

I stare up at him and oddly enough, I get it. Whatever this is that's happening between us, I'm not exactly sure I could describe it in detail either, but I can understand *necessary*. And I can understand his fear as well. We both need to take this slowly, and I appreciate the reminder.

"It's enough," I assure him. "And I guess I can be relieved you don't think I'm completely revolting."

Nix laughs as intended over my little tension breaker. "I think you're only mildly disgusting. No worries."

"Well that makes me feel so much better." I smile. "Thank you for being so kind."

"My pleasure." Nix is smiling again as if nothing ever happened, and for some reason, that gives me hope. "Now let's get you to your bell tower safely, Quasimodo."

CHAPTER NINE

"I need details. Right this second."

I turn my head to find Lila walking toward me. Her short, black hair is spikey and wet and she's wearing one of her velour track suits, which tells me she must have just come from her water aerobics class. She's also wearing a smile that is positively contagious.

"What are you babbling about?" I turn back to my duty of wiping down tables before we open. "Details on what, exactly?"

Lila comes to stand right next to me. I notice one of her sneakered feet tapping, and when I look up, her hands are on her hips and her shrewd blue eyes are sizing me up. I know what she wants. Over the last couple of weeks, Nix and I have spent almost every minute of our free time together, but I'm sorry–very, very sorry–to report I have no juicy details to discuss.

"I've been trying to keep my cool," Lila explains. "But I can't stand it any longer. So please give this old lady a break and fill me in on the gossip. Has there any been talk of marriage? You two would make beautiful babies."

"Lila!" I smack her upper arm as we both start to laugh. "For starters, you're not old."

"I'm fifty-three. That's old."

"Age is a state of mind," I remind her. "Secondly, Nix and I are just friends."

I can't help the frown that slides across my face with the word "friends". Unfortunately, Lila notices it and has no intention of ignoring it.

"Does he know how you feel about him?"

"What do you mean?"

Lila gives me a look as if I'm nuts for thinking she can't see right through me, but I don't care. I'm not ready to admit any of this out loud. I haven't even had that conversation yet with myself.

With a resigned sigh, Lila shrugs her shoulders. "I won't push you on this, but I've been around a long time and I see the way that boy looks at you. So if you have any feelings for him at all, I don't see any reason the two of you shouldn't be a couple."

"You're sweet, Lila, but I'm not sure Nix thinks of me that way."

I stare at my friend, wondering if she could be right—secretly hoping that she is—but in reality I have no idea what's going on in Nix's head. Sometimes I still get the feeling that there's something there, something *more*. But regardless of the time we've spent together, I still know very little about him and that includes how he feels about me. Telling me I was "necessary" a couple of weeks ago was the first and last time he's mentioned anything at all about his feelings for me and I haven't pushed. Selfishly, I keep hoping I won't have to.

"How do you know how he feels?" Lila challenges. "Have you asked him?"

"No." My answer is quick and firm. "And I love you, Lila, but this conversation is over. Nix and I are friends. And I'm fine with that."

"For now."

"Forever, if necessary."

I'm lying and Lila knows it, but thankfully, she agrees to give it a rest.

"Okay then. Suit yourself." She pulls her purse strap up higher on her shoulder and gives me a wink before walking away.

I go back to wiping tables, but look up when Lila calls my name from the doorway.

"You know I just want you to be happy, right?"

"I know." I smile at my friend. "And I am happy. I promise."

"For now." Lila gives me another wink and is down the hall before I have a chance to reply.

Her persistence is frustrating, but I know she's right. In only three short weeks, I've found I miss him when he's not around. I crave his company, his familiar scent, the sound of his voice. But then at night, I toss and turn in my bed, scared to death by my growing feelings for him. I know he's worth it. It's risking my own heart again that scares me the most.

When I finish up with my opening duties, I head toward the front to unlock the door. Within the first hour, I can tell it's going to be a slow night, so I plant myself in David's office to try and organize his neglected paperwork. After I finish that, I spend the rest of the evening trying to find enough menial tasks to keep my mind occupied so I don't spend all my time analyzing my feelings for Nix. Of course none of it works, and by the time the night is over, my brain is exhausted from the effort.

David insists I head home as soon as I'm finished closing up the dining rooms, but I protest, refusing to leave him alone to finish up in the kitchen.

"I've got this," he tells me. "You just go on home and get some rest. Have a good night, angel."

With a resigned sigh, I give him a kiss on the cheek and say goodbye. I do hate leaving him, but a hot shower and my bed are sounding really good right about now.

However, when I walk out the front door, I'm surprised to find a sleeping Nix in the driver's seat of his Jeep. I have a feeling this may be why David rushed me off this evening, but I'm so relieved to see Nix, I don't take the time to think about anything else.

He must have come here straight from the airport, obviously exhausted from his second trip out to California in the past three weeks. He was probably worried that he wouldn't make it here in time to follow me home, like he has almost every night since we've met.

I wrap my arms around my middle to try and keep myself from bursting apart with affection for him. I've never had a man in my life treat me with this much care and kindness. I used to think all of his compassion—coming at a time when I needed it the most—was the cause of my growing feelings for Nix, but now I know that's not the case. As I watch him sleep, I think about all of the time we've spent together—decorating his place and slowly making it his own, eating together, watching movies together and even when we're not together, I'm thinking of him and smiling. Always smiling.

I walk toward the Jeep as quietly as possible so I don't wake him, watching his broad chest rise and fall with even breaths, enjoying the sight of his peaceful face as he rests. As always, the doors and top of his Jeep are off, so I can see his long legs are bent, straddling the steering wheel while his arms are crossed loosely over his stomach. His face is pointed in my direction as if he were watching the front door, waiting for me to come out and simply fell asleep.

When I'm close enough, the urge to reach out and touch him is so great it's hard to deny myself the pleasure. But the rare opportunity to stare at him like this, openly, shamelessly, is well worth the torture. He's so beautiful, and it's more than his face and body that keep me riveted. It's all of him. It's everything. He listens to me. He takes care of me. When I'm around him, I feel important. I feel like myself again—someone who could put a positive spin on anything, who saw the world with love and hope instead of caution and regret. With him, I matter. With him, I feel worth it.

Without thinking, I lift my right hand to his face and cup his cheek. His skin is warm and prickly from what looks like a couple of days without a razor, but it feels amazing. As always, that familiar current is there when I touch him, and to my surprise, he doesn't jump at the contact. Instead, he nuzzles into my palm and takes a satisfied breath.

"*Rose...*"

I startle, assuming I've woken him, although his eyes aren't open. But the longing in his raspy voice when he said my name has me caressing his scruffy cheek with my thumb instead of removing my hand as I should. Nix nuzzles even further in as I gently stroke at his skin, and I shake my head in wonder. He'd never allow me to touch him like this if he were awake, so he must still be sleeping.

"Rose..." My name is barely a whisper from his lips, but the night is as quiet as it is dark, so I can hear him perfectly. "Rose...I missed you..."

My hand is trembling now against his cheek. "I missed you too," I breathe into the darkness, and his eyes suddenly open.

For a brief moment, I see it. That look. All of the emotions that have been stirring inside me since I've met him, I see them reflected in his chocolate-brown eyes. But it's one of those moments that flashes by so quickly you're not sure if what you really saw was truth or just what your crazy in love mind wants to see.

Then to add insult to injury, after our short but lovely moment in time passes, Nix's eyes widen to the size of silver dollars before he jerks his face from my hand and sits up straight in his seat. He grabs the steering wheel so forcefully his knuckles go white, as I wrap my arms back around my middle, trying to act like yet another rejection from him doesn't hurt like a knife to the gut.

I notice Nix's arms are shaking, either from me startling him or how hard he's gripping the steering wheel. He's obviously exhausted and disoriented, and suddenly, I feel bad for what I did. I've found Nix can be jumpy on a good day. I shouldn't have abused his trust by touching him like that.

"I'm sorry." I look down at my shoes, hoping he's not too angry with me. "I didn't mean to scare you."

I keep my eyes on my feet, but I can hear Nix taking long, slow breaths. I must have really spooked him, and the embarrassment and awkwardness on my end are becoming more unbearable by the second.

By the time I muster up the courage to risk a glance, his weary head is leaned back against the seat and his palms are spread flat on his thighs. I wish he would look at me so I could see his eyes, but their currently focused intently on the windshield in front of him. God, I wish I knew what he was thinking.

"I really am sorry," I say again, my voice small and weak and I hate it, but I can't help my vulnerability in this moment with him. "You must be so tired from your trip. I appreciate you coming here tonight, but maybe you should head home and get some rest. I'll be fine, really."

"Stop it." Nix interrupts my nervous prattling. "Stop apologizing. You didn't do anything wrong."

"I shouldn't have done that," I admit with a shaky breath. "I know how you feel about...I shouldn't have taken advantage..."

I can't make myself say it because I'm not sure if I am sorry. I'm sorry for abusing his trust, but not for touching him. I could never be sorry for that. And the way he whispered my name, dreaming or not, made it all the more worth it.

Nix closes his eyes briefly then turns back to me. "Let's just get going, okay?"

I nod and walk quickly over to the van. The second my behind hits the seat, tears start trickling down my cheeks. It's ridiculous I know. I can't really be upset with him. This was my fault. I took the risk, knowing the consequences. Nix has never led me on. He's an honest man. And all of those gentlemanly acts? They're not exclusive to me. The same rules apply everywhere and for everyone, as if they're a part of who he is, how he's made.

By the time we make it to my house, my tears have dried up and I'm feeling a little better. I can always justify Nix's rejections by realizing they could be worse. Some may hurt more than others, but he's still around. He still follows me home every night. He still asks me to help him fix up his cabin, go to the hardware store with him and have lunch or dinner with him. We've been to the movies together, hiking together, swimming together. He even volunteered to spend more time with my mom in an effort to get her to warm up to him. It hasn't worked, of course, but I'm still hopeful.

The bottom line is that if he were as turned off by me as his frequent denials make me feel, he wouldn't still be around. Nix is a nice guy, but I don't get the impression he does things to please other people. I think he's been through enough to know that life is too short to waste time on insignificance. Personally, I couldn't agree more.

And I think it's about time I challenge that philosophy.

Instead of heading to the front door tonight when I arrive at my mom's house, I turn and walk toward Nix's Jeep as it idles in front of the driveway. In the dim glow of the streetlight, I can see his brow furrow in confusion, but I keep walking until I'm standing at the passenger's side. Determined to start practicing some level of honesty with him, instead of being afraid of my feelings, I climb into the seat and turn to face him.

"Is something wrong?" he asks and I shake my head.

"I wanted to tell you something."

"Okay. What's going on?"

Nix seems a little nervous, and that's okay because so am I, but I swallow back my anxiety and take a deep breath.

"I missed you."

Nix blinks, opens and closes his mouth a couple of times, but nothing ever comes out. And he's so positively adorable, I could cry.

"I realize you weren't awake, so you probably don't remember, but you said you missed me," I explain. "I have no idea if you meant it or if you were dreaming, but either way, I want you to know that I missed you and I'm glad you're back."

Nix's eyes glide over every inch of my face, heating my already flushed skin.

"And I'm not sorry for touching you like that," I continue, ignoring my racing pulse for now. "I know touching makes you…uneasy, and I shouldn't have violated your trust, but I'm an affectionate person by nature and sometimes I just can't help it."

Nix still hasn't said anything, and I keep quiet a moment, allowing my words to fully sink in. I don't regret what happened tonight. I did miss him. Tremendously. It's important that he knows that, even if I'm not ready to confess exactly how much.

Eventually realizing I'm most likely not getting anything more out of Nix this evening, I give him a smile and hop out of the Jeep. "Goodnight Nix."

I wave before turning to walk away, and I'm not sure why, but the fact that I left him speechless feels like a win in my book. I smile the entire walk to my door and I'm still smiling a half hour later when I get out of the shower and climb into bed.

Out of habit now, I check my phone one last time before I turn out the light. The first text from Nix is standard issue.

Sweet dreams, Rose.

That text is what has me checking my phone every night before bed, because the words never seem to get old, no matter how many nights I read them. But it's the next text that breaks my smile into a full blown, practically-causing-my-room-to-glow-with-its-light kind of smile.

I missed you too.

He missed me. Probably not nearly as much as I missed him, but any amount, big or small, is enough. Just the idea of him thinking of me once while he was away has me giddy. So giddy in fact that I know I'll never go to sleep tonight, but I hardly care. Nix is back. And he missed me. For now, that's all I need to know.

CHAPTER TEN

I toss and turn for an hour before deciding to give up on sleep for the evening.

I quietly make my way into the kitchen, open the door to the refrigerator and grab the orange juice from the middle shelf. I pour myself a glass and stand in the dark as I enjoy my refreshing beverage, then head back to my room, opting for my Kindle over watching TV. But after only a few pages in, I quickly realize there's no book in the world that could hold my attention right now. I put my Kindle back in the drawer of my nightstand and throw myself into my pillows with an aggravated sigh. Immediately, I know what I need and when I glance at my clock, I'm relieved to see that, due to the time difference between here and California, she'll most likely still be up.

I quickly grab my phone and dial my best friend. She answers on the second ring.

"Hey Rose! It's good to hear from you!"

"Hi Sam. How are you?"

"I'm great! Wait..." she pauses on the other line, and I know she's looking at a clock. "Why are you calling me this late? Is everything ok?"

"It's fine," I quickly reassure her. "I just needed to hear my bestie's voice."

"Awww. I miss you too."

Her sentiment brings me back to the reason for my call. "Sam, I kind of need your advice."

"Of course."

Sam and I are good about staying touch, but I haven't told her about Nix. I've thought about it, but I wasn't sure what to say. Until now.

The way I missed him this last time he was gone, only solidified what I've known all along. For me, he's more than just a friend– much, much more. Now I'm scared and need some sort of validation, and who better to get that from than your best friend.

"I've sort of met someone," I tell her. "But it's complicated. I need your help."

"Someone new? What happened between you and Vick?"

I wince, forgetting I hadn't told Sam about that either. "Well, we went on a few dates. I thought everything was going well, but he quickly proved me wrong by never calling again."

"Oh Rose." The sadness in Sam's voice makes my heart hurt all over again. "I'm so sorry. I had no idea."

"It's not a big deal," I promise her. "I think I miss his friendship more than anything. As you know, we had gotten really close. For a while, he made living without you a little more bearable."

"I miss you so much, Rose. You know that."

"I know." We both laugh sad little laughs. "But I also know how happy you are, and I wouldn't trade your happiness for anything in the world."

I wipe the tear from my cheek, and Sam sniffs into the phone, both of us obviously feeling a little emotional this evening.

"So, tell me about this new man?" Sam says excitedly. "He better be good to you. Is he a hottie?"

"He is good to me, and he's definitely a hottie." I laugh. "Let me send you a picture."

I pull my phone from my ear so I can text her my only a picture of him. Nix isn't really big on having his photo taken, so I had to sneak it.

I sit and admire the photo a moment after I press send. It was taken last weekend when Nix and I went for a long hike at Red Creek Mountain. I realized my boot was untied just as we reached the top, so I bent to tie it as Nix walked ahead. When I stood back up, he was standing on the crest, his stance wide, his arms crossed over his broad chest as he gazed out over the scenery. He looked like a god safeguarding his kingdom, and I immediately reached into the back pocket of my shorts, took out my phone and snapped a picture, knowing it would be an image of him worth revisiting.

"*Wow.*" I hear Sam breathe, so I quit gawking and pull my phone back to my ear. "Are those tattoos I see? And is he really that huge, or does this picture just do him all kinds of justice? Good gracious, Rose."

"Yes, those are tattoos. And yes, he's a pretty big guy," I laugh again. "He has piercings too."

"Oh really?"

"He has one under his bottom lip, and..." I hesitate, wondering what Sam will think, but I know her well enough to know she'll probably think it's as sexy as I do.

"And *what*, Rose?" Sam questions before I have a chance to finish.

"His nipples are pierced."

"Seriously?"

I smile at the obvious appreciation in her tone. "Seriously."

"And how do you know this?"

The excitement in Sam's voice keeps me smiling. "I've seen him without his shirt on, but it's not what you think."

I pull my phone from my ear so I can look at his picture once more. Just the thought of him shirtless has me all hot and bothered, but even better are his...

"I wish the picture was at a better angle," I tell Sam. "I wish you could see his eyes."

"Oh, his profile works just fine."

"It's not bad," I agree. "But he has these incredible eyes, so dark brown they're almost black. And in the sun they have these flecks of gold in them. Really unique."

"Oh my. Listen to you, my little smitten kitten." Sam's teasing voice breaks me from my lust-filled Nix haze. "You really like this guy, don't you?"

"I do, but that may be a problem."

"Well, with the tattoos and piercings, I know your mom's probably not a fan. I hope she's been cordial."

I tell Sam about the first time he and Mom met, and we both have a laugh over Mom thinking he was robbing the place.

"Good for him for not getting his feelings hurt too badly," Sam says. "But something tells me your mom isn't the main problem."

"No." I sigh. "She's not."

"Talk to me, bestie. What's going on?"

"The problem is we're friends." I relax into my bed with another sigh. "And sometimes I think that's all we may ever be."

"No way." Picturing the defiance on Sam's pretty face makes me smile. "He's not blind, right? So there should be no question on whether or not he's attracted to you."

"He may be attracted to me, but I was hoping for a little more than that."

"How long have you known him?" she questions. "It sounds like you're already in deep, so I assume you've known him a while? And if so, why am I just now hearing about this guy?"

"I've actually only known him a few weeks," I admit. "But it wasn't until just recently, when he went out of town for a few days, that I realized I couldn't ignore the way I feel about him any longer. Honestly, I think I've had feelings for him since the second I laid eyes on him."

"So what's his problem? You're smart, beautiful, single...oh no, Rose. Is he married or something?"

"He's single," I quickly confirm, but then realize I have no idea if Nix is seeing anyone or not. "Either way, nothing has happened between us so it doesn't matter."

"Does he know how you feel?"

"Not really, and after everything that happened with Vick, I'm a little hesitant to tell him. I don't want to lose his friendship."

"Tell me more about him," Sam urges. "What's he like?"

I tell Sam everything I know, which isn't much. I tell her how we first met, his relationship to David, his brief mention of being in the Army and everything he does for me, including following me home every night to make sure I'm safe. Sam's quiet for a moment or two after I'm done.

"That's very interesting," she finally says. "And I don't want to overstep my boundaries, since I'm not there, but based on what you're telling me—and what an incredible person we all know *you* are—I would say it sounds like he has feelings for you too."

"But he won't let me touch him," I blurt out, then immediately wish I hadn't. That little issue seems private for some reason, something that should be kept between Nix and me.

"What do you mean?"

"He doesn't want me to touch him. At all," I explain. "And you know how I am, hugging and touching without thinking twice about it. I've had to tamper all of that down around him and it's killing me, in more ways than one."

"Rose, is he...okay?"

I know she's asking whether or not he's stable enough for me to be around, but the worry in her tone tells me she's not being judgmental. She's only being a good friend.

"Outside of the no touching rule, he's wonderful," I tell her. "Since he doesn't ever tell me anything about himself, I assume maybe his time in the Army has something to do with his fear of affection."

"I don't know, Rose. Now that you're telling me all of this, I'm a little leery of this guy. You said so yourself. You barely know anything about him."

"Okay, that's enough worrying," I say calmly, trying to reassure her. "And remember, David has known him his whole life."

Sam knows all about David from me and has come to trust him like I do. "Okay, I forgot about the David connection, but I'll still say that secrets are never a good thing, Rose. I would try and keep your guard up until he's willing to open up to you. He's good looking for sure, but he's potentially full of baggage and more trouble than he's worth."

"I think he's worth it," I counter, always quick to defend him. "But I agree I need to keep my guard up. I've been telling myself that over and over, but it helps to hear it from someone else."

"I'm just worried for you," Sam soothes. "What does David say about him?"

"He has only nice things to say about Nix and his family, but I haven't really asked for many details. I think David may actually want us together, and I don't want to lead anyone on."

"I understand," Sam agrees. "But I don't think there's any harm in asking David a few questions. And I'm sure if you let David know your concerns, he would keep it to himself."

"Maybe, but probably not."

Sam laughs. "Yeah, I guess you're right. David seems like the kind of person that may twist the information to get what he wants, especially in this scenario, but maybe that works to your advantage as well."

"I don't know." I sigh, feeling discouraged. "I think I violated Nix's trust tonight with my inability to keep my hands off of him while he slept."

"You did *what*?"

I put a hand over my eyes as I tell Sam the story. "I still can't believe I did that."

"Well at least he admitted he missed you too," Sam reminds me. "I think he likes you more than you know, but promise me you'll be careful. I can't bear the thought of you getting hurt again, especially when I'm thousands of miles away."

"I'll be okay." I try to force some confidence into my voice. "By the way, have I mentioned I miss you like crazy?"

"I miss you too," Sam laughs. "And speaking of missing my friends...I spoke to Sydney a few days ago."

"Awww, how is Sydney?" I smile, thinking about our vivacious friend. "Still touring with Simon, or are they back?"

"They're currently in Paris, so you know Sydney's most likely shopping like a fiend."

"Oh, she must be in heaven. Simon's poor bank account."

"Whatever. We both know Simon would buy Sydney the moon, if she wanted it," Sam declares, and I have to agree.

"So is she coming back to Atlanta soon?" I ask Sam. "I thought I remembered her saying the last stop was Germany."

"The tour ends the first week in September. She told me they had planned to spend the few weeks before the wedding back here in L.A., but since they're having the wedding in the Bahamas with only the two of them, I asked her about maybe doing a wedding shower in Delia before they leave."

"No way! What did she say?"

My friends back in Delia? This may be the best news I've heard in months!

"She thought it was a fabulous idea," Sam tells me. "This way she gets to have her wedding cake and eat it too."

"Sounds like Sydney," I laugh. "I still can't believe Sydney wanted a private ceremony with only she and Simon. I guess I understand the sentimental appeal of the Bahamas for both of them, but I always assumed Sydney's wedding would rival that of British royalty."

"I know, right?" Sam laughs too. "But love changes everything, and I think it's definitely changed Sydney for the better."

"I completely agree," I say, trying to ignore the pinch in my chest as I selfishly wish for the kind of love my friends have found. "Just make sure to keep me updated on the details."

"I will," Sam promises. "Sydney mentioned late September. We just need to think of a place to have it."

All of a sudden, the most fabulous idea pops into my head. "How about *Geoffrey's*? I told you Nix has been doing some work on the place. I'm sure he can have the new deck finished by then, and it would be the perfect spot for this. What do you think?"

"I think that sounds amazing!" Sam agrees. "We'll have to chat again soon and figure out the details. I'm sure Sydney will love it!"

I smile, feeling happy about the possibilities this may bring for David, and of course I can't wait to see my friends again. It's been too long and their faces are exactly what I need right now. Just a couple of months. I can work with that.

We say our goodbyes and I toss my phone on my nightstand before turning off the light and sinking down into my bed. I close my eyes and immediately think of Nix as the quiet darkness settles in around me. I wonder what he's doing right now. Is he sleeping, or is he wide awake like me, wondering what to do next? Maybe he's wondering if he should tell me how he feels. Or maybe he's thinking about what it would be like to be together in his bed, his arm wrapped around me as I nuzzle into his warm chest and inhale his woodsy scent.

My eyes pop open to the sound of my phone vibrating on my nightstand. I don't rush to check the message, assuming it's Sam sending me a text to tell me something she forgot to say earlier. Instead, I rub my tired, restless eyes and stretch before reaching for my phone. To my surprise, it's from Nix.

And it's just perfect.

Wanted to be the first to say good morning.

In the midst of trying to get the butterflies in my stomach calmed to a dull roar, a giggle bursts from my lips, so I decide to give up the fight. I haven't felt this way about someone in what seems like centuries, and unrequited feelings or not, he makes me happy. Just the thought of him, sitting with his phone in his hands, texting me, thinking of me at the same time I was thinking of him…I have no idea what it all means, but I know it makes me happy.

And as hard as it is to not reply, I know his text was intended to be read in the morning and not in the middle of the night. So I put my phone back on my nightstand, slide back under my covers and fall asleep with a stomach full of butterflies and a smile on my face.

CHAPTER ELEVEN

Still feeling bold from my truth-telling conversation with Nix last night, I decided to call him this morning and invite myself to come help him work on the dock. He's never asked me to join him in the mornings before, so I wasn't sure if I would be facing another rejection or not, but I was so anxious to spend time with him that I really didn't care.

"You want to come and work on the dock with me?" he asks and I'm relieved he sounds shocked, but not at all disapproving.

"If you don't mind." I smile into the phone, just happy to hear his voice. "I'm not terrible with a hammer and nail, and I'll bring breakfast."

"Well then I look forward to it," Nix laughs. "I'll be there in about a half hour. See you then?"

"See you then."

Nix's Jeep is already in the driveway when I arrive, so I gather our coffees and breakfast then head toward the backyard. I find Nix sitting at the edge of the dock, his long legs dangling over the side. It doesn't appear he's aware of my presence, but I know better.

Sneaking up on Nix—when he's awake—is practically impossible. The man misses nothing.

"Coffee?"

He turns toward me and I have to remind myself to breathe. His smile has a tendency to take my breath away. This morning is no exception.

He pops up in one quick, fluid movement that makes me envy his powerful body, while lusting over it at the same time. His black tank-top leaves his colorful arms exposed and already glistening in the blazing summer sun. And shadowed by his favorite San Francisco Pirates ball cap, I can't see his eyes as he approaches me, but that beautiful smile is enough to increase my body temperature by what feels like a few hundred degrees.

"A little hot for coffee, isn't it?"

Dumbfounded by the perfection that is Nix Taylor, it takes me a second to realize he's spoken. "Yes, but that's what iced coffee is for."

I hand him one of the two iced, blueberry coffees I picked up for us at Dunkin' Donuts. It's my favorite drink there, and I hope Nix likes it as well. Believe it or not—even with the amount of time we've spent together over the past few weeks—I may have finally learned his last name, but I still don't know a lot of his preferences. He so rarely talks about himself that it's trial and error until he decides to start helping me out.

He stares at the drink a moment then looks back over at me. "I've never had iced coffee before."

"Seriously? It's amazing. Try it."

He takes a cautious sip, pauses then goes back for more. "It's delicious."

"Told you so."

Nix gulps down half the cup before realizing I have a box of goodies with me as well. "And what's for breakfast?"

I smile as I hand him the box. "I wasn't sure what you liked, so I just got us the sampler box of Munchkins. Not exactly the most wholesome breakfast in the world, but the sugar should keep us going for a while."

"I love donuts."

Nix gestures for me to follow him out to the end of the dock, and we take a seat side-by-side. I watch as Nix puts his coffee down and digs into the tiny donut holes. I immediately notice he has a preference for the blueberry ones, making me even happier about my coffee choice. Plus, the blueberry ones are my favorite as well, and I can't help but to be excited we have something in common, no matter how big or small.

"You've done so much already," I say to Nix as I look around, admiring his work. "It's going to look amazing."

"Thanks." Nix smiles again as he pops another donut into his mouth.

"Are you going to cover the deck?"

Nix has already redone the dock and built the foundation for what will be a huge deck off to the side. Lila, with her shameless spying, told me he's had some guys out here to help him a few times. I have no idea where David got the money to hire anyone, and I don't ask because it's none of my business.

"As much as I hate to cover it because the stars are incredible out here at night, I think it's necessary." He passes me the last blueberry donut with a shy smile. "I'm guessing they're your favorite too."

I take the sugary goodness from his hand with a grin. I notice he doesn't jerk away from me when our fingers touch in the exchange and that makes me grin a little wider.

"How about partially covered?" I suggest. "It looks like there will be plenty of room to leave a small area uncovered. That way we could have the best of both worlds."

"Great idea," Nix agrees, watching me bite into my donut.

My heart skips a beat as he stares at my mouth with unmistakable desire. I've seen this look before. I've always thought it was in my head, but after what happened last night and the sweet text I received early this morning, I wonder...

Testing the situation, I pull the remaining bite of donut from my mouth and offer it to him. "Do you want some? I'm willing to share."

Nix eyes the donut in my proffered fingers then looks back up at me. I can see the hesitation in his eyes, but I extend my fingers a little further in his direction anyway, knowing this is a dangerous game, but I have to know.

I watch, captivated as Nix's brown eyes turn impossibly dark. His tongue slides slowly across his bottom lip, as if he's licking away his final bit of control, then he leans over and takes the last bite from me with his mouth. He grabs my hand to steady it and his eyes close with the contact. I can hear and feel his soft, vibrating groan as his smooth lips slide leisurely over the tops of my fingers.

Dear God, give me strength.

Nix takes one final swipe with his tongue across my fingertips, then releases my hand and his eyes find mine once again. I remain motionless, my hand still raised in offering, my lips parted as I try desperately to find my breath.

"Sorry." Nix has the nerve to smile as he chews. "I couldn't decide what I wanted to taste more, you or the donut, so I went with your idea. Got the best of both worlds."

Nix is good at hiding things, but I can tell what just happened between us put a crack in his carefully constructed walls. He's trying to seem unaffected, but his eyes are gleaming with a barely contained need that I happen to be very familiar with, especially where Nix is concerned.

However, as much as I love seeing that look in his eyes, I drop my hand in my lap and give myself a good mental slap. Sam's right. I'm in way too deep with this man after only knowing him a few weeks and I fear I'm setting myself up for disaster. I shouldn't have goaded him like that. Attraction isn't enough. I'm not interested in having only part of him. I want the whole package. I want him to talk to me. I want to know him. So until he decides to open up, I have to ignore the chemistry between us, no matter how impossible that may seem.

"All right, funny guy." I stand and look down at him with a smirk. "Let's get to work. What can I do to help?"

It's tough acting as unaffected as he seems, but I give it my best shot. My heart can't afford another break, and definitely not from him.

Nix eyes me curiously as he stands. "You don't really have to help me." He takes a step closer, weakening my resolve. "Your company is more than enough."

"And my donuts?" I tease, but Nix quickly puts me in my place with that drop-dead gorgeous smile of his.

"Nope. Just you. The donuts were a happy surprise."

I close my eyes briefly, trying to slow down the emotions, currently spinning out of control inside my head. I wish I knew what he was thinking. I wish he would talk to me.

"I want to help," I tell him, anything to get my mind off his mouth on my fingers. "Believe it or not, I happen to know a few things about construction. My dad built houses for several years and used to take me to job sites with him. I'm no expert, but I know enough to be dangerous."

"Okay then," he concedes. "I plan to finish the flooring of the deck over the next couple of days. I'll grab you a hammer from my tool box. I'm not sure I can trust you with the nail gun quite yet."

I roll my eyes at his teasing then shamelessly admire the back of him as he walks away. Despite the near heart attack I suffered earlier from the donut incident, I have to admit I'm enjoying his good mood this morning. He's been so sad and broody lately, which I assume has to do with his grandfather's declining health, but I can't know for sure. Of course he hasn't said anything to me.

Of course, he hasn't.

Nix walks back to me and hands me a hammer and a box of nails, his pretty white teeth still fully exposed. "Come on. I'll show you where to start."

I sigh deeply before following him. I must be crazy for thinking a man like Nix will ever give me his whole heart, but I refuse to accept anything less. With my chin held high, I kneel beside him on a small part of the deck flooring that's already complete.

"So, give me some direction, boss man."

Nix looks over at the pile of wood stacked next to him. "Rose, could I ask you for something?"

"Sure." I scan the area around us. "You need another tool?"

I move to get up so I can head back over to his toolbox to retrieve whatever he might need, but a large, warm hand on my thigh stops me. His rare touch has the same effect on me every time—stopping everything in motion except my racing heart.

"I don't need another tool." He moves his hand away from my leg and back to his side.

"Then what do you need?"

Nix takes a deep breath. "Patience."

"*Patience?*" I question, begging for an explanation, but as usual, he gives me nothing. "Patience, as in you're a bad teacher? I told you I know a little about construction. Just give me the basics and I'll---"

"I'm not a bad teacher." Nix interrupts me, seeming frustrated.

I'm about to tell him he can't possibly be as frustrated as I am, but then his determined eyes snare mine, leaving me defenseless.

"That's not what I meant," he continues. "I'm asking for patience...with me...in general. Just...be patient. Please."

Nix's face is desperate, practically begging me with his eyes to understand so he doesn't have to say it. Selfishly, I would love to hear him say it. I would love to hear him say anything at this point, but I won't torture him over this. I'll just have to keep drawing my own conclusions for now and hoping for the best. You never know.

"I can do patient," I assure him and watch as his shoulders relax. "But if you ever get the urge, I'm a really good listener."

Nix nods with a smile. "Thank you, Rose."

"Anytime."

Nix grabs a two-by-four from the pile next to him. "How about we build a deck?"

"I thought you'd never ask."

Nix lays the board down for me and gives instructions on how and where to place the nails. He's right. He isn't a bad teacher, and I'm beginning to think there isn't anything Nix Taylor can't do. Other than trust me. That seems to be number one on his list of impossibilities, and no matter my feelings for him, his lack of trust in me will eventually become a problem.

And that's only one of many reasons why I should be careful.

Every time I look at him my heart flares in my chest like a warning signal, a cautionary reminder that he has the power to break me. But warning or not, I know I won't be careful with Nix. I will take the chance. I will foolishly risk my heart again because deep down, I know this man is worth it.

CHAPTER TWELVE

Patience.

Nix asked me for patience, and for the most part, it's been a surprisingly simple request to fulfill. I think it's because I needed the slowdown myself. It's easy to get seduced by Nix's good looks and charm. Even more attractive is how comfortable I am...how happy I feel when I'm around him. And he's getting more comfortable with me every day. Not enough to fully open up yet, but he's shared some tidbits here and there about his family, being in the Army and his time overseas. Nothing groundbreaking, but I cherish every detail.

I've had to keep reminding myself I can't afford to jump into this with both feet. I've tried to focus on my past, remember what's at stake, remember to protect my heart. But the more time I spend with him, the harder it is to ignore my feelings or the burning chemistry between us. I'm constantly fantasizing about what it would be like to have him hold me, what it would feel like to have his strong arms around me or his fingers laced with mine. I crave his rich, masculine scent like a drug. I dream about kissing him, knowing his full lips would taste and feel like heaven as they moved slowly, softly against my own.

I'm trying. I'm pushing back as hard as I can, but lately I've been slipping more and more—my body instinctively reaching out to his, overpowering my exhausted mind and taking matters into its own hands. A poke in his side when he's teasing me. A hand on his arm to get his attention. I even fell asleep on his sofa a few nights ago while we were watching a movie and woke up with my head on his shoulder. My first instinct was to panic, but after a couple of blinks to get my bearings, I realized Nix was asleep as well. His hand was resting on the top of my thigh, his nose buried in the top of my head, breathing me in as he slept. It was everything I could do not to snuggle into him even further, to drown in his warmth, get drunk off his intoxicating scent. But I managed to untangle myself without waking him, leaving him completely unaware that anything ever happened.

I'm trying, but I don't know how much longer I can do this. I don't know how much longer I can hide. It's not me, and I'm beginning to realize that no matter what kind of heartache I've been subjected to in my past, I can't resist putting my whole heart out there. It's the hopeful romantic in me. It's who I am. I can't help falling in love. And with Nix, I may be falling harder than ever before.

Patience.

Mine is wearing thin.

And to top it all off, last night on my way home from work, the minivan breathed its final breath. Thankfully, my faithful bodyguard was following me home and helped me contact a tow service. Nix has helped me with the van a couple of times before, adding mechanic to his long list of talents, but since it was dark out this time and he didn't have any tools on him, he suggested having it towed to a local auto repair shop.

As soon as the owner called this morning to let me know it was the transmission, I knew my money would be better spent on a new car rather than putting anything more into my mom's old clunker. Nix agreed and insisted on taking me car shopping today, since he's convinced I'll get steamrolled if he's not there to help me negotiate. Personally, I think I would have been fine handling the whole car buying process on my own, but I love being around him. And as much as I would prefer to call him something other than "friend", I'm ashamed to say I've settled for taking him any way I can get him. At least for now.

Patience, Rose. Patience.

"Well, I only have around five-thousand to spend," I tell the very slimy sales guy at the first used car dealership we came across in Bristol. "So this one is a little out of my budget."

Despite his many protests, I made Nix promise to stay in his Jeep and give me a chance to handle things on my own. Now I'm second guessing that decision.

The slimy sales guy ratchets up his khaki pants, adjusting himself as I try not to gag.

"I'll tell you what, gorgeous..." Good Lord, this guy is creepy. "I'll cut the price down on this beauty so we can fit that budget of yours. How's that sound?"

I study him with wide eyes. "You're going to cut the price in *half*?"

He gives me a head-to-toe-curling once over then brushes a hand down my arm. "For you? Absolutely."

I'm about to push past the guy and get the heck out of Dodge, when I notice my savior approaching.

"Let's have a look under the hood," Nix demands, and I smile as the salesman turns to size him up.

"Uh...I'll uh...I'll be with you in a moment, sir." The salesman tugs at his shirt collar as he clears his throat. "Just as soon I finish with the lady here."

"Actually, he's with me," I inform the salesman and his face instantly pales.

"I see. Well then...I'm sorry, sir. What was it you requested?"

Nix crosses his arms slowly over his broad chest, walks a couple of steps closer and looks down at the salesman with a smile that promises nothing short of broken bones if he's given anything other than the answer he's looking for.

"I'd like to look under the hood," Nix repeats in a low, confident tone. "You see, I need to make sure my friend is safe, completely protected at all times. And if you sell her a junker that breaks down every other mile and leaves her stranded, then she's not very safe now, is she?"

"Well...I uhhh..."

It seems Nix has left the poor man speechless, which I didn't think possible. I pull my lips between my teeth, fighting back a smile.

"I happen to know a little about cars," Nix continues. "And I know that this piece of shit you're trying to sell her isn't worth a thousand dollars, much less five, unless you're going to surprise me with a Hemi under the hood. So I'll ask you one more time...can I take a look, or should we maybe go check out some other options that might be more suitable for my lady friend here?"

Nix looks over the guy's shoulder and gives me a wink. Then it's another few collar tugs and throat clears before the man can speak again.

"You know what?" His index finger is shaking as he points it at his own temple. "I just remembered that we got a couple of new arrivals in this morning. I'm thinking one of those may be perfect for your friend and meet her budget."

"Sounds like a plan." Nix smiles and punches one of the salesman's shoulders, probably a little harder than necessary. "Let's go take a look, shall we?"

As the salesman rubs at his shoulder, Nix gestures for him to lead the way and then falls in step beside me.

"Thank you," I whisper with a smile. "My own personal negotiator to the rescue."

"Any time," he says with this charming, lop-sided grin of his, and I barely have time to catch my breath before we reach the first of two cars the salesman mentioned.

"Still not good enough." Nix grabs my elbow and turns us away from the salesman, then he leans down and whispers, "If you could have any car on this lot you wanted, what would it be?"

He pulls away from me with a smile, and I take a quick peek around the lot. I immediately notice an older, convertible Volkswagen Beetle. It looks beat-up enough to be in my price range, but possibly still in good running condition.

"I like that one." I point so only Nix can see. "The silver Beetle."

"That's worse than the first one he showed you."

"Probably," I agree. "But I like it, and I happen to know a really good mechanic."

Nix gives me that adorable grin again as he studies me. "It's yours," he concedes with a sigh. "But let me do all the talking, okay?"

I nod enthusiastically as I picture myself driving around in my new convertible. "You got it."

Nix turns us around to face the salesman again. "My friend likes the VW Bug you got over there."

He tosses a thumb backward in that direction, and the salesman has the decency to look nervous.

"Umm...I'm sorry sir, but that's a bit out of her price range."

Nix rubs his chin. "Is it, now?"

I'm about to speak up because the poor sales guy looks like he may have a stroke at any moment, but as if reading my mind, Nix gives me a discreet poke in the side.

"The way I see it," Nix continues, glancing at his watch, "there's still plenty of time left in your day for you to rip off at least a handful of people, but I'm sorry to tell you that my friend won't be one of them. I can see from here that car's seven, eight years old and if I had to guess, probably sporting around a hundred thousand miles. Now we can go test drive it, see if my friend likes it and if she does, and it meets my safety standards, then we'll give you her five-thousand in cash and call it a day. If you don't like that offer, we'll take her money and go elsewhere. Simple as that."

Nix and I both wait for an answer, although Nix seems much more optimistic than me.

"I can guarantee she's gonna love it," the salesman says as he gestures toward the car. "It is a 2006 model, with a little under a hundred thousand miles, but she still drives like a dream. You guys head on over, and I'll go grab the keys from the office."

"Sounds good."

Nix winks at me again as we walk toward what will hopefully be my new car, and I give him a wide smile. "Have I told you lately that you're the absolute *best*?"

"Yes." I love the sound of his laugh–so deep and pleasant. "But you can tell me again, if you'd like."

"You're the best!"

"I'm sorry, I'm not sure I heard you." He cups a hand to his ear. "Could you please repeat that?"

"Seriously?"

"Yeah, still nothing. Maybe a little louder?"

"You're pushing it." I nudge his arm with my shoulder. "But I do appreciate your help today, so for the last time...you're the best!"

"Glad you think so," Nix smiles at me. "But you're better."

Thankfully, we reach the car so I don't have to react to another one of his puzzling remarks.

"I love it even more up close!" I squeal, brushing off his comment for now. "Do you think it's redeemable?"

"I'll give it a look under the hood." Nix walks around the car, giving it a thorough assessment. "And you can tell a lot from a test drive, but from what I can see, you'll be getting a pretty good deal."

Completely caught up in the moment, and not thinking clearly, I rush toward Nix with a huge smile on my face and wrap my arms around his neck. It's not until I hear his breath catch and feel his entire body go tense that I realize I've made a horrible mistake. But this time....

This time I decide not to let go.

This time, I decide to throw caution to the wind, and you can't imagine my shock when I feel his heavy arms wrap around my waist. And when he pulls me close and nuzzles his face into my hair, my heart is beating so wildly I worry it may burst.

With a shuddering breath, I slowly move my hand up and over the back of his head. His short-trimmed hair is impossibly soft and cool to the touch, even with the summer heat, and suddenly I'm lost, dizzied by his heady scent and the feel of his silky hair gliding through my trembling fingers. And just when I think I can't take anymore, a warm hand slides up my back and around my neck, pushing me even further in.

I don't dare let go.

Instead I breathe in a little deeper. I push up on my toes, move my hand to the top of his head and press in a little closer. Nix nuzzles me and sighs, and when I feel his soft lips brush against my neck, I know then my heart is lost forever.

"You guys ready?"

Nix and I pull away at the same time, and I can tell by the shocked look on his face he was just as lost in that moment as I was. Still in a haze, I let my hands slide from around his neck. They hang limply at my sides, and the only things keeping me upright now are Nix's strong arms, still wrapped firmly around me, one hand still clasping the back of my neck.

"Ready for what?"

I assume Nix is asking this question of the salesman, but his eyes are glued to mine...that is until they travel deliberately down to my mouth.

Nix slowly leans in, and I stop breathing completely when his lips are less than an inch away from mine. But at the last minute, Nix shifts and his kiss lands on my cheek instead. His lips linger for a bit, then he takes one last deep inhale before releasing me.

He gives me a sad smile before turning back to the salesman and repeating his question. "Ready for what?"

The man smiles and dangles the keys in front of his own face. "Ready to fall in love, of course!"

Nix shakes his head, mumbling something as he heads for the backseat.

Wait. What was that?

I'm obviously still delirious from whatever that was that just happened between Nix and me.

Completely confused.

Totally irrational.

Because if I did in fact hear what I thought I heard, it sounded a lot like..."I think I just did."

CHAPTER THIRTEEN

Nix and I spent the remainder of the day joy riding in my new-to-me convertible, and even though we didn't speak a word about what happened at the car dealership earlier, there was a positive charge in the air around us that was impossible to ignore. Nix was happier than I'd ever seen him—laughing, teasing and showing me a side of himself I've never seen before. We ate tacos together at *Murphy's*, then drove back to Delia and sat in the driveway of *Geoffrey's*, staring up at the stars as Nix made up ridiculous constellations that had me laughing so hard I was in tears. As always, he followed me home that night and my usual "sweet dreams" text was preceded by one that had me smiling myself to sleep.

Breakfast tomorrow? I look forward to sharing donuts with you.

Needless to say, I woke up this morning still smiling. I showered and dressed in shorts and a tank-top then headed out a little early so I could grab donuts on the way to *Geoffrey's*. With the help of a few contractors, that I'm now fairly certain Nix has been paying for all along, the dock and accompanying deck are almost complete. Nix has chosen to take on the last few details himself, but he's promised that I can help choose the seating and décor for the space. I envision wrought iron and white twinkling lights that will look beautiful reflecting off the dark water of the lake. It will be so romantic and perfect for Sydney's wedding shower. I can't wait to send her and the other girls pictures of the finished product.

It's hard to believe how well everything is coming together. Hope is alive and blooming in my chest as I arrive at *Geoffrey's* around nine with coffee and donuts in hand. I'm so excited to see Nix I can barely keep from running to meet him, but when I reach the backyard, he's not there. I walk closer to the dock, thinking maybe he's behind a railing and out of sight, but he's nowhere to be found. I walk back to the front of the restaurant and realize in my haste to get to him, I hadn't even noticed his Jeep wasn't in the driveway.

I put everything back in my car and climb into the driver's seat. I pull my phone from my purse, hoping to find a text to explain his whereabouts, but there's nothing. I decide to call him instead of texting, wanting a response quickly, before my growing anxiety starts forcing images into my head of him dead in a ditch somewhere on the side of the road. He doesn't answer his phone, which isn't unusual, but I can't shake the gnawing feeling inside that something is wrong. I glance up at David's bedroom window, wondering if he's awake. I decide to try him first since I'm here, rather than drive to Nix's house in a panic.

David answers on the second ring. "Good morning, angel."

The somber tone in David's voice is highly unusual and fuels my fear. "Good morning. Is everything okay?"

"I'm afraid not." David sighs deeply on the other end. "Got a call around six this morning. Nix's grandfather passed away last night in his sleep."

"Oh David, no." I clutch at my chest as a tear slides down my cheek. "I'm so sorry."

"He was such a good man." David's voice is thick with grief and unshed tears. "But we can't live forever. Mr. Taylor led a full, happy life and now he's at peace. God rest his soul."

I sit silently and let a few tears fall before I speak again. "Have you spoken to Nix? I came to meet him this morning, but he didn't show up. I knew something must be wrong."

"Why didn't you tell me you were here?" David scolds. "Come in and let me fix you some tea. You want waffles? I'll make them with powdered sugar and strawberries, just the way you like."

I smile through my tears, thanking God once again that he brought me to David. "I appreciate the offer, but I would like to check on Nix if you think it would be okay."

"I haven't spoken to him," David confesses.

"Does he know about his grandfather?"

"Yes. His mother spoke to him this morning before she called me. She's worried about him too, but I assured her he'll be fine. He's been doing so well since he's been here—stronger and happier than I've ever seen him. He just needs some time."

"I tried calling," I admit. "But he didn't answer. I hope he's okay."

"He'll be fine," David repeats. "This is going to be hard for him. The two of them were very close, but I know Nix would never want his grandfather to suffer."

"Do they have funeral arrangements yet?"

The idea of Nix leaving again makes my heart hurt, especially after the incredible day we shared yesterday. I had even planned to talk to him at some point today to finally confess my feelings. But all I want him to know now is that I'm here for him, willing to support him however he needs. Hopefully, he'll give me the chance.

"They're making funeral arrangements today," David tells me. "I assume we'll hear something back this afternoon."

"Do you plan to go?"

"Probably not." The remorse is obvious in his tone. "I can't really afford the trip right now, but I may be traveling out to visit my aunt in Sacramento this Christmas. I'll make sure to pay my respects then."

I consider offering David the money for a plane ticket, but I don't want to insult him.

"Are you sure you don't want some breakfast, angel?" David asks and I sigh.

"No, thank you. I appreciate the offer though."

What I really want is a way to make it through the day without worrying about Nix to the point of hysteria, but I doubt David could help me with that.

"Rose?"

"Yes?"

"I'm sure he'd love to see you, but I'd give him a little time alone. I doubt he's heading out before tomorrow morning. Come in and grab one of my casserole's from the freezer, take the night off and go take care of him for me."

"I-I can't take the night off," I stutter, shocked by the offer. "Who will help you tonight? You can't do it all alone."

"Lila is perfectly capable. Now come on in. I'm making you waffles, whether you eat them or not."

I look up and smile when I find David staring at me from the front porch. We both pull our phones from our ears at the same time, and I toss mine on the seat before getting out and heading over to him. I give him a big hug and once again express my condolences.

"I'll be just fine," he soothes. "And so will Nix. He's probably fishing, if I had to guess. No point in even driving out to see him until this afternoon. I imagine he'll be out there all morning."

I type a quick text to Nix, letting him know I'm sorry for his loss and I'm here if he needs me, then I manage to force down a few bites of waffles with David before taking a chicken casserole as requested and heading back to Mom's house. It's the last place I want to be, but I need to put the casserole in the refrigerator. I stuff the dish in the fridge, then head back to my room to change into shorts and my running shoes. I decided a few miles at the park is exactly what I need right now.

Of course I'm checking my phone every five seconds, praying I'll hear from Nix, and my prayers are answered just as I'm pulling out of the driveway at my mom's house to head for the trails.

I'm okay. Please don't worry.

It's short, but it's enough to ease some of the tension in my chest. I pull back into the driveway so I can text him back.

I'm so sorry, Nix. I'm here if you need anything.

I'm dying to see him, but I don't want to push. I'll wait and use the casserole as an excuse to visit later on. I'm sure I'll be desperate by then.

I wait for a minute or two in my driveway, hoping for a response that doesn't come. I'm stretching next to my car when Nix finally replies.

Thanks.

Now I'm left wondering if even the temptation of David's cooking will work.

Feeling heartbroken, I hit the trails at high-speed. The next thing I know, I'm four miles in, but I barely feel the burn. I go another four, mainly trying to kill time before I go into work. I've resigned myself to the fact that Nix won't want to see me at any point today, so I may as well go in and help David. There's no way I can spend the night at home alone with my mother. I'll go crazy.

After nearly ten miles worth of trails behind me, my legs are past the point of exhaustion, but my brain is still working in overdrive. I make my way back to my car, checking my phone as I walk. Unfortunately, he hasn't called or texted, so I head back to Mom's house to grab a shower and rest for an hour or so before I head to *Geoffrey's*. It isn't until I'm dressed in my uniform and getting ready to head out the door, that I receive another text from him.

Looking forward to following you home tonight.

Relief flows through me as I drop my purse on the table by the door and fall down into the sofa.

Actually, David's given me the night off and a chicken casserole. Interested?

Best news I've heard all day. See you soon.

I rush back to my room, change out of my work clothes and into the shorts and tank-top I was wearing to meet him this morning. I grab a hoodie and the casserole and I'm out the door in less than ten minutes.

It's around five o'clock when I pull into Nix's driveway and at this point, the worry feels like it may eat me alive. I have no idea what to expect, although I can't imagine I'll find him sobbing in a corner somewhere. He's not exactly the vulnerable type.

I knock on his door a couple of times then decide to try the handle when he doesn't answer. It's unlocked.

"Nix?" I call for him. "Nix? Are you here?"

I put the casserole in the fridge then start walking around the small space, getting more anxious by the minute.

"Nix?" I try again, but still no answer.

In a matter of minutes, I've checked every room and still no Nix. I walk out onto the back porch and breathe a sigh of relief when I see him sitting on the ground at the edge of the creek.

"Nix?" I call from the porch.

His shoulders straighten before he turns his beautiful face in my direction. He gives me a small wave and I have to focus on keeping my pace slow and even as I walk toward him. It's hard not to run. It feels like I've been waiting years to see him.

"Hi." I take a seat beside him, resisting the urge to wrap my arms around his waist and never let go. "Thanks for asking me over. I was worried about you."

"Thanks for coming over." His voice sounds tired, but his eyes are brighter than expected. "I hated to bother you, but I wanted…"

Wanted what? Wanted me? Say it. Oh please, Nix, just say it.

As usual, Nix leaves me to draw my own conclusions, but not willing to bother him today of all days, I decide to change the subject.

"When will you be leaving?" I ask. "David mentioned you may leave as early as tomorrow."

"Probably tomorrow morning," Nix confirms with a nod. "Mom's supposed to call back tonight with the funeral arrangements."

"I'm so sorry, Nix."

"Me too," he sighs. "I feel awful for not being there when he died."

I reach toward his hand then think better of it. "There wasn't anything you could do for him that wasn't already being done, right?"

"Yeah. I know you're right. And I know he understood. It was his idea for me to come here in the first place."

"It was?"

"He was career military. Airforce. He knew what I was going through when I came home. Suggested that maybe I needed a fresh start."

"So that's why you came here?"

"Being home again was hard for a lot of reasons." Nix takes a breath as he gazes out over the creek. "My grandfather sat me down one day and all but forced me to talk to him. I'm glad he did. He explained to me that I was changed and that home would never be the same again, so I either needed to accept that or try something new. I decided to try something new."

"He sounds like a wonderful man, and I'm glad he was there for you. I'm sure that was a hard time in your life. I can only imagine."

Nix nods as he stares out over the water, but doesn't say anything further. I stay beside him, letting him have his silence.

"How about something to eat?" he eventually asks. "You brought a casserole, right? You want to have dinner with me?"

Only every night, for the rest of my life.

"I'd love to," I say instead, as Nix extends a hand to help me off the ground. "And you should probably call David. He was really worried about you."

"I will," he promises. "I'll call him when we get inside."

He calls David as soon as we enter the cabin, and I wait on the sofa while they chat. As soon as he's done, Nix is back in the living room, taking a seat next to me.

"Do you want me to make dinner?" I offer, noticing how tired he looks.

"That would be great."

Nix smiles over at me, and I give his knee a gentle pat before standing and heading off to the kitchen. I turn on the oven then get the casserole out while the oven preheats. I go back to his refrigerator and see that he has enough ingredients on hand to make a salad, so I pull those out as well and put them on the counter. Since I helped him organize his kitchen, I'm pretty familiar with the space. I quickly grab plates, a bowl for the salad and all of the utensils I need.

Nix stands and comes into the kitchen as I'm dicing up some tomatoes for the salad. "I really appreciate you doing this."

"I don't mind." I glance up at him with a smile. "So you just sit and let me look after you for a change."

With a smile, Nix takes a seat in one of the two chairs at the table in his kitchen. He doesn't say anything, and neither do I, but I can feel his eyes on me as I prepare dinner. And I like it. I love it, as a matter of fact. Especially when I catch him looking a few times, and he lifts up one corner of his mouth, knowing I keep busting him and not caring one bit.

"Almost ready," I tell him as I check on the casserole one last time. "You want the salad now or with the meal?"

"Come here."

I look over at him in confusion. "What?"

"Come here," he repeats, and my feet immediately start moving in his direction, as if they were made to follow his every command.

"Sit with me," he says next, so I move toward the other available chair, but he stops me. "Not there. Here." He pats his lap, and I freeze. Is he serious?

I try to control my breathing, but it's no easy task. And before I have a chance to rationalize things, my obedient feet follow his command once again. Nix takes my arm and pulls it around his neck as I ease myself gently down onto his lap. I'm barely settled in before both of his arms are wrapped around my waist and his head is on my shoulder. I feel his nose pressed against the side of my neck, and as he slowly inhales, my body reacts instinctively, aching to comfort him regardless of how shocked I may be by this unusual turn of events.

I raise my other arm and run my fingers through the back of his soft hair. He has to hear my heart pounding against my chest, but I don't care. He's in my arms. And right now, that's all that matters.

"Thank you," he whispers against my neck as he nuzzles in even further.

I don't say a word. I just hold him close, and when he eventually pulls away, the look in his eyes tells me he wants more but doesn't know how to give it to me. That's okay. I'll settle for the wanting for now.

I grab his face in my hands and kiss his forehead before getting up and heading back to the kitchen, but I'm fighting back tears as I pull the dish from the oven. Maybe I'm not okay with settling after all. Either way, I pull my shoulders back and suck it up as I put the finishing touches on dinner. My job tonight is to be here for him in his time of need. As a friend. The rest can wait.

By the time I turn back around, Nix has left the table. I look around and eventually spot him through the window above the sink in the kitchen. He's outside on the back porch, shoulders slumped, his hands braced on his hips as he stares at his shuffling feet. I know how hard all of this must be for him, and I certainly don't want to be one more worry to add to the pile.

He turns the minute I open the door to the porch and gives me a sad smile, which I ignore.

"Dinner's ready." I try and sound as upbeat as possible. "Come and eat with me."

Nix nods and comes inside. He goes to fix his plate in the kitchen, but I tell him to sit down and I'll bring it to him. I make two plates and carry them over to the table, then move back to the kitchen to grab us a couple of glasses of sweet tea.

"Thanks again," he says to me when I sit down. "This looks great."

"You're welcome."

We both dig in to the casserole, which is magnificent, of course. David truly is a gem in the kitchen.

"So, you're leaving tomorrow?" I ask Nix in between bites.

"Yes."

"I'll miss you."

I'm not sorry for saying it, or embarrassed. It's the truth. I will miss him.

Nix puts his fork down on his plate and leans back in his chair. "Will you come with me?"

His question stops me mid-bite, my fork suspended in front of my mouth, as I try and grasp what he's just said. I still feel like I barely know anything about him or his family, outside of what David's told me, and he wants me to go with him? To California? To his grandfather's funeral?

I quickly decide I'm probably reading too much in to this so I relax, lower my fork to my plate and answer him. "Of course I'll go. That's what friends are for."

Nix gives me a bitter look. "I don't want you to feel obligated. I just thought…"

What did I do wrong now?

I lower my head to hide the disappointment, but then he reaches out and lifts my chin so I'll look at him.

"Please go. I would really like to have you with me."

"S-Sure," I stutter, not sure what's affecting me more—his fingers on my chin or the desperation in his eyes. "I'll go with you."

Nix exhales and leans back in his chair, as if he's relieved. "I'd like to try and leave early tomorrow. I'll buy our plane tickets tonight."

"I can pay you back for the ticket. It's the least I can do."

Nix shakes his head. "You going with me is more than enough."

"Well then why don't I go home so you can get some rest," I suggest, since he seems absolutely beat. "I'll clean-up for you first."

Nix submits with a nod, but insists on helping me. So we finish up the last few bites of dinner, then together, we have the kitchen cleaned and the leftovers put away in no time. He asks me to sit with him on the sofa for a bit when we're done, and I willingly comply. I know I should leave so he can get some rest. I know there's nothing I can do to make things better but selfishly, I'd rather be with him now than have him be alone.

I pull a leg up on the sofa and turn to face him. "So, I get to meet your family?" I ask, the excitement obvious in my voice.

"Yes, although I do wish it was under better circumstances," he admits. "Either way, they're good people. And I'm sure they'll love you."

"I hope so. I'm excited to meet them."

A yawn escapes as Nix smiles, and I offer to go home again but he refuses.

"Stay a little longer," he says, and as I seem to be a slave to his wants more so than ever this evening, I keep my seat next to him on the sofa.

He leans his head back and tilts his face toward me. "Could I ask you a favor?"

"Sure."

"Promise you'll do it."

"That's not how favors work," I inform him with a smile.

"Just promise."

"Okay," I sigh. "Tell me."

"Sing to me."

I blink at him, confused. "Why do you want me to sing to you?"

"Because I like it. Please?"

I stare at his face, gauging whether or not he's serious. Seems he is.

"What do you want me to sing?" I ask, and he shrugs.

"Anything. You can even hum, if you prefer. I just like the sound of your voice."

Shockingly, I don't feel as embarrassed by this request as I probably should. Maybe it's because I'm flattered by his compliment. Or maybe it's because I would do most anything right now if I thought it would make him feel even the slightest bit better.

I rest my elbow on the back of the couch and place my head in my hand. Nix turns his face from me, takes a breath and closes his eyes. The first song that comes to mind is an old favorite, and it's been popping into my head from time to time these days when I'm around Nix. Since the words to this particular song would give away my feelings for him, I opt for humming instead of singing, but Nix doesn't seem to mind. He relaxes deeper and deeper into the sofa as his breathing slows and evens out, and within minutes, he's sound asleep. But I keep singing, and when I feel it's safe, I switch to singing the words instead of humming. I quietly sing the verses as if I'd written the song just for him—part of me wishing he was awake to hear and the other part of me treasuring this secret moment with him.

I sing the song a couple of times through, then I take the blanket from the back of the sofa and drape it over him. I give him another soft kiss on his forehead, grab my things, then leave as quietly as I can, locking his door behind me.

I take a long, hot shower when I get home, and I'm surprised to hear my phone vibrating on my nightstand when I walk back into my room. Or maybe I'm not all that surprised.

Are you home?

I smile down at my phone as I type my reply.

Yes. I'm here. Go back to sleep.

His reply is quick, as if he was holding his phone, waiting for me to get back to him.

Good. Glad you're safe.

I'm typing back when another text from him comes through.

And thanks for tonight, for dinner, for everything.

You're very welcome. Now get some rest. I'll see you tomorrow.

Sweet dreams, Rose.

Sweet dreams, Nix.

I lie back in my bed with a heavy heart, but I can't deny the excitement I feel at the idea of spending the next couple of days with Nix and his family. If they're anything like Nix, I'm sure I'll love them instantly. Let's hope they feel the same way about me.

CHAPTER FOURTEEN

The plane ride to Sacramento was awkward to say the least. Nix and I barely spoke. I tried multiple times to start up a conversation, but I kept getting one word answers. After a while, I gave up. Nix was radiating tension, but I knew he wouldn't talk to me about it, so I put my earbuds in and stared out the window for the most of the flight.

Now I'm trying to figure out why we're riding in the back of a very nice Land Rover, complete with a driver who was waiting for us in baggage claim with one of those signs like you see in movies. Ever since our fateful shopping day in Bristol, when Nix first moved to Delia, I've had reason to believe he has money. But he doesn't flaunt it, and I respect him for that. So I was a little surprised to find a car and driver waiting for us at the airport.

"I should warn you that my sister is a little…headstrong."

I look at Nix with a smile, happy to finally have more than a word or two out of him. "I'm sure she's great. David talks about her all the time. She's younger, right?"

"She's three years younger," Nix replies. "And she's full of fire, never afraid to voice her opinion. She loves being in my business.

She'll probably have plenty of things to say about you being here with me."

"Oh..." And things just got awkward again. "She doesn't know I'm coming?"

Nix shakes his head. "I didn't really have time to tell anyone."

"Well, we're friends," I remind him. "And we sort of work together. I'm sure they'll understand, right?"

"They'll understand," Nix sighs. "But they'll definitely be surprised."

"Why? Because they're used to you showing up with a harem instead of only one girl hanging off your arm?"

Suddenly Nix seems more nervous than ever, and I feel bad for teasing him. He looks down at his hands as they tangle restlessly in his lap. "Let's just say it's been a while since I brought a girl around, or brought anyone around, for that matter. I lost contact with a lot of people while I was away."

I wait for more, hope for more, but it doesn't come. I try not to be disappointed.

"Well then maybe this will be a good time to reconnect. The circumstances aren't ideal, but it's times like these that you need your friends and family the most."

Nix nods, but something is off about his smile. "I think you may have to do," he tells me, and once again cuts off the communication.

We have several more minutes of uncomfortable silence before we reach what I assume is his parents' house. I watch out the window as we move up a narrow drive with huge trees lining either side. Then all of a sudden, the line of trees ends and it's like we've entered another universe—an impossibly beautiful, completely breathtaking universe.

The horizon is full of low, rolling hills and blooming orchards, seemingly never-ending from every angle. I sit and admire the incredible view as we continue down the dirt road, until I can finally see the house in the distance. I try to control my reaction, but a quiet gasp escapes my lips.

"It's their dream house," I hear Nix say, and I turn to find him staring wistfully at the sprawling mansion before us. "My dad and grandfather basically built it from the ground up. They used only recycled materials and it runs on solar energy. It took a while, but they finally finished it a few years ago. I'm glad my grandfather got to see it through to the end."

His face is so sad, so mournful that it takes everything inside of me not to reach out and hug him, but with the mood he's been in today…I cross my arms over my chest and turn my attention back to the house. I suppose the car and driver make more sense now. People with this kind of money probably don't take taxis from the airport.

When we finally pull up in front of the house, an attractive woman with long blonde hair steps out onto the enormous front porch. She's barefoot, dressed in wide-legged pants and a flowing white top.

"That's my mom." Nix nods his head in her direction as we step out of the car. "Her name is Alexia, but most people call her Lexi."

Nix grabs our bags from the driver and Lexi walks over to us with tears in her eyes. The car drives away, and I try not to frown at the uncomfortable looks on both their faces. I'm not sure why, but something other than his grandfather's funeral is causing him grief over being at home. As for his mom, I can tell she wants to reach out and hold Nix, to comfort him, but she refrains. I feel bad for her, as I know the pain of that rejection all too well.

"Hi, Mom." Nix leans in and kisses her cheek just as a tear falls from her eye.

"Hello, my baby boy. Did you have a nice trip?"

Nix nods then turns to introduce me. "Mom, this is Rose. She's a friend from Delia. She works with David."

Lexi looks between Nix and me several times, trying–but failing–to conceal her surprise. I extend my hand and speak to try and ease the tension.

"It's a pleasure to meet you," I say, as I wait for her to take my hand, but she doesn't. Instead, she pulls me in for a hug, squeezing me nice and tight.

Tears are coming out of both of her eyes by the time she pulls away and she's staring at me with admiration. Confused, I glance over at Nix and find he's trying to fight a smile, his face the perfect picture of "I told you so".

"Thank you so much for coming, Rose. My name is Lexi."

"Thank you for having me, Lexi."

Nix suggests we go inside, and I'm grateful for the reprieve.

"Yes. Yes, of course." Lexi shakes her head and smiles as Nix grabs our two bags and we follow him back toward the house. "I apologize, Rose. I'm just so happy to have you both here."

"I'm honored to be here," I tell her as we climb the few stairs of the porch to the front door. "And you have a beautiful home, by the way."

"Oh, thank you." Lexi looks at me with a new light in her eyes. It's obvious she's very proud. "It was a long time coming, but it was well worth the wait."

The inside of the home is positively stunning. It's massive for sure, but they've done a great job making it feel comfortable with its simple, rustic décor.

"We have extra bedrooms upstairs," Lexi gestures toward the huge staircase on the left as we enter. "Or you can stay in the guesthouse."

"Rose would prefer the guesthouse," Nix quickly interjects. "I think she'll be more comfortable there."

Lexi eyes her son, as I process the familiar confusion and rejection that often accompanies my relationship with Nix. Is he really concerned about my comfort or does he want me as far away as possible? After the awkwardness of today, I can't be sure.

"The guesthouse will be perfect." I try and paste a smile on my face as I turn to his mom. "I appreciate you making the room, since I know you weren't expecting me."

Lexi gives me a look I don't understand. Her eyes are blue instead of brown like her son's but unfortunately, they're just as hard to read.

"You are most unexpected," she tells me, then glances at Nix and I'm completely lost in the exchange. "But you are more than welcome. Come and let me show you out back. I'm sure you'd like a minute to freshen up before dinner."

Lexi links her arm with mine and grabs my shoulder bag from Nix. I try and take it from her, but she refuses as she starts leading me toward the back of the living room.

"Nix, we'll see you later," she calls over her shoulder, and I turn to give him a small wave before we walk out the huge glass doors.

We walk in silence to the guesthouse, but I barely notice the lack of conversation as I gawk at my surroundings. The back yard is basically a built-in oasis that most people would pay thousands to visit for a weekend retreat. The place is covered in natural ponds, cedar wood and exotic flower gardens spread all over and in between.

Then, at the back of the oasis is a house that is definitely small compared to the main house, but it's nearly the size of my mom's, so I hate thinking of it as *small*.

"This backyard is incredible," I tell Lexi as we near the door of the guesthouse. "I would spend so much time out here. I'd never get anything done."

"Exactly," she agrees. "I probably should have thought of that when we were building it. We still have a few years before retirement, but I plan to practically live back here when the time comes."

The guest house is decorated much the same as the main house, but whoever decorated the bedroom must be a baseball fan.

"This is where Nix stayed when he came home," Lexi sighs. "I tried talking him into staying with us in the house, but he preferred being alone."

"Looks like not much has changed," I mumble to myself, but Lexi hears me and laughs.

"I guess you're right. Nix hasn't ever been overly social, but he was better before the war." Lexi's face is sad and withdrawn and I can't imagine what it must be like as a mother to have your child overseas, fighting for our country. I'm not sure what would be more overwhelming, the pride or the anxiety.

"Nix and I have become friends over the past couple of months, but I wouldn't say we're close," I admit to her as we have a seat on the sofa in the living area. "He doesn't make that process very easy."

Lexi laughs again. "Yes, I know, but you should feel special. You're probably the closest Nix has come to having a friend in a long time."

"What do you mean?" I know I shouldn't push, but I'm so thirsty for knowledge about this man, I'll take it any way I can get it. "Was it something that happened overseas? I know war has been known to change people."

"That, among other things, but I'm afraid to give you any details. Nix already keeps me at arm's length these days. I can't risk his trust."

"I understand and I'm sorry," I say. "It wasn't right of me to ask you to talk about him. He keeps me at arm's length as well, and like you, I fear if I push him any further away, I'll lose him completely."

Lexi and I share a sad smile. "It's quite the double-edged sword, is it not? Wanting to help him, but afraid of losing him if you do? My boy is strong-willed. Always has been, but he has a good heart. He just needs some time to heal."

"He has a heart of gold," I agree. "I see it in the way he treats David. And me. He's very chivalrous. You should be proud."

"I'm glad to hear the chivalry hasn't gone by the wayside along with his social skills," Lexi smiles. "But I can assure you, he doesn't show his manners to just anyone. And I'm still trying to wrap my head around the fact that he brought someone home with him. You must be special, Rose, and I can speak for the rest of the family when I say, we're glad you're here."

"Thank you." I can feel the heat in my cheeks, and with my pale skin, there's no hiding my blush. "Nix is a good man. So is David. I'm glad to be here to support them both."

"Well then..." Lexi rises and extends a hand to me. I take it and she pulls me up from the sofa. "Dinner should be ready in about an hour. Take your time."

"I will. Thank you, Lexi."

"You're very welcome, Rose." She gives me another hug. "I look forward to getting to know you better over the next few days."

As soon as she leaves, I plop back down on the sofa to take a breath. The journey here was definitely a little awkward and unsettling, but I'm glad I'm here. Regardless of how Nix feels about me, coming home is obviously hard for him and the fact that he asked me to be with him is a huge step. I need to try to keep that in mind over the next few days because if they're anything like this trip has been so far, it's going to be a long week.

CHAPTER FIFTEEN

When I come back to the main house, I follow the scent of roasted tomatoes and garlic toward the kitchen. I come across the dining room first and since it's currently empty, I take the opportunity to look around. This house is truly amazing and the dining room is no exception. The table looks like a slab of some enormous tree, bark still intact, and the chairs are the same–all twelve of them. Everything here looks like it was merely borrowed from nature, no polishing necessary or desired.

As I stand there admiring the furniture and décor, a man walks into the room that has to be Nix's father. They're practically identical–same height and build, same color hair, the same coffee-colored eyes.

"You must be Rose." The man walks up to me with a smile I would love to see on Nix's face more often. "We're glad to have you."

Now that he's next to me, I can say he's maybe a tad shorter than Nix, but the other similarities are uncanny.

"You must be Mr. Taylor."

"My father was Mr. Taylor," he rectifies with a sad smile. "You can call me Joe."

"It's nice to meet you, Joe." I take his extended hand. "Thank you for having me. You have a lovely home."

"Thank you, Rose. How about a proper tour? I don't think dinner is quite ready, so we have a few minutes."

"I would love that."

Joe and I are about to leave for the tour when someone else enters the room.

"I got this, Dad."

I shake my head at a smiling Nix standing in the doorway. How can the man look that amazing in something as simple as jeans and a gray ARMY t-shirt?

"Go on then," Joe sighs. "Steal all of my fun."

Joe gives me a wink as he moves back toward the kitchen, and I turn toward Nix, hoping he got some rest and is feeling a little better.

"Shall we?" He gestures for me to exit the room then comes to walk by my side. "I hope you don't mind me taking my dad's place. He looked pretty disappointed I stole you away."

"I guess you'll do."

"I appreciate that," Nix chuckles, and it's such a lovely sound. "So, I think you've seen most of the front of the house. Let's head toward the back."

Nix takes me upstairs first and we peek into bedrooms and bathrooms as they pop up. I lose track of how many rooms there are after the first few, but every one of them is just as lavish as the rest of the house. It's obvious a lot of planning and care went into building this home, and Nix confirms as we walk that most everything inside is made of all natural materials and left as untouched as possible. From the bed frames to the linens, everything would fit outside in the middle of the woods, just as well as they fit in here.

"When you said your parents were farmers, I thought..." I don't want to say something to insult him, so I pause to think before I finish my statement.

"They are farmers," Nix winks. "Very successful ones."

"Obviously," I laugh.

"It wasn't always that way," he tells me. "This land has been in my family for a long time, but believe it or not, it was never used for farming until my grandfather retired from the Airforce. He started small, a few fruits and vegetables here and there, but before he knew it he had built an empire. Most of the farming is done elsewhere now, but my grandfather would never sell this land. It meant too much to him. The land, the business—it means a lot to all of us. This house was actually my dad's idea. He and my grandfather started building it about fifteen years ago. I used to love to come help them."

"And that's how Nix the Handyman, was born."

"You got it." Nix smiles at me. "Most everything I know about building things, fixing cars, fishing, it all came from my grandfather."

My hand instinctively reaches out to comfort him, but I manage to catch myself before Nix notices. "You were lucky to have him in your life."

"I was." Nix nods in agreement as we make our way back downstairs. "He was a great man. And Lennix is a legacy to be proud of."

"Wait..." I stop walking and Nix stops with me. "Did you say *Lennix*? As in *Lennix Organics*?"

"Yes. That's my family's business."

Nix is eyeing me skeptically, but all I can think about is how much I love their fruits and veggies!

"This is so cool!" I gush. "You guys have the freshest strawberries, even in fall and winter, and your greens? That spinach is to die for!"

"Are you..." Nix crosses his arms, his face amused as he studies me. "Wait a minute...are you *fangirling* over me?"

"No. I'm fangirling over your produce."

"Story of my life." Nix shakes his head with a sigh. "Damn strawberries. They get all the girls."

I give him a smack on the arm and he gives me a heart-stopping smile before resuming the tour. He continues to explain everything with enthusiasm and obvious admiration as we walk around the parts of the first floor I haven't seen.

"So that's basically it." Nix shoves his hands in his front pockets as we turn down a long hallway. "What do you think?"

"Honestly, it's unbelievable. I've never seen anything like it."

Nix gives me a shy grin. "And how about my parents? I'm happy to see they haven't scared you away, but I guess there's still time."

"Well, I can't say I know a lot of farmers," I admit with a laugh. "But so far your family has been very welcoming. And by the way, you and your father could be twins."

"Yeah," Nix nods with a smile. "People say we favor a bit."

"Just a bit." I hold up two fingers indicating a tiny amount and Nix playfully bats them down.

"I hope he was nice and didn't make too many embarrassing remarks."

Nix opens a door at the end of the hallway that leads to the back yard, but the guesthouse is several yards away to the left, proving how huge this main house really is.

"He was very pleasant," I assure him. "And no embarrassing remarks."

"Yet," Nix adds. "I'm sure he's just waiting for the right time to strike."

"I'm kind of looking forward to the possibility of hearing embarrassing stories about you," I confess and Nix mocks me with a raised eyebrow. "What? I hardly know anything about you, so embarrassing stories or not, it will be something."

The minute I said it, I knew it was wrong. I try so hard to be careful around him, careful of what I say, what I do. But I'm starting to wonder if I can really push him any farther away than he already is. Maybe I don't have as much to lose as I like to think.

Either way, this is not the time or place to push things. "I'm sorry," I start, but Nix shakes his head.

"Stop apologizing." He places his hands on his hips with a sigh. "Look, I know I don't give you much. Hell, I don't have much to give." He rubs a hand over his short, dark hair and turns toward me. "But there are so many times, Rose...with you, there are so many times I want to spill my damn guts. I want you to know everything. I'm just...I'm just so afraid of what might come out."

Nix looks away from me, his eyes roaming everywhere and over everything except for me. I know now this is a sign of the walls coming back up. He gave me a peek into that beautiful head of his, but now he's closing himself back in and that's okay. The tiny glimpses are enough to keep me going, to keep me around. Truth be told, I'd stick around without them because even if I can't admit it out loud or even to myself, it's becoming more and more obvious every day that I'm falling in love with him.

"I understand," I assure him. "And I don't want you to think I would ever pressure you. I guess I got caught up in being here with your family, and I care about you...." *Careful, Rose.* "I care about our friendship, and I got excited about getting to know you better."

Nix's eyes continue to roam over the surroundings, but I can tell he wants to say something. He draws his lips in between his teeth as if he's trying to stop himself, then his eyes eventually settle back on mine.

"Well, there's no stopping my dad, so I'm sure a few stories will slip whether I like it or not." He gives me a forced smile then starts walking toward the guesthouse. "I assume you're comfortable out here," he says over his shoulder, as I start to follow him.

"Yes. It's perfect. Thank you." Nix nods and keeps walking. I catch up to him and walk by his side. "Are you okay?"

"Other than the fact that I'm here for my grandfather's funeral, I guess I'm doing fairly well."

Ouch. Looks like I've pushed a button.

"I'm sorry," Nix sighs. "I shouldn't have snapped at you like that."

Nix shoves his hands in his pockets, as I wrap my arms around my waist. If I didn't know any better, I'd say we were both resisting the idea of touching each other.

"It's okay."

"No, it's not."

He stops again and turns to me. He stares into my eyes so long this time it starts to make me uncomfortable. I wind my arms tighter around my waist and look over his shoulder at the guesthouse in the distance until I hear an exasperated sigh from Nix.

"I'm glad you're here, Rose."

His voice is so low. "What did you say?"

When he looks up at me, his face is covered in something similar to regret. "I want you to know how happy I am that you're here. I'm sorry if I don't know how to show it, but please know that I'm better…I'm better because you're here."

I nod and smile, having no idea how to respond to that without crying like a baby.

Nix and I start walking through the backyard oasis, toward the main house. We walk in silence, but for the first time today, it's not uncomfortable.

He's glad I'm here. And I'm happy to be here.

With him.

For him.

I only wish I could find the nerve to tell him how much.

CHAPTER SIXTEEN

Nix's dad refrained from telling embarrassing stories over dinner, but I have a feeling they'll come out at some point. His parents are wonderful, and in spite of the somber reason for bringing everyone together, the table was full of smiles and laughter as everyone took turns sharing their favorite memories of Nix's late grandfather. After dinner, we were all led into the living area where the stories and laughter continued, but without Nix this time. He left the table as soon as he finished eating and said he was going for a walk. I was going to ask if I could join him, but I could tell by the look on his face he wanted to be alone.

Nix's unwillingness to let me in is hard enough on a good day. Being here, watching him grieve and not being able to help, is making me feel positively useless. I wish there was something more I could do.

Feeling tired and slightly awkward, I decide to head back to the guesthouse for the night. But before I can excuse myself from the group, someone rings the doorbell then comes bursting in without waiting for an answer.

"Anyone home?"

I look up to find an absolutely beautiful woman that I immediately know is Nix's sister, Lennon, but not because she looks anything like him. As Nix is the spitting image of his father, Lennon is an exact replica of her mother. And dressed in flared jeans and a flowy tank-top, it seems they even share the same fashion sense.

Joe and Lexi rush to give hugs and kisses, and I stand as well but keep my place near the sofa. I don't want to intrude on the happy family reunion.

Everyone says their hello's before Lennon finally realizes I'm in the room. "And who do we have here?"

"This is Nix's friend, Rose," Lexi points out and Lennon shakes her head.

"Mom, that's impossible. Nix doesn't have any friends."

"Stop it, Lennon." Lexi rolls her eyes at her daughter. "They work together with David."

Lennon walks toward me. "So David invited you? That makes more sense, and any friend of David's is a friend of mine."

"Nix invited her."

Lennon gapes at her mother before turning her shocked face back in my direction. "For real?" I nod and she gives me a warm smile. "Well then I am extremely happy to meet you, Rose."

Where Nix is against any affectionate gesture, it seems the rest of his family is about as touchy-feely as they come. Lennon pulls me into a hug so tight I can barely breathe.

"Maybe something good *will* come out of this weekend after all." She pulls away with an optimistic smile. "Now where is that brother of mine?"

"He needed a break," Lexi says in a sad voice. "But hopefully he'll be back to join us soon."

As if on cue, Nix walks into the room. "Hey Lennon."

"Hey, Nix!"

Seemingly unaware or unafraid of Nix's aversions, Lennon rushes him and gives him the same bear hug she just gave me. It's briefer but just as tight, and she completely ignores Nix's obvious discomfort as she gives him a kiss on the cheek. Normally, it makes me sad that he doesn't like to be touched, but in this case, it's quite comical.

I think I'm going to like Lennon.

"It's good to see you again," Lennon tells him. "I've missed you."

Nix's face softens instantly. "I've missed you too, Len. How's school?"

Lennon takes a seat on one of the sofas, and everyone follows suit. Except Nix sits on an ottoman, leaving me solo on the loveseat, and when Lennon looks between us, I suddenly wish there was some dark hole I could crawl into so I could die from embarrassment in peace.

And then, as if I needed any more of the spotlight, Lennon gets up from her seat and plops down next to me.

"I don't want Rose to think everyone in this family shares your special brand of asshole," she says to Nix, and he scowls at her as she cuddles up next to me. "Now Rose, tell us about yourself. We need to know why you would ever agree to take a four hour plane ride with Mr. Grumpy Ass over there."

"That's enough, Lennon," her mother scolds with a smile. "Let's have a cease fire this weekend, okay?"

"Fine," Lennon huffs, as she rolls her eyes at Nix. "But I do want to know more about you, Rose. Are you originally from Delia? I've been there a couple of times to visit David, and I thought it was such a charming town."

"I was born and raised in Delia," I tell her. "I lived in Atlanta with my best friend for a short time, but I recently moved back home to be with my mom."

"Oh no. Is she sick?" Lexi asks and I shrug.

"Sort of," I admit. "My father left her, and it was kind of a messy situation. It's been tough, but we'll get through it eventually."

"I'm sorry to hear that," Joe pipes in. "Are you an only child?"

"Yes sir," I nod. "I'm happy I can be there for her, though it's been hard seeing her suffer."

"I'm sure it will take some time," Lexi says. "It was nice of you to go back home to be with her."

"Thank you. She's been a little better lately, so that's good to see."

"Probably not an easy adjustment," Lennon gathers. "Going back to Delia after living in Atlanta must have been tough."

"Coming home has been hard for a lot of reasons," I admit. "I love Delia, but it hardly feels like home anymore."

"Why not?" Lennon asks.

"Well, most everyone I care about has moved away. Delia's become this sad reminder of the way things used to be. It's dull and lonely, and honestly, I've been counting down the days until I can make my escape."

I force out a laugh to try and make light of my sad situation. This group certainly doesn't need anything more bringing them down at the moment. But then I catch the look on Nix's face and I quickly realize my mistake.

"Of course I love David and working at *Geoffrey's*," I start, hoping to make up for my thoughtless blunder. "And I know you must miss him terribly, but we all really enjoy having Nix around. He's been working so hard to help David fix the up the restaurant. The new deck is going to be beautiful."

Nix smiles at me, but it doesn't reach his eyes. Hurt and regret are clearly evident on his face, and I make a mental note to apologize the first opportunity I get. But when I break away from Nix's sad eyes, I find the rest of the eyes in the room are trained on the two of us. The tension is thick and as sticky as molasses and I have the sudden urge to run from the room, never to return again. Thankfully, Lennon swoops in and saves the day.

"Ugh. I can't imagine anyone wanting to voluntarily spend time with my brother, but to each her own." Lennon smiles as her mother scolds her once again. "Any time you need a break, feel free to come visit me in California," she offers. "Sun and sand work wonders on the soul, and I'd love to have you."

"Thank you," I smile. "I've never been to California."

"Then it's settled!" She claps her hands excitedly. "We won't leave this weekend without making a date. You can even bring my sad lump of a brother with you if you want, but a girl's weekend would be preferable."

She winks at me, and I don't dare look at Nix. He's been in a rotten mood all day and Lennon hasn't stopped teasing him since she walked in. I'm sure he's fuming.

"So tell us how's school going, sweetheart?" Joe asks Lennon, and I sigh, grateful the focus has moved from me.

Lennon starts to tell him all about school, and I find out she's currently at Berkley working on her PhD in environmental science. Her goal is to work in D.C. as a lobbyist to help get chemicals out of the food supply. I'd say she's chosen the right path. She seems outspoken and positively fearless, which will serve her well in politics.

"Maybe I'll even run for president one day," she says at one point, and no one in the room discourages the idea.

Of course it's only me, Lennon and her parents left at that point. Nix excused himself about fifteen minutes after our awkward stare down, claiming he was tired and turning in for the night. Feeling pretty beat myself, I'm relieved when Lexi finally cuts the conversation off around midnight saying we have the next couple of days to catch up, and everyone will need their rest for tomorrow.

"Do you want me to walk you to the guesthouse?" Lennon asks, but I decline, although it was nice of her to ask.

She gives me a hug goodnight, and I'm learning that it's apparently Lennon's goal to try and squeeze every last drop of air from your lungs with each embrace. I think I could learn to love them all the same.

As I walk through the backyard toward the guesthouse, I think about tomorrow and how I can help offer some comfort, but I keep coming up blank. With a sigh, I go to open the door to the guesthouse then pause when I see movement to my right. I know without looking who it is, but I look anyway because I want to see him. I always want to see him.

Nix is standing several yards away, near the door we came out of when he gave me the tour earlier. His bare chest is on display and gleaming in the soft glow of the moonlight, and I grab at my own chest as I drink him in. God, he's beautiful.

As I stand there fixated on his stunning form in nothing but a pair of faded jeans, he starts walking toward me, and the hand on my chest clutches at the thin cotton of my shirt. *Why is he coming over here*? I'm not sure I can handle him up close right now. Maybe it's being here, surrounded by everything he loves, but my feelings for him are getting stronger by the minute. It's starting to scare me. I'm afraid I'm going to do something I'll regret, something to ruin this already delicate relationship we have, and I don't want to lose him.

But it looks like I'm safe for another day because Nix stops suddenly after closing half the distance between us. I still can't see his face clearly, but I see him shake his head slightly before he holds up a hand and gives me a small wave. I take the hand from my chest and wave back, wishing now I could have had a chance to see him up close, but it's probably best I didn't.

Nix crosses his arms over his chest, and I know he's waiting for me to go inside before he turns to leave. Confused and heavy hearted, I open the door and walk inside, leaving my faithful protector to fend for himself in the dark.

CHAPTER SEVENTEEN

This morning has been something I would describe as quiet chaos.

I couldn't sleep last night, so around seven this morning I finally gave up and got in the shower. Less than an hour later I was making my way toward the main house, where Lexi, Joe and Lennon all greeted me when I walked in. The sadness was already hanging in the air, much heavier than yesterday, as we chatted and ate a delicious breakfast that Lexi had prepared.

Afterward, everyone went their separate ways to either get dressed for the funeral or to work off some nervous energy by doing aimless chores and activities around the house. Feeling somewhat useless and out of place, I decided to go back to the guesthouse, where I've spent most of my morning worrying about Nix. He wasn't at breakfast. As a matter of fact, I haven't seen him all morning, but his family didn't seem too concerned. Joe mentioned he had probably gone fishing, which wouldn't surprise me, since fishing is Nix's favorite escape back in Delia as well.

The funeral starts at noon, but the family wanted to get there early to greet the guests, so I was told we'd be leaving at eleven. Around fifteen minutes 'til, I still haven't seen or heard from Nix, so I give myself a last look in the bathroom mirror before grabbing my clutch and making my way back up to the main house.

I'm surprised to find Nix sitting on a wooden bench near the house. He stands when he sees me approaching, and I know it's inappropriate at a time like this, but I can't help but notice how handsome he is. I've never seen him in a suit before.

"Hi." He tucks his hands in his pockets, looking like a young boy in grown up attire.

"Hi." I give him a smile, which he doesn't return. "You look nice."

"Thanks. So do you," he replies, then clears his throat. "I'm sorry I missed you at breakfast. I just needed some time alone this morning."

"That's okay. Your family's amazing. I've enjoyed getting to know them."

Nix nods, as if he's thinking of a way to keep the conversation going but coming up blank. I decide to put him out of his misery, but I do want him to know...

"I'm here for you today if you need me," I tell him, and his eyes snap to mine. "No expectations. I just wanted you to know that I'm here."

"That means a lot," he breathes. "Thank you, Rose."

Nix is looking at me like I'm the last drop of bourbon in an alcoholic's bottle and I can't take it. Not right now.

"Well, I guess we should probably get going," I suggest, but I barely give him a chance to respond before I'm moving past him and walking toward the house.

I can still feel his eyes on my back as I walk away, and when I catch his reflection in the glass doors in front of me, he seems undecided on whether he should follow me or not. Right as I approach the doors, I catch him rubbing his hands over his face then through his hair before he finally trails after me. I can feel his grief as if it were my own. I know today's going to be hard for him, and I wish there was something more I could do. At least he knows I'm here if he needs me. I think that's what's most important right now.

Everyone is waiting for us in the kitchen when we walk inside. Nix and I follow his family out the door and Nix once again avoids being close to me by allowing Lennon to get in the limo ahead of him, putting her in between us. I pretend not to be heartbroken and smile at Joe, who's eyes are already glistening with tears. Seeing a big man like Joe break down makes it hard for me to keep my composure, but I do. I want to stay strong for Nix, even though I'm pretty sure he doesn't need me for that.

I look over at him and he's staring out the window seemingly calm, but I can see the tension in his shoulders and the constant ticking of his jaw. Lennon puts a hand on his forearm obviously noticing it too, but Nix flinches. I understand this is tough for him, but she's his sister. I really wish he'd try, at least for today.

Deciding I need to help someone in this car before I go mad, I reach out and grab Lennon's hand. She turns to me with a sad smile, but I can tell she's grateful for the support, and by the time we reach the funeral home, Lennon is crying softly with her head on my shoulder. Lexi was trying to be strong for her husband, but the minute the first tear slipped down his cheek, she lost the fight. Nix and I are the only two not in tears when we finally reach our destination, but he looks as white as a ghost—like he may pass out at any minute.

"Will he be okay?" I ask Lennon, as she helps me out of the limo.

"It's going to be a rough day for him for a lot of reasons." Her voice is quiet as she stares at her brother's back, watching him clench his fists at his sides before shoving them in his pockets. "Losing Grandfather is hard enough, but then you add in the crowds and the likelihood of running into Maggie, and Nix is basically entering his own personal hell on Earth."

The sound of screeching tires roars through my head. "Who's Maggie?"

"You don't know about Maggie?" she asks, and when I shake my head she shrugs. "I guess he wouldn't have told you about her. The man isn't exactly a pro at sharing his feelings."

"You don't have to tell me about her," I say, trying not to be nosey. "If Nix wanted me to know, he would have said something."

"No he wouldn't have," Lennon corrects me. "He would probably rather forget about Maggie all together, and I'll gladly tell you everything, but not here." Lennon looks around the foyer we're standing in and when she finds what she's looking for, she grabs my hand and walks up to her mom. "Rose and I are going to the ladies room. We'll be back shortly."

"Don't be long." Lexi kisses Lennon on the cheek. "I'm sure guests will start arriving soon."

Lennon promises Lexi we'll be back soon then starts pulling me toward the restrooms. I glance over my shoulder at Nix and there's a question in his gaze. I shrug my shoulders, acting as if I have no idea why she's dragging me away, and Nix buys it. He gives me a small nod then turns back to whatever conversation he was having with his parents before Lennon interrupted.

The ladies room is small, only a few stalls, but there are two wingback chairs on the left as we enter that Lennon and I decide to occupy. I have no idea what I'm about to hear, but I'm so thrilled to get another glimpse into Nix's past that the nervousness hardly registers.

Lennon sits and crosses her legs. "So, *Maggie*..." She says her name like it's a disease she may catch if she gets too close. "Maggie and Nix were high school sweethearts. Everyone suspected they would get married right after graduation, but Nix had always wanted to join the military and follow in our grandfather's footsteps. He got his undergrad degree, and even though Maggie was practically begging him to put a ring on her finger before he left, he insisted on getting through officer training school before he made any kind of commitment." Lennon leans toward me and narrows her eyes. "Personally, I think Nix had reservations then, but he was blinded by his love for that woman. When he graduated from officer training school and Maggie gave him an ultimatum—marriage or bust—he conceded. He was scheduled to deploy before they had a chance to have the ostentatious ceremony that Maggie was planning, so they ended up having a small ceremony the weekend before Nix left for Afghanistan the first time. They spent a few days at my parents' beach house for their honeymoon, and that was the last time he would see his wife in person."

"Wait, she died?" I gasp, but Lennon laughs.

"I wish. She lasted about three months before she cheated on him. With his best friend, no less."

"Oh God."

"Yeah, and that's not the worst part."

"It gets worse?"

Lennon gives me a sad smile. "The marriage was officially annulled and we didn't see Nix for years after that. He would write or call periodically, but we didn't see him again until his first turn was up. He came home, undecided on whether or not he was going to re-up or stay and help Dad and Grandfather with the farm. What we didn't know then, is that he and Maggie had been writing to each other. She claimed things had fallen apart with her and Jacob, claimed she'd made a huge mistake, and part of the reason Nix was coming home again was to see if the two of them could have another go at things. If only we would have known, we could have told him she was full of shit, but I'm not sure he would have listened to us anyway. So, here comes the bad part." Lennon takes a deep breath, as if this is as hard for her to remember as it would be for Nix. "Nix's friends used to have this party at the lake every year the day after Thanksgiving. Nix knew Maggie would be there, so he planned to surprise her, but he ended up being the one surprised."

Lennon stands and goes to check herself in the mirror. I follow her, not wanting to miss any of this, as hard as it may be to hear.

"Long story short..." Lennon pauses to apply some lip-gloss. "Things between Jacob and Maggie were still going strong, and Nix got an up close and personal look at the situation when he walked in on them wrapped around each other at the party. He blew up, confronted them both, then left the party and re-upped the next day. He left less than a week later without a word to any of us about what happened, but word travels fast in a small town. The next time we saw him was a little over a year ago when he came home for good, but he'd changed so much. Nix has always been a quiet, private person, but he came back completely withdrawn. He barely spoke. He flinched every time we tried to touch him. He spent most of his time in the guesthouse, only coming out to get tattooed or pierced or to help Dad with the farm and to do odds and ends stuff around the house. He was better for a while when he finally started talking to Grandfather, but it was like he couldn't get comfortable here. He'd changed so much being overseas, and when you add that to his existing trust issues and the bad memories this place drags up, I think he just wanted a fresh start."

I shake my head with a sigh, realizing Nix and I have more in common than I thought. I understand his move to Georgia now more than ever.

"He told us at breakfast one morning he was going to spend some time in Delia with David," Lennon continues, "and we all thought it was a great idea. I know Mom and Dad have missed him, and I know Nix hated leaving with Grandfather sick and Dad handling all of the business with the farms, but our parents have always insisted our happiness comes first. Mom says that when she speaks to Nix these days, he seems better, but I think being here now...there are too many memories, and Nix is about to be confronted with a lot of faces he hasn't seen in years. I'm sorry to say Maggie and her now husband, Jacob, will probably be two of them."

Lennon puts her gloss back in her purse and turns to me. "I'd like to think she'll act like an adult and leave him alone, but Maggie is a drama connoisseur and she's always been an expert at pushing Nix's buttons."

"Does Nix still have feelings for her?" I don't really want the answer to this question, but I feel like I have to know.

"Hell no," Lennon quickly interjects. "Nix left any love he had remaining for her at that party all those years ago, but I'm afraid she did some permanent damage. The boy is so closed off emotionally, I don't think he'd know love now if it came up and punched him in the face."

I turn from her to try and hide my reaction. I don't want her to see how that last line affected me, but I'm too late.

Lennon grabs both of my hands. "Look at me, Rose," she commands, and I slowly move my eyes back to hers. "I'm going to be brutally honest with you for a second. I can tell you have feelings for him, and I don't blame you. We may tease and bicker, but my brother is an exceptional man and I love him dearly. However, I feel obligated to warn you this will be no easy road to travel, so as his sister, all I ask is that if you're even the slightest bit uncertain, please let him go now. There's so little of the old Nix left as it is. Another broken heart and we may lose him forever."

I wish I could say I'm surprised she realized my feelings for Nix, after knowing me less than twenty-four hours, but I'm not. Not at all. What troubles me is that her brother seems clueless, or even worse, he doesn't care.

"I understand your concern," I assure her. "But I don't think you have anything to worry about. I do have feelings for your brother, but I'm fairly certain my heart is the one at risk here. Not his."

Lennon tilts her head, her light blue eyes scrutinizing me. "Well, I would prefer any and all broken hearts be avoided." She puts her purse back on her shoulder then opens the bathroom door. "But I wouldn't be so sure about Nix being completely absent from the equation. I see the way he looks at you, the way he watches you."

"He's got this thing with protecting people. Maybe it's an Army thing."

"Maybe," Lennon shrugs. "Or maybe it's a *Rose* thing. Don't count him out. Just be careful."

She smiles and pulls me in for one of her insane hugs, and I once again wonder over how the strength of a thousand men seems to reside in Lennon's willowy frame.

"I'll be careful," I promise her as we walk back toward the lobby, and she surprises me with a kiss on the cheek.

"Well, I'm in love with you already," she tells me. "And if my idiot brother hasn't caught on yet, I'm confident he will. It's only a matter of time."

We're both smiling as we enter the lobby, and a small crowd has already formed near the entrance to the sanctuary. Lennon and I are looking around for her parents and Nix, when she grabs my upper arm so hard I nearly yelp.

"I spy a narcissistic bitch," Lennon whispers in my ear, as she points in front of us and to the right. Nix is standing with his back to us, blocking the view of whoever is standing in front of him.

"Maggie?" I question, and Lennon nods.

"Go save him."

"How?"

"Make her jealous." Lennon gives me a mischievous smile. "It's the fastest way to shut her up for good."

I shake my head as Lennon walks away. How am I supposed to do this when the man barely lets me touch him? But then I think of how I promised to start being more honest with myself and with Nix. The sad circumstances surrounding us today shouldn't change that. I said I would be here for him, and if getting him out of an uncomfortable situation is my only opportunity to help, then I'll take it.

I move slowly in his direction, knowing this is definitely a risk, because if he refuses to play along in front of Maggie, she'll see right through the façade. But as I get closer, I can feel Nix's anxiety pulsing out of him like a radio wave. He's practically crying for help, so maybe the risk will pay off.

Maggie sees me coming before Nix does, but the surprise on her face when she realizes I'm heading for them causes both Nix, and who I assume is Jacob, to look my way.

Nix's eyes are wide as he takes me in, but I give him a sincere smile that seems to set him at ease. Then it's the moment of truth.

CHAPTER EIGHTEEN

I walk up beside Nix, take his hand in mine and lean in to kiss him on the cheek. Even those small acts of intimacy nearly take my breath away, but somehow, I'm able to maintain my focus.

"Hi." I smile, as I lace my fingers through his. "I've been looking for you."

Nix's eyes are darker than I've ever seen them, his lips parted in stunned silence, and I start to think this isn't going to work.

Then a miracle happens.

Nix turns his body to face mine and with his free hand, he slides two fingers down the curve of my cheek. "I've been right here," he whispers. "I've always been right here."

I blink, wondering for a moment if I may be dreaming, but Maggie's shrill voice quickly brings me back to reality.

"Nix? Aren't you going to introduce us?"

You'd have to be deaf not to hear the hurt in her tone. I know Nix hears it because he gives me a small smile before turning back to face her, and when he does, I have to remind myself that this is just a show. He's simply playing along, and I don't need to read too much into this. *Act cool, Rose. Play your part.*

"This is Rose," Nix tells them then turns back to me. "Rose, these are my friends, Maggie and Jacob."

Maggie's face sours at the word "friend", while Jacob seems genuinely touched by the term.

I release Nix's hand so I can shake theirs. "It's a pleasure to meet you both," I say with a smile, and to my surprise, Nix immediately grabs my hand back in his the minute it's free.

"So how long have you two been seeing each other?" Maggie asks, and I look at Nix, deciding to let him handle the details.

"We met about a week after I moved to Georgia," he answers her, while his eyes stay linked with mine. "Sometimes it's hard to believe it's only been a few weeks. I feel like I've known Rose my whole life. Or maybe I've just been looking for her that long and haven't found her until now. Either way, I know she's been in my heart for a very long time."

Keep breathing, Rose.

It's not real.

It's just an act.

And now I feel like crying.

"Congratulations, man." Jacob extends his hand to Nix. "I'm really happy for you two."

"Thanks." Nix shakes Jacob's hand. "Well, it was great to see you both again, but we should probably go. I'd like to speak to a few more people before the service starts."

"We understand." Jacob gives him a light-hearted pat on the shoulder. "And it was great to see you too, both of you. We're so sorry for your loss."

Jacob seems genuinely happy that he and Nix have made some small progress, while Maggie is just standing there looking like she's swallowed a box of nails.

"Thank you," Nix says again. "We appreciate you coming."

Without even a final glance in Maggie's direction, I smile to myself as Nix walks away with my hand still linked firmly with his. He pulls me along through the crowd, until he's finally stopped by his dad and asked to speak with a couple who are apparently long-time friends of the family.

Nix lets go of my hand, but when I try and step away from him and give him some space, he wraps his fingers around my forearm and pulls me back to his side. And that's where I stay for the next twenty minutes or so as Nix speaks to several people in the now packed lobby. He never takes my hand again, but he makes it clear either with his eyes or a slight touch of his fingers against my skin that he wants me close. And that's perfectly fine with me.

Nix and I are speaking to an old Airforce buddy of his grandfather's when the funeral director asks for everyone to start finding seats, so Nix excuses us and we leave to find his parents. The family will be following the casket in right before the service starts, and although I told Nix I would be happy to sit by myself, he insisted I walk in with his family.

We're directed to a room where we'll wait for the director to come and get us when it's time. Lennon is already in the room when Nix and I get there, crying softly in a chair in the far corner.

"Have you been in here the entire time?" Nix asks when he sees her, but she shakes her head.

"I spoke to a few people, but I only lasted about ten minutes or so. It was just too hard talking about him in past tense."

I immediately walk over to her, knowing she'd probably rather have her brother, but I'll do what I can to try to help.

I don't say anything when I sit next to her. I simply wrap my arms around her and let her cry on my shoulder. I stroke her long, blonde hair and rock her gently until she starts to relax. When I look up, Nix is still standing near the door, his face torn. I pull one arm from around his sister and hold out my hand to him, beckoning him over. He shakes his head at first but I curl my fingers, begging him to let me help. My heart softens in my chest as he walks slowly toward us and takes my hand. He gives my fingers a squeeze, just as Lennon raises her head to see what's going on. She notices Nix's hand in mine, and the most unexpected smile stretches across her face.

Lennon lets go of me, stands up and wraps her arms around her brother. It takes him a minute, but Nix finally starts to hug her back, and that's when my first tear of the day finally falls.

Joe and Lexi walk in on their children hugging and both immediately look to me. I give them a small shrug as Lexi walks over and puts a hand on Lennon's arm. Lennon looks up at her mom and kisses Nix's cheek before letting him go to hug her mom. Joe walks over and puts a cautious hand on Nix's shoulder, and to everyone's surprise, Nix doesn't flinch. Tears fill Joe's eyes as he looks at his son, and when Nix wraps his arms around his dad, there's not a dry eye in the room.

Nix eventually lets go of his dad and turns to his mom and Lennon. Lexi reaches up as if she's going to touch his cheek, but she hesitates. Then Nix takes her hand and places it on his cheek himself, and after that, there is no hesitation. She buries herself in his chest and weeps openly, and I suddenly feel like I should probably leave and give them some privacy as they reconnect, but

Nix has a hold of my arm before I even take the first step toward the door.

"I just thought I should give you all some privacy," I explain. "I thought you may need a moment as a family."

Nobody says a word, but Lexi lets go of Nix to come give me a hug. "Thank you," she whispers in my ear, then kisses my cheek before pulling away. "Today, you're part of this family, and we're happy to have you here with us."

"Very happy," Lennon adds with a smile, and when I look at Joe, he gives me a small nod in agreement.

"Thank you." My voice shakes as my heart swells with love for this sweet family, but before I can say anything further, the funeral director comes in telling us it's time. Everyone wipes at their eyes before exiting the room. I fall in step beside Nix and when I look over at him, I notice he must not have been crying along with everyone else as I had originally thought. His eyes are a little red, but his cheeks are dry. I guess I'm not that surprised. I can't imagine what it would take for a man like Nix to cry and even if he did, I'm sure it's not something he'd do in front of an audience.

We stand near the doors to the sanctuary and watch as they bring out the casket. Joe glides his fingers along the side as it passes, and I can feel my eyes fill with tears once again as we walk toward our seats. It's a huge room, with a lower level and a balcony, both filled to capacity. There are even several people standing along the walls in the back, who were unable to find a seat in the pews. Nix's grandfather must have been a great man.

"I wish I could have known him," I lean over and whisper in Nix's ear as we walk, and he surprises me by taking my hand in his once again.

"He would have loved you," he says to me, then raises my hand to his lips and kisses the backs of my fingers.

If I wasn't already so moved by our surroundings and the miraculous turn of events that have transpired over the past hour, I probably would have been appropriately shocked and awed by the gesture. Instead, I lean over and place a kiss on Nix's shoulder, returning his intimacy. And when we sit, I stay close to him whether he likes it or not because right now, I need some comfort as well. Luckily, he doesn't object. As a matter of fact, he keeps my hand in his and rubs various patterns on the top throughout most of the service. Nix also keeps me close during the burial and even sits next to me in the limo on the ride back to his parents' house.

Even throughout the afternoon, as he and his family accept guests into their home for refreshments and fellowship, Nix never lets me out of his sight. And when Lennon tries to borrow me to help in the kitchen, Nix tells her I'm a guest and shouldn't have to help with clean up. Lennon gives me a look like he's not fooling her, but I'm not sure what to think. Nix is definitely acting differently toward me, toward everyone for that matter, but I'm trying not to read too much into things. Instead, I've decided to enjoy this side of him while it lasts.

The crowds eventually clear around seven and Nix and his family seem absolutely beat as we all plop down onto the sofas in the living room. Lexi takes her shoes off and Joe pulls her feet into his lap for a massage. Lennon curls up in a ball in the big fluffy chair in the corner, and I take the same seat on the loveseat that I had the night before. The only difference now is Nix comes and sits beside me, so close his thigh is pressed firmly against mine.

"So what are we doing tonight?" Lennon says from her spot in the corner, and Nix stares at her in disbelief.

"Aren't you exhausted?"

Even though Lennon currently has her eyes closed, she shakes her head. "I'm going to head back to my room and take a thirty minute power nap. Then I'm taking a shower, and we're going out."

"No way," Nix refuses. "We can go out tomorrow. I don't want to go anywhere tonight."

Lennon sits up and narrows her eyes at him. "You're going and so is Rose. I promised my friends I would meet them somewhere tonight, and I think we could all use a little fun."

Nix raises an eyebrow—a challenge for her to come up with something better than the excuse she just gave him, and Lexi and Joe watch the showdown with small smiles as if they've witnessed it a million times.

"Okay fine," Lennon concedes. "I never get to see you anymore and I want to spend as much time with my big brother as I can while I'm here. So will you please go out with me? Pretty please?"

Nix sighs, but I can see it in his face he's going to give in. It's obvious he's a complete sucker for his sister, and that just makes him all the more attractive to me.

"Fine," he agrees. "But I'm not going to one of those crazy techno clubs you and your friends used to go to. I'll go someplace like *McLean's* or *Rusty's*. At least they have decent music and we can play pool."

"Deal." Lennon hops up with an excited smile on her face. "And you'll go too, right Rose?"

I look at Nix to make sure he wants me to come, and he answers for me instead.

"Oh you're coming." He elbows my side with a smile. "Misery loves company."

I roll my eyes at him then look over at Lennon. "I'd love to go. Thanks for inviting me."

Lennon claps and skips her way back to her room, and now I'm doubting that nap is going to happen.

"Do you want some time to rest before we're dragged out this evening?" Nix asks me and I smile.

"I'm not much of a napper, but I think I will take a shower. Maybe that will help rejuvenate me."

"I think it may take more than a shower to wake me up." Nix yawns. "Come on. I'll walk you to the guesthouse then come get you when she's ready to go."

"You kids have fun," Lexi says from the sofa, looking like a little shut-eye may be in her near future as well. She and Joe give us a wave before we walk through the glass doors and into the backyard.

"You look tired," I say to Nix. The dark circles under his eyes are noticeable, even in the dim lighting of the oasis. "Are you sure you want to go?"

"I am tired," he admits. "But my sister can be ruthless, and I'm too tired to fight her."

"I'm sure she'd understand."

Nix shakes his head in disagreement. "You don't know her well enough yet. What Lennon wants, Lennon gets."

"I think she just wants to spend time with you."

"I know."

"I think she misses you very much."

"I miss her too."

"I think she loved being close to you today."

Nix tenses his jaw, and I fear I've stepped over the boundary once again. Why can't I just leave well enough alone? *Dammit, Rose!*

We walk a minute in silence before Nix speaks again, but all he says is "Thank you."

"For what?"

"For today." We both stop in front of the door to the guesthouse, and Nix turns to face me. "Thank you for helping me."

Helping him? Oh. Maggie. Right.

"It was no problem. Lennon told me about Maggie, and when I saw how uncomfortable you seemed talking with her and Jacob, I just thought--"

"I'm not talking about Maggie, and you know it."

"I'm sorry?"

Nix's eyes are dead serious, and all I can think about is that our friendship–or whatever this is between us–would be so much easier if looking at him wasn't like getting a private tour of the Louvre. Talk about a work of art. Scholars could spend years on those eyes alone.

"Rose, you know this isn't easy for me," he says, and the sadness in his voice snaps me back to reality. "But today, it felt good to be close to my family again. It's been a long time."

"I wasn't responsible for that," I gape. No way am I taking responsibility for that blessing. "Tragedy has a way of bringing people together."

Nix looks down at his shoes, trying to hide his smile. "Say what you want, but me wanting to be closer to my family today had a lot to do with you."

"It did?"

Nix looks back up at me, his eyes serious once again. "I needed their support today. That's a given," he says. "But part of me felt like if I could let them back in, maybe I'd have a better chance of letting other people in too...letting *you* in."

Okay. That was unexpected.

"There's no pressure here," I reassure him, my hands trembling at my sides as my fingers fidget with the seams of my dress. "Your family is more important, so work to repair those bonds first. I'm not going anywhere."

"I hope not."

I can't fight the smile that spreads across my blushing face. Where is all of this coming from? What in the world is going through his head right now? I'd give anything to know.

"I should probably go and let you rejuvenate," Nix teases.

"I'm hoping the shower does the trick," I admit. "I may need some coffee as well."

"I'll be back as soon as the queen beckons."

Nix starts to walk away, and I know I shouldn't, but all of this forward progress has me feeling bold.

"Nix?" I beckon, and he turns back to me with a smile. "Could I ask a favor?"

"Sure."

"You can say no, and I promise it won't offend me." That's a lie.

"You're freaking me out, Rose."

"It's not that serious," I wave off his concern. "I just wanted to see...since it seemed to come so easily for you earlier today...."

Yeah, maybe this wasn't such a good idea. I'm sweating. I'm actually sweating.

"Spit it out, Rose."

"Okay..." *Deep breaths.* "I wanted to see if you would...if I could..." *Oh good grief, Rose. Just say it!* "I wanted to see if you would mind if I gave you hug?"

Nix seems to contemplate my request, but then shakes his head.

"I'm not sure that's a good idea right now," he says, and I swear I feel my heart literally deflate like a balloon.

"I understand." I try laughing off the humiliation. "I guess that wasn't really fair of me to ask. I mean, I just told you that you need to work on your family relationships first then I go and get selfish on you. Just forget I asked. I'll see you later, okay?"

Nix is staring at me open-mouthed, clearly uncomfortable with this situation, so I quickly push open the door to the guesthouse, saving us both from any further awkwardness.

"Rose, wait."

I close my eyes and dread turning around. I don't want to hear some story about how he's afraid it will ruin our friendship or how he just doesn't feel that way about me. Rejection from him hurts so much more than it probably should, which is even more reason why I need to end this before I lose myself completely.

"Rose, please look at me."

With a dejected sigh, I turn to him. "You don't have to explain."

"Yes, I do. You deserve an explanation."

I cross my arms over my chest and wait for the words I don't want to hear. "If it will make you feel better, I'll listen."

Nix takes a step back from me, as if he needs the extra room to breathe. "It's just that sometimes...it's hard being close to you."

I watch and wait for more but grow impatient after a while. "It's okay," I lie once again. "Like I said, I shouldn't have asked that of you. It's not a big deal. I promise."

"It is a big deal," he amends. "The reason I have a hard time being close to you is a very big deal, Rose. But after I tell you this there's no going back, so are you sure you want to know?"

"Is it good or bad?"

"That depends on you."

"Well then I want to know," I quickly reply. "Because nothing you say could ever change the way I feel about you."

Nix's scowl makes me regret my last statement, or at least saying it out loud. "That's what I'm afraid of."

"Please just say it," I plead, as I uncross my arms and take a step toward him. "I'm not sure I can take much more of this."

Nix is quiet for what feels like days. Or maybe it's the way he seems to be sizing me up and not the silence that has me on edge. Either way, by the time he finally speaks my heart is pounding like thunder in my chest as I await my fate.

"The last thing I want to do is lose you, Rose, but the truth is..." He puts his hands low on his hips and studies his shoes. "I would love nothing more than to hold you right now."

When he looks up at me, I exhale with a smile. "So what's the issue?" I tease, but he doesn't smile back.

"The issue is..." Nix comes a little closer, a fierce look of determination on his face. "If I hold you right now...I don't think I'll ever want to let you go."

Nix watches my face for a reaction, and frankly, I have no idea what he sees there because I can't stop replaying his words in my head long enough to concentrate on anything else.

When I don't say anything, he turns from me, seeming frustrated. "Jesus, Rose. Do you have any idea how much I hold back? How hard it is to keep my mouth shut? How hard I have to fight to keep my hands off of you?"

Wait. *What?*

"I don't...why would you...why are you fighting?" The words sound distant to my own ears, so I wonder if I even spoke them out loud. But then Nix turns around and the look on his face...

"I think about you all of the goddamn time," he confesses, taking a cautious step closer to me. "That first day we met...how you felt in my arms, those soft lips on my neck. I could kick own ass for the way I acted that day, but I knew it was the right thing to do. Getting close to you was too risky because I knew...even then I knew it has to be all or nothing with you, Rose. That's the only way."

Nix takes another step closer, and I remain perfectly still. I'm not sure I can move. I'm not sure if I'm even breathing.

His hand is shaking as he brings it up to my face and softly trails two fingers down my cheek. "Are you ready for all or nothing, Rose?" Nix is standing so close to me now I can feel his body heat, feel his warm breath brush across my face as he speaks. "Maggie may have left me broken, but you have the potential to ruin me for good. So I'm warning you now that the next time I have the privilege of holding you in my arms, it will be for a very, *very* long time."

I continue staring in silent vigilance, waiting for the words—any words, any thoughts at all—to come to me, but they never do.

Nix leans in close to my ear. "The choice is yours, Rose, but please be sure." He places a soft kiss on the edge of my jaw. "For me. Please."

That last plea leaves me reeling as I watch him walk away. Okay, so it was more than that last plea that has me reeling. Did I just stand here and listen to Nix tell me I could have him, all of him, if that's what I want? Did he just give me an open invitation to hold on to him and never let go?

I watch Nix until he's out of sight, then stumble my way into the guesthouse and fall down into the sofa. After everything that's happened today, I'm not sure I have the brain power to think about this right now. The one thing I know is that I want him. *God*, I want him, and if that conversation was in fact real and not a dream, then it seems Nix wants me too. But the fear hiding behind those dark eyes...I need to think this through. I won't be responsible for hurting him. In any way.

CHAPTER NINETEEN

I'm sitting on the sofa, completely lost in thought, when I hear my phone beep somewhere in the distance. I look around in a daze, wondering how long I've been sitting here, staring into space.

I stand to find my phone and it beeps again before I can pull it from my clutch. It's a text from Nix.

Twenty minutes. See you soon.

Twenty minutes? I look at the clock on my phone and realize I've been on the sofa over an hour. I haven't even taken a shower yet. *Holy Moses*!

I toss my phone and clutch back on the small table near the door and rush to get ready. I manage to take a shower, but I skip washing my hair. It's so thick and takes forever to dry, so when I get out of the shower, I toss it in a messy bun, freshen up my make-up and move to the bedroom to find something to wear. I grab the first thing I see, which is a pair of dark jeans and a flowy, green halter top that Sam bought me last year for my birthday. I search around for my brown sandals, which thankfully aren't too hard to find, and by the time I slip them on and add a little lip gloss, someone is knocking on the door.

I feel my heart trying to jump from my chest as I walk from the bedroom to answer the door. I know it's Nix. And I know I still haven't figured out what in the world to do about him, about me, about *us*. But the minute I open the door, all I can think is how lucky I am just to have the opportunity to stare at this man all night. He's simply stunning, standing there in jeans, a dark t-shirt and boots, accessorized only by the colorful swirls of ink covering each arm and that sexy piercing stuck in the soft skin under his bottom lip. He wears it all so well...so, *so* well.

He smiles as I'm admiring the piercing below his lip, and I realize I'm checking him out with total disregard. I ogle Nix all the time, but I usually try my best not to get caught. This time, however, it's like the idea of getting caught never even crossed my mind.

"You look incredible." Nix leans in to give me a kiss on the cheek. "As always."

A slow smile spreads across my face as I take in the change that's happened between us. Yes, I'm still spinning from Nix's earlier confession, but that ever-present barrier between us seems to have vanished. And the fact that Nix is leaving himself vulnerable like this is enough to make me want to jump in his arms right now. But I don't. Not yet. When the time is right.

"Thank you." I take him in again from his feet to his pretty head. "You look very nice as well."

Nix's smile is relaxed and positively breathtaking. "Are you ready to go? Lennon's waiting for us in the main house. Not so patiently, I might add."

"Just let me grab my things."

I reluctantly turn from him—my eyes will never get their fill—to grab what I think I'll need from my clutch. I quickly stuff everything in my pockets and we're on our way.

Nix and I walk toward the main house in silence, but every time I glance over at him, he's looking at me. And smiling. I've never seen him smile so much, and that's a shame.

"I'm happy to see you smiling," I tell him as we near the house. "I know today was hard for you."

"It was," Nix agrees with a sigh. "But you made it better."

Wow. No more walls. And so many smiles. A girl could get used to this.

Nix opens the glass doors leading into the living area and Lennon pops off the sofa the minute we enter. "Are we ready to boogie?"

"*Boogie?*" Nix teases, and she comes over to punch him in the arm.

"Yes. *Boogie*," she repeats. "And you know how I love to boogie. So let's go. The car's waiting for us."

Nix and I follow Lennon out front where a shiny, black towncar is indeed waiting for us. I'm kind of amazed by all of the luxuries this family is afforded, when they all seem so down to earth.

Nix gestures for Lennon to get in the front seat, and I'm happy to see he's no longer shying away from me—quite the opposite, it seems.

I climb in the backseat and Nix slides in beside me, close enough that his thigh is pressed against mine. And all of these gestures—the kiss at the door, wanting to be close to me, the secret smiles meant only for me—may seem small and insignificant, but the impact most certainly is not. I've wanted this for so long now that every touch, every smile is momentous and my reactions come naturally. I return his smiles and let him catch me checking him out every chance I get.

I allow my fingers to lightly graze his leg or arm when I shift around in the car seat. I'm flirting with him, and as foreign as that concept is for me, judging by Nix's reactions, I must not be too terribly bad at it.

Lennon and I chat for most of the ride, while Nix stays quiet in the seat next to me. The tension between the two of us is building rapidly, and I have no idea how this night is going to end, but I know I'm happy now. I decide to try and concentrate on that.

Nix tells the driver we'll text when we're ready to go home, then the three of us make our way into the bar. Judging by the outside, the place looks typical of a bar you'd see in a small town like Pollock Pines—a gravel parking lot crowded with various types of trucks, neon signs lighting the dusty windows and the smell of sawdust hanging in the air.

"There's not a lot of options when it comes to going out in this town," Lennon tells me. "But *Rusty's* is better than it looks. Plus The Gin Willies are playing tonight. Awesome cover band. Lots of classic rock."

I nod and smile as Nix opens the door for us to enter. The band must not be on yet because the noise level seems modest and the crowd is light and not at all what I expected. Most everyone is our age, rather than the middle-aged crowds that usually frequent places like this back home.

"Like I said, our options are limited," Lennon says, explaining the age range of the patrons. "We either have house parties or *Rusty's*. That's about it."

"Reminds me of home," I tell her. "There aren't a ton of options there either."

Lennon gives me a smile, then waves at someone over my shoulder. "I see some friends. I'm going to say hello. Be back in a few."

Nix watches her walk away, and I start to realize how much I really love the protector in him.

"You want something to drink?" he asks and I nod.

"A beer would be great."

Nix tilts his head in the direction of the bar, asking me to follow him. Someone vacates one of the barstools right as we walk up, so Nix pulls it out and offers it to me. I sit and he squeezes in next to me, leaning his elbows on the dark wood of the bar. His hip is pressed against my thigh, and the fact that he's purposefully staying close to me in his own way is making my stomach do funny things.

The bar is crowded, but Nix must know the bartender because with just a simple wave, the guy comes rushing over.

"Holy shit! Nix Taylor! How you doin', man?"

Nix leans in to give the guy a one-armed hug. "Been doing well, Davy. You?"

"Can't complain. What can I get you?"

"I'll take a Dead Man's if you've got it and a Sweetwater for the lady."

"Is Lennon here?" Davy starts scanning the area, a very excited look on his face.

I glance over at Nix and he's watching Davy with a shrewd grin. "Yeah, she's here, but you know she doesn't do beer." Nix looks over at me then. "Davy, this is Rose."

Davy's brow raises in surprise, then he gives Nix a nod of approval before extending a hand to me. "It's a pleasure to meet you, Rose."

"Nice to meet you, too."

Davy grabs my hand and kisses the top. To my surprise, Nix pushes Davy's face away. "Enough," he growls, getting a good chuckle out of Davy.

"Still threatened by me?" Davy teases. "You should be. I still got it, my friend."

He may be teasing, but in my opinion, Davy definitely still has it. I'm not sure how old he is, but if I had to guess, I'd put him in his early to mid-thirties. He's very tall, well over six feet, with green eyes and shaggy black hair that hangs in his eyes in that sexy, surfer kind of way. He's not as well built as Nix, but his toned arms are on full display in the snug t-shirt he's wearing, making it obvious he stays in shape. Yeah, I seriously doubt Davy has any trouble with the ladies, but the way he reacted to the possibility of Lennon being in the room makes me think he may have eyes for only one lady this evening.

Davy waves to someone over Nix's shoulder, and I turn to see Lennon approaching, waving back at Davy with a huge smile on her face.

"Davy Crockett!" she squeals. "You better jump over that bar and give me a hug right now!"

I'm not surprised one bit when Davy does exactly as she says. He wraps her up in a huge bear hug, and gives her a kiss on the cheek.

"How about I put you to work?" Davy releases Lennon, but it's obvious he didn't want to. "This place will be slammed later and I'm short again tonight. What do you say?"

"Really?" Lennon seems genuinely excited about the proposition. "I'll totally do it, but only if you promise to pay me this time."

"I was kidding, Len." Davy shakes his head at her with a smile. "You guys need to have a good time, and it's on me, so take advantage."

"Thanks man." Nix pats his shoulder. "It's good to see you."

"Good to see you too, brother."

Nix and Davy share a look that tells me they've been friends for a while, then Davy hops back over the bar and goes to make our drinks. He brings three, although I didn't hear him ask Lennon what she wanted.

"Thanks, D.C." Lennon grabs her cocktail from the bar and winks at him. "And you let me know if you need help tonight. You know I don't mind."

"Will do." Davy gives her a smile and watches her as she walks back into the crowd. Yep. That man is definitely hooked.

"Are there any open tables?" Nix asks and Davy nods.

"Yeah. I always keep number one reserved for a rainy day."

The two of them share another private smile and another manly hand shake before Nix grabs both of our beers from the bar and gestures for me to follow him to the pool tables in the back.

The place is getting more and more crowded by the minute, so Nix puts both bottles in one hand, then reaches back and grabs my hand to help me through the crowd. He leads me to an empty pool table in the back, right corner of the bar and places our beers on a high-top table near the wall, before pulling out a stool for me to sit down.

"Do you play pool?" he asks me, as he pulls a rack and a set of balls from the slot at the end of the table.

"Not really," I try to lie, but my smile gives me away.

The truth is my dad is an excellent pool player, and I've been playing with him on our table in the basement from the time I could walk.

"Why do I have a feeling I'm about to get played?" Nix narrows his eyes at me as he racks. "Go find you a stick then, big money. Let's see what you got."

I go to choose a cue stick from the display on the wall, and I feel Nix walk up behind me. He's standing close, so close I can feel his heat, smell his clean, woodsy scent.

"Take your time," Nix says and I tremble when his breath touches the bare skin of my shoulder. "I'm going to kick your ass no matter what stick you choose."

"I wouldn't be so sure about that." I turn to him, my grin spiked with challenge. "I'm pretty good."

"Of that I have no doubt, but you're not as good as me."

His gaze falls to my mouth then back to my eyes, and I'm not sure how much more I can take of this new Nix—no walls, no fear—like a man that knows what he wants and he's coming to get it. I can see how much he's been holding back. He's in complete control now, and it's completely sexy.

I turn back to the display and choose the best cue stick this place has to offer. When I turn back to Nix he's nodding in approval.

"The woman knows her sticks," he teases, and I shake my head. The innuendos are getting more interesting by the second.

"So how long have you known Davy?" I ask, as I take a sip of my beer. "You guys go way back? And please tell me his last name isn't really Crockett."

"No. It's not Crockett." Nix laughs as he appraises the stick collection for himself. "It's Maguire, and we all grew up together.

Davy's a vet like me, but he went in right after high school. Joined the Army the day after graduation."

Sorrow flashes briefly across Nix's face before he pulls a stick from the wall and heads back in my direction.

"Davy was hurt in an explosion after a few years in," Nix continues. "He was discharged and about a month after he gets home, his entire squad is killed in a raid. He was already suffering from a little PTSD, but when that happened, the guilt of leaving men behind hit him like a freight train. He was hospitalized for a while then he moved to Colorado for a few years and fell completely off the grid. He showed back up here out of the blue just a few months before I came home. He bought this place from the previous owner for God knows how much money, but Davy always loved this bar for some reason." Nix pauses with a thoughtful look on his face, as if he's remembering his own time here. "Anyway, he fixed the place up a bit and he's been running it ever since. He's happy from what I can tell, so I'm happy for him."

"He seems like good people."

"He is," Nix agrees. "I wish I would have known his situation when I first came back. He probably would have been someone good to talk to, but I didn't find out his story until a couple of months ago. Lennon came home to visit and met some friends at *Rusty's* one night while she was here. She told me she ended up behind the bar serving drinks because Davy was in a bind and needed her help. He treated her to dinner the next night as a thank you and told her his story."

"Has he always had a thing for her?" I ask, and Nix looks up at me and laughs.

"For several years now. He thinks he hides it well."

"He doesn't," I smile. "Does she feel the same?"

"I don't think so," Nix says. "But I'm not sure if she even knows. Lennon's IQ may be impressive, but her common sense could use some work."

"I adore your sister. I bet she was fun to grow up with."

"We fought like brothers and sisters do," Nix admits with a smile. "But she's definitely one of my favorite people, and I'm proud of her and her accomplishments. When we were younger, I was always afraid Lennon would choose the easy life, live off our family's money and never do anything for herself, but she proved me wrong. I couldn't be happier about that."

"And you? What made you want to join the military? Was it only your grandfather's influence?"

"I used to love listening to my grandfather's stories about the Airforce." Nix takes a drink from his beer and leans his cue stick against the wall. "I had originally planned on joining right after high school like Davy, but I decided to go to college first. Starting as an officer sounded more appealing, even though it ended up being just as much of a culture shock, I guess."

"Do you miss it?" The wistful look in his eyes has me asking.

"Sometimes," he admits. "But only certain parts. I miss the routine and the comradery. Relationships in the Army are a lot easier in a way. Everything is based mainly on loyalty and trust. You have each other's backs without question and after all of that shit with Maggie, those relationships for me became the better alternative–the only kind that mattered."

Nix looks at me as if he wants to add something then decides against it. He takes another sip of his beer then grabs his stick. "You wanna break?" he asks, and I guess the conversation is over.

"I'll let you have the honors. It may be the only chance you have to hit the pocket."

Nix gazes at my sassy mouth with reverence. "You talk a big game." He extends a hand toward the table in invitation. "Show me what you've got."

I take another drink from my beer and hop off the stool. My nerves kick up for a moment, but then I remind myself this is just another game of pool, like the thousands I've played over the years. I'm not confident about many things, but when it comes to pool, my self-confidence is as solid as a rock.

"What's the game?" I ask as I approach the table.

"Eight ball."

I line-up the cue ball and pocket two solids on the break. "Solids it is."

I make another shot—one into the side pocket—then sink the three into the corner before missing what should have been an easy shot for me. I looked up and caught Nix staring at me as if he wanted to eat me alive and it shook my concentration. He's not playing fair.

Nix makes three shots in a row. He's a good player, but I can confidently say he's not as good as me. He misses a corner shot and moves back to the high-top table to watch me work.

I try not to look at him again, and I manage to knock the five into the side pocket, but then he moves to stand next to me as I'm lining up my next shot. "You're gonna miss," he says so confidently that I pause to look up at him.

"Are you questioning my skills?"

"Never."

The smile on his face is telling me otherwise.

I turn back to the table and line up again, paying no attention to his lack of confidence in me, but it's hard to ignore his physical presence when he's standing to close.

I pull back the stick a couple of times, testing the power I need to make the shot, and just as I'm about to take it, I feel a finger trail slowly down the length of my spine. I miss the six ball I was aiming for by a mile as I arch into the table and my eyes close briefly in shock.

Shock...and something else entirely.

"You missed." Nix's voice is quiet but victorious, and I can tell he's smiling, even though I haven't found the strength to right myself and look up at him.

"You cheat," I accuse, then turn to find his black eyes blazing. "I refuse to play with cheaters."

"What was I supposed to do? You were kicking my ass."

I narrow my eyes at him. "Is it because I'm a girl?"

"No." Nix shakes his head, his eyes back on my lips again. "I just don't like to lose."

I'm thinking I may need something stronger than beer to get through this evening, and just then—like the saving grace she has so far proved to be—Lennon bounds over to us with a small try in her hands.

"Hope you like Jäger," she says to me, then hands me and Nix each a shot from her tray. "Bottoms up!"

I've never had Jägermeister before, and when I do the shot, I vow to never have it again.

"That was awful," I choke as Lennon and Nix both laugh at me.

"They start to taste better after the first few," Lennon says, giving me another shot, but I shake my head profusely. "Come on, Rose.

We have no responsibilities and nowhere to be. Let's enjoy it while we can."

I consider the small glass she's waving in front of my face for a moment then reluctantly take it from her hand.

"That's my girl," Lennon smiles at me, and we all toast each other before taking the second shot. "I'm thinking something fruity for the next round. Or should we stick to Jäger?"

"No more for me," I try and plead, but I catch Nix shaking his head at me.

"She's ruthless," he reminds me with a smile and Lennon nods in agreement.

"I'll come find you again soon," she sings to Nix and me before bouncing away with her empty tray.

"That was truly horrible." I wipe at my mouth, wishing I could get rid of that after taste. Gross.

"Have some beer," Nix suggests, going over to grab my beer for me. "And don't feel obligated to participate in Lennon's foolishness. She may seem impossible, but I can handle her."

"It's okay," I smile. "I'm having fun, and she's right. I don't have anywhere to be tonight other than right here."

Right here with you, I think to myself. *Right where I want to be.*

Nix puts our beers back on the high-top table then grips my hand tightly in his. "Come with me," he demands with a seriously sexy smirk that guarantees I'd follow him anywhere.

He pulls me through the crowd, toward the middle of the dance floor, and the music is louder out here than it was in our dark corner from before. The deep, thump of the bass drum in the floor beneath our feet is making my entire body vibrate. It's not an awful sensation, especially with Nix's rough hand squeezing mine.

When Nix finally stops, there's barely a foot of space around us on any side. The dance floor is so packed, I'd be forced into standing close to him, whether I wanted to or not. But I definitely want to, and it makes me happy to see Nix must feel the same. He pulls me against his chest and I grab on to his arms as he whispers, "Dance with me" so close to my ear, I can hear him perfectly even over the blaring music and roar of the crowd as they dance around us.

The music is fast, but Nix sways us slowly to the beat. I turn my face into his neck and close my eyes, giving my other senses a chance to appreciate this moment. I squeeze his biceps as I inhale his rich scent, but before my tongue can reach out for a taste, I'm being spun around and pulled backward into his solid chest.

Nix places his hands on the front of my hips, dangerously close to a part of me that I'm not ashamed to say is silently begging for his touch. And I can barely control my breathing as those determined hands move down to the tops of my thighs and back up to my hips, again and again as we move together. His chin is resting on my shoulder and his sweet-smelling breath is skimming across the sensitive skin of my neck, making me lightheaded.

"I'm sorry, but I can't resist." Nix's hands roam over me tenderly, seductively from my hips, across my stomach. "It feels too good to touch you, Rose. So soft. So *perfect*."

I want to respond. I want to tell him I feel the same way about him, but then he lifts may arms, placing them around his neck, giving him better access as he continues his sweet caresses and I can't seem to hold on to my train of thought.

Pretty soon, every inch of my skin feels damp with sweat and alive with energy, as his hands slide over my body, even grazing the sides of my breasts a few times, making me shiver in ecstasy. I can feel

Nix's smile against my neck with each tease, but I don't mind. I'm thoroughly enjoying the torment.

By the time he turns me back around to face him, I'm completely lost in sensation. Without a thought, other than knowing it's imperative I have my hands on him in some way, I slide my arms around his narrow waist. I look into his eyes, soaking up their warmth, and suddenly, we're standing perfectly still in the middle of the dance floor. Nix reaches up and places a hand on either side of my face and God, I want him to kiss me. *Please kiss me.* But with a mind clouded by lust, and not thinking rationally, I decide to take matters into my own hands.

I grab the back of his neck and pull his mouth to mine, half expecting a pause as Nix processes the shock of my attack. But to my delight, he kisses me back with surprising enthusiasm. His tongue sweeps through my mouth, claiming it with slow, hypnotizing movements until suddenly, he stops.

"Jesus, Rose…" He dips his head low, his breath wild and labored at my ear. "What are you trying to do to me?"

My answer is a kiss on his neck, on his jaw, that soft spot right below his ear, as Nix clenches the loose fabric of my blouse at my waist. I can almost feel his self-control weakening with each touch of my lips to his warm skin, and the fact that I played a part in that has adrenaline building up in my veins like a rocket engine before take-off. I can barely feel the alcohol anymore. I feel completely awake, alive, exhilarated.

And I want more.

CHAPTER TWENTY

"Nix?"

He lifts his head, and the sight of those dark, alluring eyes causes my breath to catch in my throat.

Rose, what are you doing?

I look up at him, wondering how I'm ever going to get the words out. How am I ever going to tell him what I want when what I want could possibly ruin us forever? But he said it was up to me, and I want him. I want all of him, and I know this with undeniable certainty. But before I can tell him exactly how much, his sister is next to us somehow balancing another tray in her hands, even with the crowd of bodies bumping into us from all sides.

"Looks like you two could use something cold to drink," she yells over the current guitar solo, then gives us a wink.

"That sounds like a great idea." I grab one of the shot glasses and toss it back.

Hmmm. Lennon's right. After the first couple, the Jäger starts to grow on you.

"How about you, big brother?" Lennon offers him a glass, which he gulps down in one swallow while glaring at her the entire time. "And this last one is for me, but don't worry. I'll be back again soon."

Lennon takes her shot then waves as she slips away, leaving us alone again on the dance floor.

Nix leans into my ear as I watch her walk away. "How about another game of pool?"

He pulls back to catch my response, so I nod, but then lean in to add, "Maybe I'll let you win this time."

Nix laughs and narrows his pretty eyes at me. "I'm gonna punish you."

Punish? It may be the Jäger talking, but I kinda like the sound of that.

Nix takes my hand and starts pulling me through the crowded dance floor. Lennon catches us at the edge before we can make our way over to the pool table with yet another tray of shots.

"You'll thank me for this later," she winks, but I'm not sure I can handle any more. It's been a while since I've drank, and my head's already feeling a little fuzzy.

"I don't think I need another," I admit and she frowns.

"Come on. It's the last one." Lennon makes a show of crossing her heart with her index finger. "I promise."

Nix rolls his eyes at his sister's plea. "You don't have to do another one, if you don't want," he tells me, but I decide one more surely won't hurt.

"It's okay. I'll do it."

I take a glass from Lennon's tray and gulp it back. I barely feel the burn at this point, which I know is probably not a good sign.

Lennon takes a shot as well, but Nix declines his. "Someone has to make sure you ladies get home safely," he says, and I turn to him with gooey eyes. *My protector.* So noble.

And so damn gorgeous.

Nix gives me a slow smile as I stare at him, probably seeing that I've definitely passed from buzzed to slightly wasted at this point, but I don't really care. I just want to stare at him. I love staring at him.

"You still up for a game of pool, Jäger Queen, or do we need to call it a night?"

He brings my hand to his mouth and kisses my knuckles softly. I may be drunk, but the competitive side of me refuses to let him win this time. I square my shoulders, with every intention of heading over to the table and kicking his beautiful behind, but when I go to take my first step, I stumble and nearly hit the floor. Nix hauls me up with a laugh and walks me over to a nearby high-top table. He sits me up on a barstool, then pulls out his phone and starts dialing or texting, I'm not sure which. All I know is that he smells like heaven and I love the way his forearms are flexing while he messes with his phone.

When he finally looks up at me, his face is a tad blurry, but my favorite brown eyes are perfectly clear as they take me in.

"Your eyes..." I trail off as I get caught in his stare.

"What about them?" That teasing smile he's wearing right now is making me dizzy. Or it could be the alcohol. But I'm thinking it's his smile.

"Your eyes are so pretty."

"Thank you," Nix chuckles. "Yours are pretty too."

"You think my eyes are pretty?"

Nix reaches up to tend to a stray lock of my hair, and I suddenly wish my head wasn't so fuzzied by all of that alcohol. I would prefer to remember this moment with perfect clarity, especially when he leans in and whispers "I think *you're* pretty," in my ear.

He kisses the side of my neck before pulling away and my body trembles as if the temperature in the room just dropped about fifty degrees, but I'm certainly not cold. Quite the contrary.

I grab both of his wrists and turn his hands facing up. "You're prettier." I can feel his eyes on me as I start to trace the colorful ink coiling up and around his forearms. "Like a work of art."

If I wasn't so tipsy, I'd probably regret that last cheesy line, but if that's what caused him to look at me the way he's looking at me now—if that's what makes him take my face in his hands and start kissing me like a drowning man in need of oxygen, then I have zero regrets. Not one. And when Nix eventually pulls his lips from mine, I feel even more wrecked than before—drunk on his kisses, high from his touch.

"Let's go, pretty girl." He kisses the tip of my nose, then helps me off the barstool, and I'm once again left with trying to figure out what's making me feel so faint—the alcohol or Nix.

Either way, I wrap both arms around Nix's waist as he helps me through the crowd toward the front door of the bar. Luckily my brain is still functioning well enough to know that we're missing someone.

"What about Lennon?" I ask him, hoping my words weren't actually as slurred as they sounded.

"I texted Davy to let him know I'm taking you home, and he promised to watch over Lennon. He'll get her a car when she's ready."

Wow. Nix must really trust Davy. I know he wouldn't leave his sister's care in just anyone's hands.

"You're such a good man," I mumble into his chest as we walk. "You make me feel so safe."

I'm not sure if he even heard me, but it doesn't matter. He has his arm around me, holding me close to his side, looking after me, as if trying to prove me right.

The car is waiting for us when we get outside, and like the gentleman that he is, he opens the door and helps me inside. Then he slides in beside me and explains to the driver why we are one less, but I have trouble following the conversation. My head is spinning like a merry-go-round, and I can feel the alcohol starting to make its way back up my throat.

"You're looking kind of pale there." Nix lifts me and sits me in his lap. "Just take it easy. We'll be home in no time."

I wrap my arms around him, close my eyes and bury my face in his neck. For some reason, Nix's scent is like a cure-all for anything that ails me. As I breathe him in, the spinning immediately starts to slow and the nausea subsides.

"This reminds me of the first time I met you," Nix says in a soft voice. "When you kissed me...."

The memory has me smiling against his neck. "And you wanted to toss me into the woods?"

"Hardly." Nix is quick to correct me. "I wanted more. I wanted you to do it again. And again. And again..."

Nix stops talking when I do as requested and kiss him right where his shoulder meets his neck.

"Again," he murmurs, and I nuzzle him with my nose then kiss a spot right beneath his chin.

"More?" I whisper, but then I'm slowly kissing along his jaw line, unable to wait for an answer.

"More," he commands, and I love that I can feel the growl in his tone against my lips.

I move my mouth over his jaw and onto his cheek, but before I can go any further, Nix has my face in his hands and he's kissing me breathless.

By the time we pull into the driveway of his parents' house, my lips feel swollen and bruised from his assault, and the rest of my body is flushed and longing for him in a way that I've never wanted anything in my life.

He walks me inside and thankfully, the house is quiet. Not a soul in sight. "How about a glass of water?" Nix offers as we pass through the kitchen, hand in hand.

"Sure."

He plants a sweet kiss on my forehead before opening a cabinet and pulling out a bottle of bourbon. "For me," he smiles as he gets out a small glass and fills it halfway.

He takes a sip before getting my water, and when he hands the glass to me I take a few grateful swallows, the cold helping to bring me back to life. I look over at Nix then as he sips at his bourbon and there's a look in his eyes that would be impossible to misunderstand. And now, with a slightly clearer head, the realization of where I am, who I'm with and what I'm most likely about to do slams into me like a wrecking ball.

"I think I may like to have what you're having," I tell Nix as I sit my water down on the counter in front of me.

He gives me a questioning look but when I nod, letting him know I'm serious, he grabs me a glass from the cabinet and pours me a drink.

I take it from him and have a taste. It's awful, but I proceed to down the rest of the glass before handing it back to him to request another.

Nix shakes his head. "What's going on, Rose? Are you okay?"

"I'm fine," I lie, as I take the matter into my own hands and pour myself another glass. I down it even faster than the first, and Nix takes the glass from me with a frown. "Take it easy. That stuff will sneak up on you."

Now, if I had any experience with drinking heavily, I would know that I've had about four too many. But I rarely drink. And never the combination I've ingested this evening. So, the next time I look at Nix, it's no surprise I feel the urge to close one eye so I can focus on his face. My head is suddenly spinning out of control and my body feels like it's turning into some version of all of the liquid swirling around in my stomach. Right before the sensation reaches my legs, I manage a smile as Nix scoops me up into his arms. He seems concerned, but I can't seem to make myself care about much of anything right now.

The next thing I know, I'm lying on sheets that smell like a walk through the woods right after it rains.

Nix.

I close my eyes and turn my face into the pillow. "Stay with me," I whisper as I inhale deeply, wishing I could carry that scent around in my nose all day, every day. "Stay with me forever."

Someone starts softly stroking the back of my hair, then the bed dips down and a new pillow is under my nose. It's firm, but incredibly warm, and smells even better than the last pillow. So with a contented sigh, I nestle in and drift off into a sweet smelling oblivion.

CHAPTER TWENTY-ONE

Oh God, my head.

I wake up to the sound of crickets chirping, and I have to blink several times before I can get my bearings. It appears I'm in the master bedroom of the guesthouse and the patio doors in front of me are open, which explains the sound and the light breeze on my face.

Thankfully, it's still dark out because I don't think I could handle the sunlight right now. My head is absolutely killing me.

I glance at the nightstand and find two Advil and a full glass of water. Nix must have put it there for me. That was really nice of him. Really, really nice.

I close my eyes again as the events of last night start filtering into my foggy head—the bar, the game of pool, the dancing, the kissing...oh, the *kissing*. And when I try and put my hand on my stomach to stop the sudden fluttering, I realize a hand is already there. I can't believe he stayed with me. Even after my irrational and completely childish behavior when we got back here last night, he still stayed with me.

I open my eyes and smile at the sight of his big, tattooed arm wound snugly around my waist. I can feel his warm breath on the back of my neck, and when I start concentrating on that sensation, I feel....

I feel like I need to get out of here.

All of the fears from last night come rushing back—the fear of losing him, the fear of hurting him, but ultimately, it was the fear of falling in love again. I spent most of last night worrying over my feelings for Nix. I wanted to make the right decision, be certain I wouldn't hurt him. But when we got back here, I realized I'd been so concerned about hurting Nix that I had forgotten my own feelings. How will I protect *my* heart? Or am I too late?

Somehow, I manage to unwind myself from Nix without waking him. I grab the Advil and water and move quickly to the bathroom to assess the damage—a little wrinkled, a lot hung-over, but not as bad as I thought it would be. I empty my bladder before it explodes, then splash some cold water on my face to wake me up and also to remove the last of my leftover eye make-up. I take the pain killers and sit on the side of the bathtub a few minutes, silently vowing to never drink again. And when the pounding in my head is down to a dull thump, I shift my hair back into a sloppy bun, brush my teeth, brush at my outfit, then open the door back up quietly, praying he's still asleep.

My plan is to go out into the living room to give the painkillers time to completely kick in so I can think, but as I leave the bathroom, I glance over at the bed and something about the image stops me dead in my tracks.

Nix is still fast asleep, but he's rolled onto his back, allowing the moonlight streaming through the open doors to spotlight his perfect form. He's shed the blanket that was covering us, and I can see he's still in his jeans from last night, but the shirt and boots are gone. One arm is close to his side, while the other is lying loosely across his stomach, and the word that immediately pops into my head is *beautiful*. He is utterly beautiful, inside and out. And as I stand still as stone, staring at the sleeping man before me, I start to reflect again on everything that happened last night. He was a gentleman. He was kind. He was caring. He was...*perfect*.

Suddenly, all of those dangerous urges from last night are back with a vengeance, but I'm no longer afraid. Why should I be? It's Nix. The man makes it his mission to protect me on a daily basis. Why wouldn't I trust him with my heart?

Without a second thought, I move toward him and slide a finger down his scruffy cheek. *Yes.* That feels good, so I continue following the trail down his neck, over his chest to one of the silver bars in his nipple. I'm in such a trance, I startle when Nix's hand comes over mine.

When I look at his face, he's not smiling. "What are you doing, Rose?"

I stare at him, not sure what to say, until I finally manage to stutter out an honest answer.

"I-I don't know."

Nix lets go of my hand and sits up slowly in the bed. His eyes never leave mine, as my heart pounds a deep bass rhythm in my chest, and I know this is right. It's so right that I don't dare question it.

He moves to the side of the bed and traps me between his legs, and I don't hesitate when he puts his arms around me and pulls me closer. I grab on to his shoulders to steady myself, but I feel stronger than I've felt in a long time.

"All or nothing, Rose. Are you sure?" His voice is low and husky and tickles me in all the right places.

"Yes," I breathe. *No question.*

Nix places a kiss on my stomach before looking up at me through long, dark lashes. "Then give me those lips."

I lean down to kiss him and his lips are impossibly soft.

So sweet.

So right.

Going with my instincts, wanting to be closer, I straddle his lap and Nix lets out this little moan of satisfaction that seems to say, "thank you" and "you're welcome" at the same time.

So sexy.

So right.

"Let me see you," Nix says with a smile, and I smile back as I raise my arms so he can take off my top. He immediately starts trailing kisses along my arms and chest as he removes my bra. "I wanna kiss every inch..." his lips slide across my ribs, "of that petal soft skin. Every...fucking...inch."

I close my eyes and lean my head back, letting him do as he wishes. And when he has his fill, he pulls my mouth back to his, and I savor him—the kiss, the quiet sounds, the skin-to-skin contact, all of it—until the kissing isn't enough and I'm fighting for control, grinding against him as I start to want more, as I start to *need* more.

"Please," I beg as the desperation finally breaks through, but I don't have to say anything further. It's obvious what I want, and thankfully, Nix seems more than willing to give it to me.

Without hesitation, he lays me gently across the bed and continues to make good on his promise to kiss every inch of my body. He swiftly removes my jeans and starts his next assault on the inside of my thighs, moving painfully slow until he removes my panties with a loud rip and his mouth is finally where I want it to be.

"*Nix*...." His name is one long syllable as it leaves my mouth, and my body twitches with each lick, each groan of satisfaction from him that vibrates my core. Oh God ...*oh God*.

My orgasm rocks me from the inside out, but I barely have a chance to regain consciousness before Nix exchanges his tongue for his fingers.

"Again," he commands, and mere seconds later, like a slave to its master, my body obeys.

The second orgasm is even more life-changing than the first, and afterward, I barely have the strength to open my eyes. But then I feel his mouth at my ear, and my body starts gearing back up for another round. And when I hear these words, "Was that enough, pretty girl, or do you want more?" I nearly experience number three.

"More," I whisper, and his mouth finds mine once again as he pulls off his jeans and moves on top of me.

My eyes are still closed, but I can hear him slip on a condom, and my body shivers with anticipation. He kisses me and teases me until I'm about to scream, but as if he already knows me better than I know myself, he enters me slowly, just before I'm about to break.

"Oh Nix...*yes*...."

And those are the last words that are spoken out loud between us. There are plenty of moans and gasps in our climb toward ecstasy. And when it finally happens, we both call out the others' name then Nix sinks his hard body down onto me and whispers "thank you" in my ear as he leaves a trail of warm kisses down the side of my neck.

I can't stop shaking. One night with this man, and I know he is all I'll ever need. I'm no longer afraid of falling in love with him because it's already happened. The connection I feel between us now is like raw power in my bones, making me feel strong and safe and alive. It's incredible. And I'm hopelessly addicted.

Nix continues his kisses and I relax into him as he moves to my side and pulls me close. I feel my eyes growing heavier and heavier as he strokes my back, my hip, my thigh and back up again. I'm just about to drift off when Nix says my name. I try and open my eyes, but it's no use.

"Yes?" I answer as his soft fingers move to my face.

"I have a confession." He runs a finger along my bottom lip. "When I follow you home every night, it's not just to make sure you get there safely. That's one reason, but it's not the only one."

"No?"

"No."

I force my eyes open and raise my head so I can see him. "Tell me," I whisper. "You can tell me anything."

Nix smiles as he pets at my bottom lip again. "On the day we met, I followed you home because I was worried about you, but it was more than that," he says. "I wasn't sure exactly what it was at the time, but then when I came back to Delia after being away for a few days, all I knew was that I had to see you. After seeing my grandfather wasting away in a hospital bed and not being able to do a damn thing about it...you looked back at me from your doorstep that night and I just knew everything was going to be okay. I've always wanted to thank you for that."

I pause for a moment, delighting in his confession. He told me once before I was "necessary" in his life, and I'm not sure I really understood what that meant until now. All I've ever wanted was to be there for him, to make sure he knew if nothing else that he had a friend in me. And now I know that all of this time, I've been that for him and maybe more.

Instead of responding with words, I kiss him again–this time nibbling a bit on his bottom lip, repaying the favor, since he was just paying such special attention to mine.

"Do that again." Nix growls his request, and I eagerly oblige.

When we get our temporary fill of each other's lips, Nix and I both agree we're thirsty and leave the bed to go find something cool to drink. Nix slips his boxer briefs back on, then picks up the t-shirt he was wearing earlier and slips it over my head. His eyes skim over my bare thighs then slowly rise up to my mouth.

"That's a sight I could get used to," he whispers, then takes me in his arms and kisses me sweetly. "I'll make sure to supply you with enough of my clothes that you can wear a piece for me every day. Deal?"

I giggle as his lips move to my neck. "Deal."

We walk hand in hand into the kitchen of the guesthouse. Nix finds some orange juice in the refrigerator, pours us each a glass and we both sigh after taking our first sips.

"Man, that tastes good," I remark, but I barely get the words out before Nix pushes me against the counter and has his mouth on mine.

"I wanted to see if yours tasted better."

"You could have taken a sip from my glass," I suggest, although I definitely preferred his method.

Nix leans in and kisses the side of my neck. "Is it bad that I can't stop kissing you?"

He drags his tongue along the ridge of my ear and I whimper. "Is it bad that I hope you never do?"

Nix lifts me up on to the countertop and pushes himself between my legs. "Are you on the pill, Rose?" His mouth is now skimming across my collarbone, and I can barely concentrate on what he's asking. "Because I don't have a condom nearby, and I want to be inside you. Right now."

I nod my head, hoping he understands without my having to say anything because the minute his teeth catch my nipple through the thin cotton of his t-shirt, words are lost on me.

Nix makes quick work of his underwear and I realize I should probably ask if he's safe, but I trust him and know that he would never do anything to hurt me.

"Come here." He pulls me to the edge of the counter, and we're the perfect height for....

Oh....God....

I wrap my legs and arms around him as he establishes a rhythm—slow, deep, hypnotic, *breathtaking*. His tongue is swirling around mine, matching the tempo of his circling hips and within seconds it seems, his name is echoing off the kitchen walls.

"Don't move." Nix remains inside me after his own release, holding me so close there's barely an inch of my body that's not pressed against him. "Just let me feel this, baby. Let me feel you, inside and out. You're so perfect."

I keep my face buried in his neck, breathing in my favorite smell in the whole world, as he lightly strokes my back, shoulder to hip. Content and well satisfied, I start to drift off in Nix's arms, but I startle awake when he finally removes himself from inside of me.

"Don't worry," he grins. "It's only temporary."

He lifts me into his arms, and I snuggle back into him as he carries me to the bedroom. The minute he has me laid out on the bed, he moves over me and I inhale a sharp breath as he enters me again. "I'm sorry," he breathes, as he starts to move. "I've waited so long to have you like this, to kiss you, to touch you. Now I can't stop, Rose. God, I can't fucking stop."

"Please don't," I plead. "Please don't ever stop."

I wrap my legs around him, allowing him even deeper inside me, as he kisses my neck, my face, my shoulders—anything and everything within reach of his perfect mouth. He explores my body with loving, gentle caresses from my arms to the tops of my thighs, kissing and teasing along the way. And every time I'm close, right as I'm about to fall over the edge, Nix forces me to hold on until I'm afraid of what may happen when he finally allows me to let go.

"*Rose....*" He whispers my name as his dark eyes trap me with their heated gaze. "Come for me, baby. Show me how good this feels."

My orgasm is instantaneous and the most powerful thing I've ever felt in my life. It ricochets through me, touching every possible surface inside, until I'm all sensation, all feeling and my entire body is humming with satisfaction.

I open my eyes just in time to see Nix find his release and another orgasm spirals down on me like a second helping of warm bliss, reducing me to nothing more than shallow breaths and a racing heart.

I try and force my eyes open again, but it's no use. Nix showers my face with soft, tender kisses before gently rolling off of me. The next thing I feel is the warmth of a blanket being pulled over us both as Nix cradles me into his side.

"Nix?"

"Yeah?"

"Thanks for the hug."

His chest rumbles under my cheek as he laughs. "Let's get some sleep, smartass," he whispers, so I snuggle in and happily do as I'm told.

CHAPTER TWENTY-TWO

When it comes to sex, Nix is insatiable.

And isn't that just the best surprise.

I woke up this morning to his hand between my legs, his fingers moving in slow circles, coaxing me, warming me up from the inside out.

I thought I was dreaming. Certainly this man can't be real. There's no way this is happening. Not to me.

But then Nix moved his warm body over mine, so I could feel his weight, feel his soft caresses along my over-heated skin. And even without opening my eyes, I knew I wasn't dreaming. I wrapped my arms around his strong shoulders and pulled him close, allowing him to drown my senses.

Nix let out a low, satisfied groan as he entered me. "Good morning."

"Morning," I murmured against his neck, as he drove deep, hitting me in places I never knew existed, places I know only Nix will ever be able to find.

We made love twice before ever leaving the bed, then once more in the shower. Now, we're cuddled into each other on the sofa, watching *The Breakfast Club*. Seems Nix and I have a shared love for The Brat Pack. As if I could love him more.

"I always thought Molly Ringwold was hot," Nix says, as he twirls a strand of my hair around in his fingers.

"Got a thing for redheads, Mr. Taylor?"

"No," he smiles. "Gotta thing for *you*."

I take his hand in mine and kiss his palm. "I kind of have a thing for you too."

"Don't care what color your hair is." Nix pulls me into his lap and kisses along my neck. "Doesn't really matter what you look like at all. It's this..." he places a palm over my heart and looks up at me. "I want this. Will you give this to me?"

I place my trembling hand on his cheek. "Take it. Anything you want, if it makes you happy, I'll give it to you."

Nix smiles the sweetest smile. "What about this?" he asks, brushing two fingers across my mouth. "Can I have this?"

I kiss him deep and slow in response. "Done."

"And these?" Nix palms my breasts and I moan. "These make me really happy."

I flush, as he brushes over my nipples with his thumbs. "Anything you want."

With a smug look, Nix trails one hand down my stomach and his long fingers slide inside my panties. "But this?" he growls against my lips as he slips two of those long fingers inside me. "This is *mine*. I'm not asking this time. I'm telling."

My head drops back, my entire body trembling in ecstasy as his capable fingers glide in and out.

"Tell me this is mine, Rose," Nix insists. "Say it."

I force myself to focus on his eyes, currently gleaming with deep, male satisfaction.

"It's yours," I pant. "Everything. All of me. I belong to you."

Nix takes my mouth with an intensity that has me orgasming on the spot. I'm still shaking from the aftershock as Nix removes what little clothing the two of us are wearing, lays us both down on the couch and slowly sinks inside of me. I wrap my arms and legs around him, holding him close as he moves. My skin tingles everywhere his beautiful, scruffy face teases me, which is basically everywhere he can reach while staying inside me.

"I love kissing you." Nix glides his lips along my neck. "Your skin's so soft, so warm."

My eyes roll back as he grabs the back of my knee, lifting my leg so he can drive even deeper.

"And kissing you would be enough," he continues and I can tell he's close, his breaths coming harsh and uneven as he tries to speak. "But then you give me everything else. You give me everything, Rose. And now...I'm overwhelmed."

I open my eyes and suddenly I'm trapped in those abysmal eyes of his.

"You own me," he whispers. "You fucking *own* me."

Our gazes remain locked until we both shatter, trembling and shaking, clawing at each other, unable to get close enough. As we come down, we stay connected in every possible way, and I swear I could spend the rest of my life joined to him like this. Tears suddenly cloud my vision with the thought.

"I'm in love with you."

The words are a whisper and out of my mouth before I can stop them. As soon as I realize what I've said, my heart starts racing in alarm, but then Nix slowly raises his head from where it was resting against my shoulder and the look on his face doesn't just slow my heart. It stills it completely.

"I love you too." His hand is trembling as he wipes at the tears that have fallen from my eyes. "So much it scares me."

"Don't be scared." I grab his hand from my face and place it over my heart. "It's all yours. You gave me an option—all or nothing. All of me for all of you."

Nix smiles then kisses me gently. "I didn't really give you much of a choice. I was coming on pretty strong at the bar last night."

"I'd already made my decision," I confess. "I made my decision the day I met you in the park, before I even knew who you were. I wanted you then just as much as I want you now. I've only been waiting for you to want me back."

Nix's face is suddenly remorseful. "I had to be sure. I'm sorry I waited so long."

"It's okay." I palm his cheek and he pushes into my hand.

"It's been torture." He sighs. "I feel like I've been waiting for you forever."

"Well, the wait is over, mister. You've got me. So what do you plan to do with me?"

"The question is..." Nix's smile is full of challenge, and I marvel at the feel of him hardening, lengthening again inside me. "...what I plan to do *to* you. And I have several ideas."

CHAPTER TWENTY-THREE

It seems Nix and I are making up for lost time. All of these weeks spent denying each other has led to a lot of cuddling, kissing and more sex in the last twelve hours than I probably had in the last year of my marriage.

And speaking of my failed marriage, it's been on the tip of my tongue more than once today. It's the one thing I've kept to myself and after last night....and this morning...and about an hour ago before we had lunch...I want to tell Nix everything. He said all or nothing, and I want to give him all of me. No secrets. I'm just so scared of his reaction. Will he think of me differently? Will he think less of me?

My divorce is an ugly stain on the timeline of my life, but I don't look back on it with regret. Danny and I had some good times together, and despite our differences, I can admit he's a good man. He just wasn't good for me.

Plus I can't regret my divorce now because without it, I may have never found Nix. It's amazing how you think you know what love is, then you meet someone that proves you wrong.

I stand corrected, Nix Taylor.

"We should probably make an appearance so everyone knows we're still alive."

I turn from my seat on the sofa to find my love walking toward me. The smile on his face is even more heart-stopping than usual. Or maybe it's the fact that he's fresh from his second shower of the day—wet hair, no shirt, in a pair of dark cargo shorts hanging low on his hips—that's taking my breath away. It's hard to say. Nix is magnificent from any angle.

"Or we could call or text," I suggest with a smile. "That way, you can remain shirtless and I can remain happy."

Nix sits next to me on the sofa and immediately pulls me onto his lap. "Well, since my goal in life is to make you happy, I'll never wear a shirt again. How about that?"

I grab his face and cover his mouth with mine. I kiss him slowly, nibbling my way across his lips, soaking up his quiet moans as I go. I run my fingers through the back of his damp hair and he pulls me close.

"Love you," he whispers, and I tremble in his arms.

Hearing those words from him...that's going to take some getting used to.

"I love you," I whisper back. "So much."

Nix smiles this beautiful, shy smile before burying his face in my neck and I revel in his happiness. Since I've known him, I've never seen him like this and to think it has something to do with me...

I hold him close, silently promising to do everything in my power to keep him forever. It's not just that I love him. It's *how* I love him, as if he's already a part of me—a part I want to nourish and grow, the part I plan to cherish most in this world. I fell in love barely knowing him at all. I didn't need to know him. The connection, the pull was there the minute those black eyes caught mine. I tried to do the right thing. I tried to deny my feelings. I was afraid of getting hurt, afraid of hurting someone else. But looking back now, I can see what a foolish endeavor that would have been. I would have broken eventually because this man is meant to be mine, and I am his. It's that simple.

We eventually (reluctantly) pull ourselves away from each other so we can go spend some time with the rest of Nix's family.

As I put my hair into a ponytail in the bathroom, I wonder what Nix will tell them about us. He told me earlier to let him handle things, and I agreed. I only pray they're as happy about the situation as I am. I can see after the past couple of days that Nix is close with his family. It's important to me that they support the two of us being together.

"Stop worrying."

I look up at the mirror in front of me and smile when I see Nix standing in the doorway.

"I want them to be happy."

"They will be." He moves toward me and wraps his arms around my waist from behind. "Did you see how happy they were that I brought someone home with me? Then you poured that Southern charm all over the place and now I may have to fight my dad for you. And possibly Lennon too."

"Whatever," I scoff, as Nix nuzzles into my neck. "Just as long as you're happy. That's what really matters."

Nix lifts his head and studies me in the mirror. "Thank you." That sweet, shy smile teases his lips. "For caring about me. It feels good."

I turn in his arms, grab his handsome face and pull his smiling lips to mine. "You make it easy. Loving you is easy."

"For you, maybe."

"Good thing I'm the only one that matters."

"You got that right." Nix tilts my chin up and kisses me again. "Now we better get out of here before I convince you to keep making me happy over and over again for the rest of the afternoon."

Nix kisses me once more before taking my hand and leading me to the front door.

No matter what he says, I'm nervous about seeing his parents. And Lennon…after the speech she gave me yesterday at the funeral, will she trust that I'll do right by her brother? Will she think it's too soon, that I didn't give this enough thought?

My insecurities are deeply rooted and eating me alive as we walk through the yard toward the main house. Nix squeezes my hand before opening the door, but he seems completely relaxed, totally content. I try to absorb some of that as we walk through the glass doors, but I barely have a second to consider it.

"Afternoon, lovebirds. We were wondering if we'd see you today."

My cheeks blaze red as Nix glares at his sister. "Hello, Lennon."

She smiles at him and he eventually smiles back, then Lennon wraps me up in one of her crazy hugs. It's welcome but kind of awkward, since Nix won't let go of my hand. Lennon doesn't seem to mind either way.

"I'm so happy right now I could die," she gushes in my ear before letting me go. "I just love this. The two of you. Love it, love it, *love* it."

"Thank you," I exhale the breath I'd been holding. "I'm pretty happy myself."

Nix looks over at me and I squeeze his hand. He dips his head to kiss me on the neck, and Lennon makes a gagging noise.

"Enough of that," she scolds, but when I look over at her she's smiling. "Now let's go get some dinner. I'm sure the two of you need to refuel after last night."

"Knock it off, Lennon," Nix growls, but Lennon only rolls her eyes lovingly at her brother, completely unfazed.

I smile at both of them. Honestly, I'm not sure I could stop smiling right now if someone paid me.

Nix and I follow Lennon to the dining room, but Nix stops suddenly at the door when he sees Davy sitting at the table. I glance at Nix and regardless of their chumminess last night at the bar, Nix is currently throwing daggers at his friend through narrowed eyes.

Davy stands as soon as he sees us and tucks both his hands in his back pockets. "Hey man. Brought Lennon home last night myself since it was so late."

"He slept on the couch, idiot." Lennon slaps Nix on his shoulder. "Let's keep the testosterone in check please. Good grief, Rose. How do you deal with this Neanderthal?"

Nix rolls his eyes at his sister then looks over at me. His lips turn up in a smile that melts my heart into warm liquid in my chest. "She loves me," Nix whispers, then dips his head and gives me a sweet kiss on the lips.

I stare into his beautiful eyes, so taken by him I forget anyone else is around.

"So, Mom and Dad..." Lennon clears her throat. "Nix and Rose are kind of a thing."

My wide eyes shift over to Nix's parents, but what I see immediately sets me at ease. Joe's smiling from ear to ear and Lexi's smiling as well with tears in her eyes.

"Happy for you, brother." Davy extends a hand in Nix's direction and Nix shakes it.

"Happy for you too...*brother*." Nix wags his eyebrows at his sister and she casually flips him the bird. But when Davy glances over at her she blushes, giving them both away. What an awesome couple. I hope it works out between them.

"Well..." Lexi stands and walks over to me and Nix. "I think this is the best news I've heard in a very long time." She gives us both a warm hug then kisses her son on the cheek. "I think a little celebrating is in order, and since we're doing breakfast for dinner, how about some mimosas? Lennon, come and help me would you?"

Lexi gives us both a final smile then follows Lennon into the kitchen to make our drinks as Nix and I take a seat at the table. That was a tad embarrassing, but I'm so grateful that his family has accepted me and accepted us. Nix pulls my hand onto his thigh, refusing to let go. He looks over at me with a wink and a smile, and I give his big hand a squeeze, returning his affections.

Dinner is full of happy conversation and a ton of reminiscing. I finally get a few embarrassing childhood stories out of Joe, but I can't decide which one is my favorite. There were several unfortunate baseball moments, since Nix apparently played most of his life. But my favorite may have been the story about the time he got his wisdom teeth removed. He was sixteen and it was the first time he had anesthesia. Joe, Lexi and Lennon took turns telling me all about the outrageous things he was saying on the car ride home, including him professing his undying love for their family dog and how he was going to be a superhero when he grew up. Nix narrowed his eyes at me as I laughed at his humiliation, but it was the dark

"I'm going to get you later in the best way possible" kind of look in his eyes that had me pressing my thighs together under the table.

As hard as it was to resist sneaking off with Nix to a secluded spot after that, we stayed at the main house and spent time with his family for the remainder of the evening. Davy stayed as well and it turned out to be a really nice time, relaxing and rejuvenating as we talked and even played a couple of board games outside on the back patio. Around nine, Lennon mentioned going out one last time for drinks before everyone went their separate ways the next morning. Nix agreed he was up for it, but then quickly leaned in and whispered in my ear, "We'll be leaving early."

I smiled as I leaned into him then and whispered back, "I look forward to hugging you later."

I kissed Nix's neck before pulling away, and when our eyes met again he mouthed the words, "all night long", which had me aching for him in a matter of seconds.

And that's how we ended up in the shower together for the third time today.

Now I'm staring at my suitcase, trying to decide what to wear this evening. It's taking forever because Nix is currently lying on the bed, distracting me in nothing but a pair of faded jeans, his lazy stare following me as I move around the room.

"Are you having fun?" I ask him as I finally decide on a light pink v-neck tee and pull it on with my jeans.

"I was." Nix sits up and moves to the edge of the bed. "Not so much now that you're fully clothed."

I shake my head as I move toward the bathroom, but Nix grabs my arm, holding me in place. He pulls me between his legs and kisses me softly on the stomach. I can feel the warmth of his lips easily through the thin cotton of my shirt, and I sigh at the contact.

"Let's stay in tonight," he suggests. "I'm sure Lennon will understand."

"No." I shake my head with a smile as I run my fingers through the back of his silky hair. "As tempting as you are, I think you should spend time with your sister while you're here."

Nix exhales a resigned sigh then pulls me closer. "I guess you're right."

"I am."

"But we're leaving early."

"Okay."

Seemingly satisfied with our arrangement, he reaches up and pulls my face to his. I grab his shoulders to keep my balance as he kisses me deeply.

"And besides...." I whisper against his lips between kisses. "We'll have plenty of time together when we get back."

"We will?"

I search Nix's face for meaning. Is he saying he doesn't want me when we get back to Delia, or is this some ridiculous insecurity of his rearing its head? The way he's frantically clutching at my hips and the hint of fear in his eyes tells me it's the latter, and to say I'm shocked would be an understatement.

I pull his hands from my hips to stop their anxious kneading and wrap them around my back. I take his face in my hands and stare hard into his eyes to make sure he feels what I'm about to say.

"I'm not going anywhere," I assure him. "Even if you beg me to leave, I won't go without a fight. I love you."

Nix closes his eyes and bows his head. I wrap my arms around him and pull him close. "I love you," I whisper again as Nix relaxes against me. "I love you, and I'll be around as long as you'll have me."

"Promise."

It's more of a demand than a request, and one I'm happy to obey.

"I promise."

I lightly stroke the back of his hair and kiss the top of his head, until I feel his arms tighten around me. The next thing I know, he has me on the bed beneath him. "I think I'd like to give you one more hug before we leave, if you don't mind."

"Nix..." His name is a breathless giggle as he kisses his way down my neck, toward my exposed collar bone. *Mmmmm.*

"I thought you liked my hugs," he teases as his mouth travels even farther down my chest. He stops to raise my shirt before tickling me with kisses all along my stomach.

"I love your hugs," I gasp, as he continues torturing me. "I just don't want to be late."

Nix kisses me into a frenzy and before I even realize what's happening, he has both of our jeans off and he's slipping himself inside of me. "I do love your hugs." I moan as his hips rock slowly into me. "I love them very much."

"And I love you," he smiles, before silencing me once again with his mouth on mine.

CHAPTER TWENTY-FOUR

Nix and I had an incredible time barhopping in Sacramento last night with Lennon and Davy. But after such an emotional few days (coupled with last night's drinking, dancing and late night "hugs" courtesy of the beautiful, brown-eyed man sitting next to me), I can't seem to keep my eyes open on the plane ride home.

"Come here."

Nix wraps an arm around me and pulls me close. I cuddle into his warm chest and within seconds, I'm fast asleep. I don't wake up until the pilot comes over the speaker, announcing our descent into Atlanta. I can't believe I slept almost the entire way home. I wipe my eyes then look over at Nix. He's smiling at me, but the seemingly ever-present dark circles under his eyes tell me he didn't nap like I did.

"Did you get any sleep?" I ask, then cover my mouth as a yawn escapes.

"Don't worry about me." Nix drags his knuckles along my cheek. "I'm fine."

I study his weary face and realize he seems sad. Sad to leave his family? Still grieving over his grandfather? Perhaps it's both. Or maybe it's something else altogether.

"Are you okay?" I decide to ask, testing out our new "all or nothing" relationship.

"Yeah, I'm good. Just tired."

He kisses me again, and I guess I can take comfort in the fact that it doesn't appear to be me who has him in a somber mood. I cuddle back into him until we land, assuming he'll talk to me about it later if he wants.

"I'm glad you came with me this weekend," he says, just as the wheels touch down onto the runway. "Thank you for doing that for me."

I look up at him with a smile. "I'll always be here for you. All you have to do is ask."

What happens next shocks me more than any of the other events that have transpired over the past few days. As I stare at Nix, willing him to believe me, willing him to understand how much I care for him, I have to stifle a gasp as I watch his eyes cloud with tears. I remain completely still, my own watery eyes focused on his as I lean in and kiss him sweetly. But Nix grabs my face and holds me against his lips, transforming my innocent kiss into something so full of urgency and passion that it's frightening.

We both pull away, wrecked from the kiss and the emotion behind it. The pain behind his eyes is barely noticeable as he smiles at me, but it's there and I can't deny it. I realize then that "all or nothing" must not apply to both of us. Nix is still holding back, and I'm not immediately sure how I feel about that, but I decide to leave things alone for now, hoping that he'll come around in time. I know better than anyone that change doesn't happen overnight, and Nix has given me more than I ever expected from him over the past few days. I shouldn't be so greedy.

As soon as the plane comes to a complete stop, Nix stands and grabs his duffle bag from the overhead bin.

"Ready?"

I look over at him and plant a smile on my face. "Ready."

Nix extends a hand to help me out of the seat and we join the rest of the people already standing in the aisle, waiting for the plane doors to open. Nix wraps an arm around my waist from behind and pulls me close, as if he can read my mind and he's offering me reassurance. I accept it by leaning into him and tilting my head to give him better access to my neck. He kisses and nuzzles until we finally start moving, and by the time we have our bags from baggage claim and are heading toward Nix's Jeep, I've wiped any uncertainty leftover from that last kiss out of my mind completely. He loves me. He told me he loves me and that should be enough. I have to trust that the rest will come in time, and for Nix…he can have all the time he needs.

****

After we arrived home yesterday, Nix and I went our separate ways, much to his disapproval. He wanted me to stay with him last night, but I thought I should probably spend some time with Mom. Even though she's been doing much better lately, this was the first time I've left her for that long of a stretch since I moved back in. I called to check on her every day while I was away, and she assured me she was fine, but I was eager to see for myself that all was well.

Mom and I ended up having a nice night together. We talked and laughed as we shared our favorite pineapple and Canadian bacon pizza from *Mario's* in the square, then we watched a happy romance on Netflix and I even talked her into having a beer with me. The only thing that was off was when I tried to talk to her about my trip to California and she basically tuned me out then changed the subject, as if she hadn't heard a word I said.

Since the first day she met Nix, there have been plenty of passive aggressive comments that have helped make it perfectly clear he's not Mom's favorite person. And up until now, I've kept my mouth closed, letting her believe what she wants about him. However, after this trip and everything that's happened between Nix and me, I'm going to have to have a talk with her. I decided to let it go last night, but I don't think I'll be able to tolerate her disrespect much longer. It may take a few more dinners, but I'm sure he'll eventually charm her with his easy ways just as he's charmed me.

I know I sure did miss all of that charm last night. I missed *him*. A lot. But I have to be careful. I don't ever want to be back in a situation where I rely on someone else for my own happiness. I've been down that road, and when that road ends, it's not easy to move in another direction when you have no idea where you are without the other person by your side.

When Danny and I divorced, that feeling of helplessness was the worst part. I had no clue who I was other than Danny's wife. I had become some extended version of him—the same likes, the same ambitions, the same desires. And it wasn't until the end that I realized I had lost myself somewhere along the way.

You Think You Know

I can look back now and see that it was an unconscious attempt to keep him, to keep him happy. I've always been that way, putting everyone else's needs and interests above my own. I used to think that was a quality to be revered, but now I know it's a weakness in so many ways. I know now that no matter what, the most important thing is to just be me.

And that's one of the things I love most about Nix.

Being myself is easy around him, and he never asks for anything more. He encourages me to make my own decisions, to speak up, to never be afraid of asking for what I want. And I listen because I respect him. I respect the soldier inside of him who is well acquainted with fighting for what he believes in, who is accustomed to protecting the ones he loves. In the relatively short time that we've known each other, Nix has taught me so much about myself. And it's hard not to love someone who brings out the best parts of you, someone who believes in you, someone who makes you stronger without even trying.

Nix is amazing, and it would be easy to conform like I did with Danny, but the beauty is I don't have to. There's no need to compromise my sense of self with Nix. He loves me just as I am, and I can't even begin to describe how incredible that feels.

That thought alone has me grinning from ear to ear as I make my way to his place. He told me last night that he was okay with me spending the night away from him, as long as he got to see me first thing the next morning. I had to laugh. Watching a big, heavily tattooed soldier pout is totally adorable.

So I agreed to meet him this morning at his house, and I even stopped to pick up some Dunkin' Donuts along the way. Nix didn't mention what we would be doing. He only told me to dress comfortably and wear plenty of sunscreen. I assume we're going hiking again, but I'm not sure and it doesn't matter. I'll just be happy to spend the day with him.

He sent me his signature "sweet dreams" text last night, which turned into us texting for a half hour, which then led to him calling me because he said that he missed the sound of my voice. We talked for hours, which made me feel like a teenager again, especially since I was curled up on the bed in my childhood bedroom, speaking quietly so I wouldn't wake my mom. Or maybe it's just Nix. The way he would find moments in our conversation to tell me how beautiful he thinks I am would make me happy he wasn't there to see my blush. And the times he would turn something I said into some kind of sexual innuendo would make me *un*happy that he wasn't there to follow through with his delicious threats.

And speaking of sexy...

I pull into the driveway of his cabin and my breath catches in my throat when I see Nix waiting for me on his front porch. He's wearing long, tan shorts, a gray tank-top and his favorite Pirates baseball cap pulled down low. I can't see his eyes, but I can see his smile, and it's positively beaming.

I grab our breakfast and coffees and hop out of the car as he starts walking toward me. He's in front of me before I can take my first step, and he keeps that incredible smile on his face as he takes the box of donuts and the tray that holds our coffees and places both on the hood of my car. Then he turns back to me, and although I'm hoping he'll toss me against my car and kiss me madly, what he does instead is even better, a million times better.

He wraps his strong arms around my waist, buries his face in my neck and holds me so tightly I can barely breathe. "I missed you," he whispers and I close my eyes with a sigh. It feels so good to be close to him. And I know now that it's too late. I already need him more than I should. But I take heart in the fact that I don't need him the same way I needed Danny. I don't need him to feed my own sense of self-worth. I need him because it feels good to be around him, because it feels good to be loved by him.

"I missed you too," I say, with my mouth right at his ear, and I can feel his smile against my skin as he pulls me closer.

We hold each other a few moments longer, nothing but the sound of the warm morning breeze shuffling the leaves on the surrounding trees, and I'm not sure I could imagine anything more peaceful. I greedily soak up every second.

When Nix eventually pulls away, I finally get a good look at his face and notice he seems tired.

"How did you sleep?" He closes his eyes as I caress his cheek. "I shouldn't have kept you on the phone so late. I know you must have been exhausted from the trip."

Nix opens his eyes and turns his face into my hand so he can kiss my palm. "Stop worrying about me." He smiles. "I'm fine."

I smile back, but I'm not convinced. Once again, I decide to let things slide. I don't want to ruin our day together by forcing him to confide in me, but I know I have to stop letting him get away with this. I'm not sure if he thinks I can't handle whatever's going on, but he can't protect me from everything. I'll just have to prove to him I'm strong enough to take it.

Maybe you can start by telling him about your divorce, Rose.

I quickly shake off the voice inside my head, but I can't ignore that one for much longer either. Besides, maybe if Nix knows I've suffered my own share of heartache, he'll feel better about putting his heart in my hands. I look up at him, gauging whether or not I have the courage to tell him. It's hard to say, but I do know that now is not the time.

"How about some coffee?" I suggest, and Nix gives me a sweet kiss on the lips before letting me go and grabbing our breakfast from the hood of my car. I take the box of Munchkins from him so I can hold his hand as he leads me to the front door. The smile I get in return leaves me weak in the knees.

When we get inside, we set everything on his kitchen counter, and both of us immediately go for the coffees.

"Did you get any sleep last night?" he asks, smiling down at me and I shake my head.

"Someone insisted on keeping me on the phone half the night."

"I'm sorry..." Nix narrows his eyes and smiles. "Actually, no. I'm not sorry."

"I'm not either," I admit, then open the box of donuts (all blueberry, of course). I go to pop one in my mouth, but Nix grabs my wrist and directs my tasty treat to his mouth instead.

"Animal," I tease, and Nix growls in response.

He then grabs another donut from the box and lifts his hand to my mouth. "Peace offering," he smiles, but I leave my mouth closed even as he presses the donut firmly against my lips.

I watch him closely as he tries to figure out why I won't accept his gift, and when I feel he's least expecting it, I quickly open my mouth and snatch it from his fingers.

"I see how it's going to be." His voice is playful, but menacing, and I bite my bottom lip to keep from laughing. "I'm afraid you're going to have to pay for that."

"Oh really?" I challenge, putting my hands on my hips, but I can't seem to stop smiling. "You think I'm scared of you?"

"You should be."

"Well, I'm not."

I reach up and wrap my arms around his neck, suddenly wanting him to know I don't fear him or fear being with him, in any way. For some reason, that seems important.

I pull his face down to mine and run my tongue across his blueberry flavored lips. He groans in response and I push my tongue inside, eager to taste more of him. Nix doesn't object. He wraps his arms around me and holds me close as I take control of his mouth. I love that he gives me this. I love that he's secure enough to give me the reigns, and I love that he's given me the strength to handle it.

But it doesn't last long.

"Uh-uh, pretty girl." Nix lifts me onto his kitchen counter. "I don't think so."

He pushes his way between my legs and devours my mouth. I'm panting and needy as he moves his kisses to my neck, pulling on my ponytail, forcing my head back giving himself more room to play.

"I think I may like your punishments," I murmur, before he moves back to my mouth.

"Good." Nix gives me a wicked grin. "Because that fight in you is sexy as hell, and I'll highly enjoy choosing the proper punishment to match each offense."

All I can do is smile, loving that he continues to validate what I already know. He encourages my power. He nurtures my confidence. He makes me stronger in ways I never thought possible. He makes me *better*. And I want to do the same for him. Although I can't imagine Nix being any better than he already is.

Nix's "punishment" this go around is a heated make-out session on his kitchen counter that has my head spinning. He works me up to the point of breaking, then pulls away, promising he'll finish the job later, but only if I'm on my best behavior.

He laughs at my pathetic excuse for a pout, but I can't help it. I can't get enough of him, especially his playful side. He's normally so withdrawn, so serious. It's nice to see him this carefree, and I'd like to keep that smile on his face for as long as I possibly can.

"So, where are you taking me today?" I ask, as he grabs another donut and pops it into his mouth. "Should I be scared?"

"No." Nix grins as he shakes his head. "I just thought I'd share something with you today, something I don't normally like to share."

My interest piqued, I give him an excited smile. "Well, are you going to tell me, or do you like torturing me?"

"Torturing you can be fun." Nix puts a donut in front of my mouth, only to pull it away right before I'm about to take a bite.

"You're evil."

"I know."

Nix pretends to put the donut in his own mouth, but then I bluster at his audacity and with a laugh, he changes direction, offering it to me again.

I let my mouth linger on his fingertips, and he tries to seem unaffected, but those smoldering eyes give him away.

"Delicious," I remark after I swallow my bite, and Nix nods his head in agreement before kissing me thoroughly.

"You most definitely are."

"So, are you going to tell me where you're taking me or not?"

Nix shakes his head with a smile. "Nope."

"So you do like torturing me then?"

"Very much."

I roll my eyes and hop off the counter, my legs shaky from either our make-out session or that salacious grin he's pointing in my direction. "Well then lead the way, punisher."

Nix chuckles then kisses me sweetly on the cheek. "I have to grab a couple of things. Meet you at the Jeep."

I gather our coffee and donuts from the counter as Nix heads out back to grab whatever he needs. I go ahead and make my way out to the Jeep and notice the boat is hooked on to the back. Oh my goodness. Is he taking me...?

"I'd like to take you fishing."

I turn to find Nix coming down the porch steps. He has a large backpack slung over one shoulder and the most adorably shy smile lighting up his face.

"I know it's probably not a big deal to you," he continues, "but it's something I normally do alone. It's always been the one thing that helps make my world right again...that is, until I met you."

I feel my eyebrows shoot to my forehead. "Until you met me?"

Nix nods as his smile widens. "Now I have two things."

I stare down at my feet, wishing I didn't feel like crying a lake full of happy tears every time the man said something nice to me. I take a breath, shoving my tears back, then look up to find him standing right in front of me.

"I thought you on a boat, out in the water..." He brushes his thumb across my cheek. "I can't imagine anything more beautiful. My soul settles just thinking about it."

I put the coffee and donuts down on the passenger's seat, then turn and wrap my arms around his neck. I close my eyes and hug him close, unable to stop a lone tear from sliding down my cheek. "I love you," I tell him, then quickly wipe the tear away before letting him go.

"I love you too." Nix kisses me softly on the lips then makes his way over to the driver's side. Once our seatbelts are on, he hands me a cord that's hooked into the console. "I thought you could be in charge of music."

I take the cord with a smile and plug it into my phone, as we pull out of his driveway.

"So, where are we fishing today?" I ask him as I thumb through my music.

"I've found a great spot." Nix smiles over at me. "I think you'll love it."

I decide on my "driving" playlist, which is a good compilation of favorites—songs that are perfect for road trips on sunny days like today. It's hard to talk over the wind rushing though the Jeep, so we ride in silence for the most part, enjoying our coffees and the music. I glance over at Nix a few times and bust him staring at me more than once. Every time we both smile and laugh to ourselves and I can't remember the last time I felt this happy.

Judging by the route and the scenery, Nix is taking me to Graystone Lake, but before we get to the main entrance, he turns down a road that only a four-by-four could navigate. I hold on to the guardrail as we bump along, the Jeep trailing downward until we reach a secluded alcove set off to the left.

Nix parks the Jeep on a huge rock jutting out over the water. Below us and to the left is a small beach—mostly rocks, with a tiny bit of dirt and sand in between—surrounded by tall, overgrown maple trees and several Georgia pines. Graystone Lake is a small lake compared to some others in Georgia, so it doesn't attract families as much as avid hikers and weekend fishermen. I'm not surprised Nix was able to find a private area like this one.

"Think you can help me?"

I look over my shoulder and find Nix already out of the Jeep and starting to slide the small Jon Boat off the trailer.

I jump out to go to help him and notice a short, dirt path leading down to the alcove. I assume that's how we'll get the boat down to the water...if I can lift it.

"Good grief," I huff as I finally get my side off the ground. "This thing is heavier than it looks. How do you do this by yourself?"

Nix laughs. "I normally go to the boat ramp, but I thought since I had you to help, I'd come straight to my spot this time."

"I think I may need to start incorporating weights into my workout regimen," I admit, and Nix laughs again.

"You're doing great," he encourages. "Almost there."

We finally make it to the water and bend to get the boat on the ground before heading back to the Jeep for the supplies. Nix has a rod for each of us, a tackle box and a small cooler. We pile everything in the boat and Nix holds out a hand to help me in, then he pushes the boat out and hops in, soaking the bottom of his shorts in the process.

"It's so hot out, they'll dry in no time." My taunting earns me a heated glare from Nix.

"Careful, pretty girl," he warns. "These oars are good for splashing."

He takes the tip of one of the oars, dips it in the water and flicks it in my direction. I squeal when the cold water dots my skin and Nix roars with laughter. I narrow my eyes at him with a smile as I dip my hand in the water and repay the favor by splashing him in the face.

"Man, you're feisty this morning. I may have to take you down a notch or two." Nix starts to put the oars back in the boat and I hold up my hands in defense.

"Fair is fair!" I claim, with a laugh. "Now we're even."

"Okay, fine." Nix eyes me skeptically as he slowly puts the oars back in the water. "I'd rather get you when you least expect it anyway."

I shake my head at what I hope is an empty threat, but the evil grin he's shooting my way from under the low brim of his baseball hat tells me that he'll definitely be following through with his evil plans. And I'm certain I'll love every minute.

As Nix rows us out into deeper waters, I stare unabashedly at his powerful arms, watching the well-defined muscles roll under his tanned skin. His broad chest and shoulders are already glistening from the effort and that mind-blowing smile of his is on full display every time he glances over at me and catches me gawking. God, he's perfect.

Nix paddles us out into the middle of the alcove and tosses a makeshift anchor (a gallon jug of sand tied to some rope) out into the water. Then he spends the next half hour describing everything in his tackle box, before pulling a container of live worms from the cooler and showing me how to properly bait a hook. He was so excited to show me everything that I didn't have the heart to tell him I've been fishing plenty of times in my life. Plus, I really enjoyed the way his hands felt over mine as he helped me with my hook and the way his eyes lit up with pride when I got the worm on the hook with ease.

The next step was obviously how to cast out, and I made sure to act appropriately uneducated about the task. However, when I caught my first fish before Nix even had a bite, my naivety became a little less believable. I reeled the fish in like a pro, just as my grandfather had taught me when we used to camp together on weekends. Fishing wasn't a sport I particularly enjoyed, but I was no stranger to the game.

I snag the small bass from the hook with ease, and in my excitement, I forgot that I was supposed to be a newbie. I glance over to find Nix giving me a curious look.

"Okay, so you're telling me..." He sits up a little straighter and rolls his shoulders back, puffing out that glorious chest of his. "You handle a pool stick like a pro, wield a hammer better than Thor *and* you can fish?"

"Beginner's luck?" I shrug, smiling sheepishly.

"Honestly, I can't figure out if I'm angry right now or extremely turned on," he confesses, and I bite my bottom lip with a sigh.

"You were so excited to teach me," I concede. "Plus, I really enjoyed your hands-on teaching style."

Nix grins widely. "Turned on it is."

I toss the bass back in the water, then lean over and pull his lips to mine. "I never thought I'd meet a man that would be turned on by watching me fish."

Nix wraps his hand around my neck and smiles. "Baby, I think I could get turned on by most anything you do."

I kiss him a couple more times, before resuming my seat on the bench opposite his. I bait another hook and after a couple of hours on the lake, I've caught four. Nix has caught one.

"I'm never taking you fishing with me again," he teases, as we carry the equipment back up to the Jeep.

"Sore loser."

Nix pinches my side, making me squeal like a little girl and when he has all of the gear settled into the Jeep, he pushes me against the driver's side and tickles me breathless.

"Stop!" I beg him, finally finding my voice. "Please!"

Nix stops, but only to pull me close and kiss me soundly. "Thank you for today." He tosses me a wink. "It meant a lot, even though you completely outfished me."

"You're welcome." I run my hands up and down his sides with a smile. "It meant a lot to me too."

Nix grabs his backpack and another small cooler out of the Jeep before taking my hand and leading me back down to the beach. "I have lunch for us," he tells me as we walk. "I hope you like chicken salad."

"Love it."

Nix smiles over his shoulder at me, then releases my hand to open the backpack. He pulls out a blanket and I help him lay it on a small patch of dry land right below the tree line. Nix places the cooler on the blanket, along with a bag of chips and a loaf of bread he pulls from the backpack, then we both take a seat.

I hide my smile as he unzips a side pocket on the backpack and pulls out a package of sanitizing wipes. He offers a couple to me, then uses a few himself to wipe down his hands before pulling two plates from the backpack and some plastic knives and spoons. The man has thought of everything. My little Boy Scout.

"I have bottles of water in here," he says, as he opens the cooler to get what he needs to start making our sandwiches. "Would you like one?"

"Yes, please."

Nix opens a bottle for each of us, and we both take a long, grateful pull.

"Anything I can do to help?" I ask, but Nix shakes his head.

"I got this. You just sit back and relax."

I gladly do as I'm told, leaning back on my hands and enjoying the gentle breeze coming off the lake. Nix has our plates finished in no time—chicken salad sandwiches, chips and some mixed fruit salad he pulled out of the cooler after finishing the sandwiches.

"This looks amazing." I watch him smile as I take my first bite. "And that is some seriously good chicken salad. Wow!"

"Glad you like it."

I'm about to ask Nix where he purchased it so I can stock up on a lifetime supply, but I notice his shy smile and wonder...

"Did you make this?"

"Guilty."

"Nix, this is *really* good." I take another bite, confident I'm going to finish this delicious sandwich with embarrassing speed. "You'll have to pass on the recipe."

"I've tweaked it a little, but the original recipe came from my grandma," Nix says, as he digs in to his own lunch. "And no. I won't share the recipe with you."

I stop chewing, thrown off by his response. "Why not?"

"Because..." Nix shrugs. "If you like it that much, then I can use it as bait to lure you back whenever I want."

I roll my eyes, lovingly. "You don't need chicken salad, sweetheart. All you have to do is ask."

Nix leans over and kisses me sweetly, then with blissful smiles on our faces, we both down our lunches in record time. I guess we had both worn off the donuts from this morning. Plus, his chicken salad is the stuff dreams are made of.

"Wanna have dinner with me tonight?" Nix asks, breaking the silence as we sit close to each other on the blanket, resting our now full bellies.

"Absolutely," I agree. "But I'd like to take a shower first, if that's okay."

"I'd like to join you."

"But I don't have anything else to wear at your place," I counter, although I do love his shared shower idea. "And if you're taking me to dinner, I'd like to look nice."

"I'm cooking you dinner." Nix leans over and twirls a lose strand of my hair around his finger. "So you can be naked for all I care. As a matter of fact, I would prefer it."

Before I can object this time, Nix moves quickly, tossing his ball cap to the ground beside us then pressing me down into the blanket, covering me with his heavy body. I don't object, especially when he dips his face to mine, nibbling softly on my bottom lip, then the top one, working his way leisurely into my mouth. I moan quietly, wrapping my arms loosely around his neck, enjoying his slow pace.

We lay like that on the blanket for a while, kissing and petting, until Nix eventually suggests we get going. He nuzzles his nose against mine and gives me a final kiss that's way too short for my taste, even though he just devoured my mouth for a good half hour.

"Come on." Nix stands and extends a hand to me. "Let's get back so we can get you cleaned up."

"I'm taking a shower at my place," I remind him, and he gives me a sarcastic grin.

"Right. Got it."

"I'm serious." I give my silly lie a good effort. "I want to be pretty for dinner."

"Sure. Uh huh."

"Nix!"

I smack his shoulder as we walk to the Jeep and he laughs before bringing my hand to his lips.

"Baby, you act like I'm giving you a choice. But I'm not."

I fake a disapproving look that's probably even less believable than me passing up an opportunity to shower with him.

"So I don't have a say in the matter?" I question, and Nix shakes his head no. "You're going to force me to shower with you against my will?"

"Oh, you'll be willing. Trust me."

"You seem very sure of yourself, soldier."

Nix stops in front of the Jeep and cocks an eyebrow at me. The next thing I know, I'm shoved against the side again, except this time there's no playful tickling. Oh no. The man is trying to prove a point. And it's a point well taken.

Nix attacks my mouth with purpose. Every pull, every nibble, every slow stroke of his tongue has me euphoric. Good God, this man can kiss.

When he finally pulls away, he presses his cheek to mine, his breath harsh and uneven in my ear and I smile. He was supposed to be seducing me, and believe me it worked. But I love that he's just as affected, giving me more confidence than I probably deserve. I'm not really sure I deserve him at all, but it's too late. I have him and I'm never letting him go.

"Shower with me," Nix commands as he pulls me close, both of us slowly coming down from that last kiss.

"Anything," I breathe. "Keep kissing me like that and anything you want, it's yours."

CHAPTER TWENTY-FIVE

After one of the best showers I've ever taken, Nix released me from his custody long enough to go to my mom's house and change. I wasn't kidding when I said I wanted to look nice for dinner, so I chose my favorite dress for the evening–an off-the-shoulder, flowy peach number that's a little shorter than what I would normally wear, but I'm thinking Nix won't mind.

I give my long, red locks some beachy waves and let them fall over my shoulders. I stick with the small gold hoops in my ears to keep things simple, and not wanting to wear heels all night, I decide on some flat gold sandals, which feel more like me any way.

My mom's in the kitchen as I'm leaving, and I pray she won't stop me to ask questions.

"And why are you so dressed up this evening?"

Seems my prayers will be going unanswered this time.

I close my eyes briefly before turning to face her. It's amazing how my mom still has the ability to make me feel like an errant child on occasion.

"I'm going to Nix's." I plaster a smile on my face, begging her to keep her opinions to herself. "He's cooking dinner for me," I add for good measure, hoping to win Nix some brownie points.

My mom purses her lips, a silent sign that she doesn't approve. "What time should I expect you home?"

I try and hide my grimace. For starters, this isn't my "home". And secondly, I'm *not* a child.

"I'm not sure." I pull my purse up on my shoulder and head toward the door. "Call me if you need anything."

"Should I wait up?" Mom calls from the kitchen, and I pause with my hand on the door knob.

You're a grown woman, Rose. So act like it.

"I wouldn't wait up." I don't turn around, avoiding what I know is a criticizing glare. "See you later, Mom."

I walk out the door and close it behind me before she can say anything further. I have to talk to her about Nix. Soon. I don't think I can take much more of this without doing or saying something I'll regret.

But I won't think about that now.

Instead, I walk to my car, my smile growing with every step, knowing I'll be right where I want to be in a little over half an hour. I plug in my phone and start up my "driving" playlist again, choosing to start with a little old school Dave Matthews Band. I keep the top down and tap my hands on the steering wheel as "Two Step" blares through my speakers.

I'm back at Nix's cabin before I know it, and I'm so anxious to get inside to see him, I fumble with my seat belt a few minutes before I get it off. *So much for not falling too hard, too fast, Rose.* But that's okay. He's worth getting this excited over.

I don't bother knocking, since Nix asked me not to before I left earlier. Instead, I let myself in and I'm immediately hit with such a delicious aroma that my stomach growls in response.

"Oh my goodness that smells divine."

Nix turns from his position in front of the stove, just as I'm closing the door behind me. His smile, combined with the smell of whatever's he's preparing for this evening has me hungry in more ways than one.

"Help yourself to the bruschetta on the table," he offers. "I'm almost done here."

"You did all of this?"

I stare down in disbelief at the spread lying before me. Nix has prepared a meal that looks straight out of a Food Network show and a table display to rival any five-star restaurant around.

"I come from a family of farmers." Nix smiles at me over his shoulder. "I may have picked up a thing or two about cooking over the years."

"Just a *few* things?" I question, still gawking at the incredible dishes he's prepared. "Nix, this looks amazing."

I'm dipping into the bruschetta when Nix walks over and places what looks to be the main course on his small kitchen table. He takes the scrumptious appetizer from my hand, puts it back on the plate and takes me in his arms. Suddenly all thoughts of eating are gone, as my senses are overcome by one Nix Taylor. I can barely concentrate as he nibbles at my neck, welcoming me to his home in that special way of his.

"Hi," he whispers against my skin, and I pull him closer, loving his warmth. "I'm happy to see you."

"You just saw me a couple of hours ago," I remind him, but then Nix goes back to his nibbling, making me lose my train of thought.

"I missed you."

I take his face in my hands and kiss his smiling lips. "I missed you too, but I wanted to wear something pretty."

Nix holds my hands out and stands away from me, surveying my dress. "Mission accomplished."

"I was hoping you'd like it."

Nix pulls me back against him. "I love it, especially this part." He leans down and takes advantage of my exposed shoulder by trailing kisses from the base of my neck down to my collarbone. "But I'd still prefer you naked."

"Of course you would." I sigh as his lips make their way back to my mouth.

"Well, at least I got to shower with you, and you look beautiful. You always look beautiful."

"Thank you." I say, ignoring my blush. "And now I am starving, Emeril, so why don't you tell me what we're having?"

Nix lets go of everything but my hand and points at the various dishes on the table as he names them. "Salt-crusted sea bass with creamy au gratin potatoes and roasted asparagus with spicy Hollandaise sauce–my own special recipe." He winks at me, and I shake my head once again at the unbelievable dinner he's prepared.

"It looks incredible," I tell him, as he pulls my chair out for me to sit. "You're spoiling me already."

"That's the plan."

He takes his seat across from me, and we both greedily dig in. The food is impossibly delicious, which I make sure and tell Nix multiple times as we eat. Even a few moans of satisfaction slip out on occasion, which is embarrassing until I realize how they're affecting Nix. He immediately stops chewing every time and focuses on my mouth as he squirms a bit in his seat. I let a few slip out not so accidentally after that.

When we finish our meals, Nix grabs our wine glasses and leads me to his back porch.

"I was thinking we'd have dessert outside."

"I'm absolutely stuffed," I confess. "But it was so worth it."

"Thank you."

"I will admit, I'm kind of upset you haven't cooked for me until now," I tease him. "Why have you been holding out on me?"

"Can't pull out the big guns too soon." Nix's playful grin has me falling more in love with him by the second. "But in all honesty, I haven't cooked for anyone in a long time."

"That's a shame. You shouldn't deprive people of your talent."

Nix rolls his eyes at me with a smile. "I used to love doing it," he tells me, as he shrugs his broad shoulders. "But it's hard to make salt-crusted sea bass on an open fire in the desert."

Nix leads me down toward a blue checkered blanket laid out on the grass with a picnic basket and a bottle of wine sitting in one corner.

"I can't take credit for the dessert." Nix gestures for me to take a seat on the blanket. "David supplied us with some of his blueberry cobbler, but we don't have to eat it now if you're too full."

"I'm never too full for David's cobbler."

"I'll have to agree."

Nix grabs the picnic basket and starts to remove two small ramekins with lids on top. He hands one to me, along with a spoon, and I notice the dish is still warm. *Yummmm.*

Nix and I eat our desserts in silence, only sharing a few glances now and then to show our mutual appreciation of David's outstanding baking skills.

"Now I'm *really* stuffed." I wrap an arm around my swollen belly as Nix takes our empty dishes and places them back in the picnic basket. "But I have no regrets."

Nix leans over and kisses me before taking the picnic basket inside. I decide I should stand and move around a little to work off some of this food, so while he's gone, I make my way down toward the creek. A light breeze stirs the water and the bright, setting sun reflects off the slow ripples. It's the perfect, late summer evening, made even more so by where I'm at and the company I'm currently keeping.

I'm still staring out over the water when I hear a door close behind me. I turn to find Nix approaching with a smile on his face that threatens to stop my heart.

"Did I mention how beautiful you look tonight?" He extends his hand and when I take it, he pulls me close and wraps his arms around my waist. "I'm a very lucky man."

I bask in his sincerity a moment before reaching up and kissing him, rewarding him for his compliment.

"Are you kidding me? Good-looking *and* you can cook? I feel like I've won the lottery."

Nix lowers his head with a smile, but not before I catch his blush.

"Are you blushing?" I try and pull his face back to mine with a finger on his chin, but he resists.

"I don't blush," he laughs, but now he's blushing even more.

"You really don't see it, do you?" My voice is incredulous as I take in his absurd insecurity. "You're pretty wonderful, you know."

"I appreciate that." Nix kisses my forehead. "But it's not really a lack of confidence."

His eyes start shifting around, as if he's deciding whether or not to say anything further.

"Tell me," I encourage him, sliding my fingers through the back of his soft hair, until his eyes finally settle on mine with a sigh.

"I haven't been close to anyone in a long time, at least not like this," he confesses. "And sometimes I feel like a teenager again, fumbling around, completely out of practice. I have no idea what the hell I'm doing."

"I think you're doing a fine job," I reassure him with a smile. "No complaints here."

Nix kisses me again, but when he pulls away his face is serious. "But the thing is…I'm not a teenager anymore." His eyes follow his fingers as they caress my face from forehead to chin. "So what I'm trying to figure out is why everything feels like a first with you, Rose, why being with you has made me forget about everyone else. It's like my life started over when I met you."

Fighting back tears, I snuggle into his chest and hold him close. I have no idea what to say other than "ditto", but he has to know that. And in case he doesn't, I'll make sure to tell him how much I love him and how wonderful I think he is every day for the rest of my life…just as soon as I can catch my breath.

"Come on." Nix kisses the top of my head and releases everything but my hand. "I have a surprise for you."

"Another surprise?" I quickly wipe away a stray tear from my cheek before Nix can see it. "I'm not sure I can handle much more."

Nix smiles as he leads me back toward the blanket we sat on earlier. He lets go of my hand to pull out his phone, then grabs a small speaker off the ground. He syncs his phone with the speaker then I see him open iTunes on his phone.

"You're making playlists, now?" I question. "Such the Renaissance man."

"What can I say?" Nix gives me a shy smile. "You inspire me to try new things."

I watch as he slides his finger across his screen until he finds what he's looking for. Then he places the phone and the speaker on the ground at his feet and moves toward me.

The music starts playing as he grabs my hand and pulls me into his chest. "Dance with me," he commands and I smile when I recognize the song.

"Nina Simone. This has to be David's influence."

"The man has excellent taste in music."

"That he does," I agree. "And this is a good choice. 'Wild is the Wind' happens to be one of my favorites."

"I know."

"Oh, do you now? I assume that's David's influence as well?"

Nix shrugs with a mischievous grin. "I may have asked him a few questions."

"You could have asked me."

"That would have ruined the surprise."

Nix leads me slow and steady as we both lose ourselves to Nina's soulful voice.

"You know…" I close my eyes, trying to gather my thoughts as Nix kisses across my bare shoulder. "Nina and I have something in common."

"What's that?"

"I believe Nina too, had a thing for handsome, brown-eyed men."

Nix laughs and raises his head. "I know that song, and if I remember correctly, she refers to us brown-eyed men as trouble."

"Trouble, maybe. Irresistible, most definitely."

"You think I'm irresistible?"

"Very much so."

I'm about to kiss him again, prove to him exactly how irresistible he is, but I stop short when the next song starts to play. It's another favorite, but David wouldn't have known about this one.

"It reminds me of you." Nix trails a finger across my bottom lip. "This song. It reminds me of the first time I saw you. It was a picture of you and Lila—the one in the blue room at *Geoffrey's*, the one on the mantel? You're wearing this pretty green dress, and your smile...man, you have the best smile. I couldn't wait to meet you."

Ed Sheeran's soft voice croons in the background as I stare up into sparkling brown eyes. He knows this is one of my favorite artists, and it thrills me to think he's been listening to his songs when I'm not around.

"And now that you've met me..." My voice is barely a whisper as I get lost in Nix's eyes. "What do you think about me now?"

"Let's see..." His adoring gaze roams my face as if he'll find the answers there. "I think your kindness and ability to love knows no bounds and that alone makes you the most attractive woman I've ever met. But then you color my world with that hair of yours and man, that smile...sometimes it feels as necessary as the blood in my veins." Nix takes one of my hands and places it over his heart. "Basically, I think you're everything I've ever wanted. And all I'll ever need."

I kiss him slowly, passionately, silently showing him how much I care and how much he means to me. He's all I'll ever need. He's all I'll ever want.

"Rose..." Nix pulls away and rests his forehead on mine. "Please don't kiss me like that. I can't think...I can hardly breathe when you kiss me like that."

"I love you." I take his face in my hands and stroke his cheek. "And I want you to feel that every time I touch you and in everything I say, with every look I give you, every smile. I don't ever want you to forget how much you mean to me. You deserve it. You deserve to be loved like that."

One minute I'm standing, holding the man I love and next, I'm off my feet and in his arms. He carries me up the stairs of his deck and through the sliding doors. I'm not sure what his exact destination was, but we don't get any further than the living room before he's pulling my dress over my head. I remove his shirt slowly, one button at a time, even though my pace looks like it's causing him physical pain. His fingers are digging into my bare hips, his chest pumping up and down with quick breaths.

"Are you trying to kill me?" he finally asks when I make it to the last button on his shirt.

I glance up at him through my lashes as I push his shirt off his shoulders. "I like to take my time unwrapping my gifts."

Nix takes over after that, his movements swift but controlled as he removes the rest of our clothing and carries me to his bedroom. He sits down on his bed and leans back against his headboard, before grabbing my hand and pulling me onto his lap. Nix wastes no time lifting my hips and pushing himself inside, but when I start to move, he stops me.

"What's wrong?" I ask, as he sits upright and pulls me close. "Is everything okay?"

Nix caresses my face, his lovely eyes open and full of contentment. "You're the gift," he whispers, as he kisses under my chin. "Priceless and one of a kind."

Nix lifts my hips again, encouraging me to move, and I do as instructed, exhaling in a low moan as I take him. The humbled worship in his expression and his own quiet sounds give me strength, urging me to please him, to please us both. It's not long before both our bodies are slick with perspiration, our hearts pounding in our chests, our breaths escaping in frantic bursts.

"Rose..." Nix growls low and deep in his chest, drawing my eyes to his. "God, I don't want this to end, but...*fuck*...I can't...."

"I know, sweetheart." I lean down and kiss his trembling lips. "I feel it too. Let go with me."

We find our release together, staring into each other's eyes, like we've done so many times now. And it never ceases to amaze me—sharing that moment with him, utterly vulnerable, completely exposed in every possible way. I know I'll never be able to share myself this way with anyone but him. There's no way I could find this kind of love twice in my life. I feel blessed beyond measure that I've found it all.

After holding each other in easy silence for who knows how long, Nix lifts a weary head from my shoulder. "Stay with me," he mumbles against my lips and I sigh. "Stay with me tonight. Please."

"Okay."

"I'll make breakfast."

"I already said I'd stay," I grin at him. "No need to sweeten the deal."

"Is there something wrong with wanting to take care of you, Rose?"

I shake my head as Nix kisses along my neck. I can't speak while he's torturing me like that with his lips.

"I like making you happy." Nix kisses my chin, my cheek, my mouth. "Like I said, I'm a sucker for that smile."

I give him one in response that probably makes me look like a close cousin of the Chesire Cat, but I don't care.

"Beautiful…" Nix whispers before pulling my face back to his.

This kiss starts out slow and sweet, but that doesn't last long. Nix has me beneath him on the bed soon enough, without ever breaking our kiss, and I let him take me. I let him claim me, although he owns every part of me already.

It feels like he always has.

And I'm pretty sure he always will.

CHAPTER TWENTY-SIX

I'm in a deep, peaceful sleep when the echo of a scream causes a sudden panic to grip my chest and I wake with a gasp.

I look quickly to my left as I try and catch my breath, hoping I didn't disturb Nix, but the panic only worsens when I see I'm alone in the bed.

I close my eyes and lean back against the headboard. I need to calm down. It must have been a bad dream. Just a dream. Nothing to worry about.

After a few calming breaths, I start to feel better and I look to my left again, wondering where Nix could be. There's no light coming from the bathroom, and when I look to the open bedroom door, I don't see lights coming from elsewhere in the house either.

I stand and grab a pair of Nix's boxer shorts from his drawer and pull on the white, button down shirt he was wearing yesterday. The man has no clocks anywhere in this house, so I walk quietly into the living room to grab my phone. I expect to find Nix somewhere along the way, but he's nowhere to be found. I pull my phone from my purse and see it's a little after two in the morning. I look around the moonlit room as the panic starts to ease its way back into my chest. *Where could he be?*

I put my phone away and move toward the sliding doors that lead to the backyard, thinking he may be on the porch. But when I open the doors and look around, there's still no sign of him. Squinting my eyes as they adjust to the dark, I walk to the railing and look out over the grass. Finally, thanks to the moonlight's reflection off the water, I find what I've been looking for.

Nix is sitting on the grass near the water's edge, and I smile with relief as I start walking toward him. But as I get closer, I notice something isn't right. He's slumped over, knees bent, his arms wound tightly around his waist, and it isn't until I'm standing next to him that I notice he's shaking. When he looks up at me, the pain in his eyes echoes the panic I felt earlier. Now I know it must have been him that had me waking up, gasping for air.

I'm not sure what's wrong, but I instinctively know I need to try and make it better and fast. Without a word, I sit behind him, wrap my arms around his shoulders and lay my head on his bare back. His skin is damp with perspiration, and I wonder if maybe he's cold and that's the reason for the shaking, but something tells me that's not the case.

"N-Nightmare," he stutters out and I pull him in even closer.

"It's okay, sweetheart," I whisper. "You're going to be fine. I've got you, now."

Nix continues to shake, and I start panicking again, trying to think of something, anything I can do to help him. Then it comes to me.

I press in close and begin to softly hum the first song that comes to mind. The shaking stops before I even finish the first verse, then Nix loosens the grip on his waist and I feel his fingers wrap around my wrists as I continue clinging to his chest. He rests his forehead on his knees and I stay curled against him, humming my favorite song to sing to him—the one that tells him that he may not have been my first, but I want him to be my last.

Eventually, his breathing calms, and I'm about to suggest we go back to bed, when Nix lifts his head and sits up straighter. He pulls on my arm, urging me into his lap and I gladly settle in. He takes my face in his hands and pulls my mouth down to his, kissing me with soft, brief caresses, cherishing me, loving me…thanking me.

When he's done, he buries his face in my hair and I close my eyes and pull him closer. "Feeling better?" I whisper in the darkness and Nix answers with another soft kiss right beneath my jaw.

I would have been content to hold him like that until the sun came up, but as his breathing starts to even out, I realize he would probably be more comfortable sleeping in his bed than out here on the hard ground.

I lift his head slowly from my neck and kiss his cheek. "Come on, baby. Let's get you inside."

Nix can barely open his eyes, but he manages a nod, so I slide off his lap and offer my hand to help him up. As soon as he stands, I pull his arm around my shoulders and let him lean on me as we walk back toward the house.

Thinking about his damp hair and skin when I found him, I lead him into his bathroom. Nix looks down at me, puzzled.

"Just let me take care of you, okay?" I use my free hand to caress his face as he leans against the sink in the bathroom. "Let me wash it away."

I may be imagining it, but I could have sworn Nix's eyes seemed watery as he nodded in agreement. Assuming it's mostly exhaustion more than anything else, I move quickly to get the water just right in the shower then move back to Nix so I can undress him. Since he's only in a pair of jeans and nothing else, I have him naked and in the shower in no time. I quickly remove my clothes, then step in behind him as he stands under the spray, letting it pound against his slumped shoulders. I go to grab the shampoo from the shelf so I can wash away his nightmare as promised, but I'm stopped suddenly by strong arms as they wind around my waist. Nix pulls me against his hard, slick body, seemingly wide awake now. In every way. Everywhere.

I stare up into his eyes, knowing what he wants and giving him my consent. Without a word, he presses me against the shower wall and slides his hands down to my thighs. He lifts me so my hips meet his and enters me slowly—a low, gratified moan vibrating through his chest as if he's finally found relief, as if I'm healing him, and I can't fight the tears this time as they slide down my cheeks.

Nix rocks into me, maintaining his slow, easy pace until he finally whispers a heartfelt "I love you" right before he reaches his climax. I'm right behind him, whispering the same three words into his ear as I give myself to him.

Afterward, I can feel Nix's arms shaking with exhaustion as he releases me slowly, letting me slide down his body until I'm back on my feet.

"Let's get you cleaned up and in the bed," I suggest, as I reach for the shampoo once again.

He lets me wash his hair this time, somehow managing to keep himself upright even though he seems to be asleep on his feet. He makes these soft, satisfied sounds as I gently knead his scalp and I smile, happy to see him relaxed and content.

I get out first, dry off a little then wrap a towel around myself before shutting off the water and helping Nix out. I'm sure he's capable of drying himself, but he lets me do it with eyes half-closed and a slight grin that tells me he may be exhausted, but he's enjoying this. Thoroughly. Of course I don't mind at all, especially when I finally get him in the bed and he immediately pulls me down with him, curling his naked body around mine.

We lay in silence for a while, and I think Nix is sleeping, until he whispers my name in the darkness.

"Yes?"

"I was just thinking..." Nix's voice is low and groggy, almost as if he's talking in his sleep. "When I was overseas, a lot of the guys had girlfriends or wives back home. Used to talk about them all the time." I try and turn in his arms so I can see his face, but he pulls me in a little tighter, hindering my efforts. "Never really bothered me until my last tour," he continues. "It was a rough few months and more than once, I didn't know if I'd ever come home again. One night, my buddy Mike and I were on watch and he kept talking about his girl. Said she had these pretty blue eyes and that sometimes, the only thing that got him through was the thought of seeing those eyes again. I don't know why, but that stuck with me. I started wondering if I had someone to come home to, what would I miss most about her?"

Nix pauses for a long time, but my eyes stay wide and watery, jonesing for more.

"I wish I would have known you then," I whisper, breaking the silence. "I would have written you every day, sent you care packages, called, texted, Skyped, whatever I could do to make sure you knew how much I missed you, to make sure you never felt lonely."

I wait for a reply that doesn't come, and I assume again that Nix has drifted off. Then he inhales a shuddering breath and I feel him nuzzling into the back of my hair.

"Your voice," he says so low I barely hear him, even in the quiet dark. "I would have missed everything about you, but your sweet voice...that's what I would've missed the most."

I try again to turn in his arms and this time he allows it. His eyes are half-closed and I have to wonder if he'll even remember this conversation tomorrow.

"I love you," I whisper, as I trail my fingers down the side of his face. He closes his eyes with my touch, and I kiss him softly before snuggling back into his arms. I bury my face in his chest and he sighs.

"Sing to me," Nix whispers into the darkness as he holds me tight, and as tired as I am right now, I find I still can't seem to deny him anything.

I lift my head and lightly stroke his face as I sing a new song this time. I sing the Nina Simone song we danced to earlier, and even though Nix is fast asleep in less than a minute, I continue reciting the lyrics to one of the most beautiful songs ever written, to the most beautiful man I've ever met—begging him to kiss me, to cling to me, to stay with me as we find our way through this wild love we've found. I know we're both scared, but if we can just hold on, I know everything will be worth it in the end.

✳✳✳✳

The next time I wake up, it's to the smell of bacon. And coffee.

Obviously, I've died and gone to heaven.

I pull on another pair of Nix's boxer briefs and one of his t-shirts before making quick use of the bathroom. I use his toothbrush, hoping he won't mind, then run my fingers through my long hair, working out the knots caused from sleeping with it wet. The end result isn't great, but as I stare at myself in the mirror, my pale skin flushes with the memories of last night, my light brown eyes are glowing with love and happiness, and I decide I like the way Nix Taylor looks on me.

I leave the bedroom, following the mouth-watering aromas into the kitchen, where I find Nix in nothing but a pair of black cotton pants as he stands over the stove, flipping bacon in an iron skillet. He turns to me, his eyes lazily appraising me from head to toe and back again before giving me a lopsided grin.

Definitely heaven. There's no other possible explanation.

Nix turns back to the stove, still smiling. "Morning, pretty girl."

"Good morning." I walk over to him and wrap my arms around his waist from behind. I press my cheek against his warm skin and sigh.

Nix pulls one of my hands from his waist and kisses my palm, then places my hand back where he found it. "How do you like your eggs?"

"I love eggs, so whatever's easiest for you."

"That's not what I asked," Nix corrects me. "I asked how *you* like your eggs, not how *I* like your eggs."

I kiss his back with a smile. "Scrambled. With cheese."

"A woman after my own heart."

"We like our eggs the same way? Uncanny."

"Obvious soul mates."

"Definitely."

I give Nix a few more kisses on his back before releasing him to go search for coffee.

"Hey, Rose..."

I turn back to see what he needs, but he only stares at me as if trying to find the words. Eventually, he turns the eye off on the stove, walks over and pulls me into his chest, hugging me tight. He doesn't say or do anything, other than lay his cheek on the top of my head and sigh contentedly as he holds me close. I realize it must be another silent thank you for last night and I close my eyes, giving this gesture the respect it deserves. Another piece of my heart? Another piece of my soul? Take it. There's nothing I wouldn't trade for these private moments with him.

"You know..." I run my hands up and down the smooth skin of his back. "It's hard to believe that a week ago you would barely let me touch you."

Nix smiles as he takes my face in his hands. "Gotta make up for lost time."

He leans down to kiss me, and I wrap my arms around his neck, giving myself over to him. I'm not sure if it's a God-given talent or a practiced sport, but Nix is an incredible kisser–firm but controlled with enough soft, tender movements mixed in to keep you begging for more. Needless to say, by the time he releases me, I'm lightheaded and hardly aware of my surroundings. Nix rests his forehead on my shoulder, and I'm grateful for the chance to gather my senses.

"If I would have known you were this good of a kisser," Nix breathes, "I wouldn't have waited so long."

I laugh, as I was just thinking the same thing about him. "Well, now you know, and you're lucky I didn't give up on you."

I meant the remark to be light and teasing, like the mood has been so far this morning, but Nix immediately tenses in my arms. I pull my fingers through the back of his soft hair and he relaxes with a sigh.

"I was scared," he whispers. "Still am."

Whoa. Where did that confession come from?

"It's okay." I try not to stutter in surprise. "Trust doesn't come easily. I understand."

Nix stares at my face, his lips parted, his eyes troubled. I wait for whatever it is he's about to tell me but of course it never comes.

"You know you can talk to me, Nix," I remind him, "about us, about your nightmares, about anything. And I promise to just sit and listen, if that's all you need, okay?"

Nix studies me, indecision flashing across his features, and I silently hope what I said is sinking in. Even if it doesn't happen today, it's important to me that he knows I'm here for him.

"Sorry..." he shakes his head as if shaking off the moment and gives me a small smile. "This is all a little heavy for so early in the morning. How about some food?"

"Sounds good," I laugh half-heartedly, and he gives me one more brief kiss before going back to finishing our breakfast.

"Coffee?" I ask him as I grab a mug for myself from the cabinet.

"Please."

I pour two cups and silently mourn yet another lost opportunity for him to open up to me. I add cream and sugar to both mugs and carry them over to the breakfast table just as Nix is bringing over our plates.

"This looks delicious." I'm practically drooling as I sit down in front of pancakes, bacon and eggs scrambled with cheese.

Nix smiles as he passes me the butter and syrup, and I smile back, not wanting to ruin our morning. I can't force things, and judging by the way he cut things off a moment ago, it looks like he won't be opening up anytime soon. But I'm certain it will come in time. I just have to be patient.

"Good grief," I moan as I take my first bite. "I still can't believe you've been holding out on me. You're an incredible cook."

I take another bite and a quiet moan escapes my mouth once again as I chew. I look over at Nix and expect him to be enjoying his breakfast as I am. Instead he's sitting back in his chair, arms crossed over his bare chest. His eyes are focused on my mouth and that sexy, lopsided grin of his stops me mid-chew.

"What's wrong?" I ask with a mouth full of food, not very lady-like.

Nix smiles a little wider. "Just taking a minute to enjoy the view."

I feel my cheeks warm as I finish my bite, and we spend the next several minutes enjoying a comfortable silence while we eat the delicious breakfast Nix prepared. Part of me is itching to ask him about his nightmare last night, curious if it happens often and why, but again, I don't want to ruin the morning. Regardless of how upset he seemed when I found him last night, he seems happy now, his full lips turned up in some fashion of a smile even as he eats.

Eventually, the conversation picks back up when he asks about Sydney's wedding shower and I suddenly get the bright idea that Nix could help with the food.

"David's amazing, but I'm sure he would appreciate your help," I say, to try and convince him. "Does he know you cook?"

"He does, and you don't have to sell me on this. I'd be happy to help."

I stand and move over to his side of the table, plopping down into his lap. I kiss him hard on the lips then hug his neck. Nix laughs at my reaction.

"If this is my thank you, then anything you ask...consider it done."

I smile as I lean down to kiss him again. The sweet syrupy taste mixed with Nix's own delightful flavor has me lingering a little longer than intended. I nip at his bottom lip, unable to resist taking a bite. He tastes too good.

"Rose..." He says my name with a growl that has me trembling with anticipation. "You up for working off some of our breakfast?"

"Absolutely."

Nix stands, lifting me effortlessly in his arms and starts walking. I have no idea where we're going and I don't care because Nix is kissing me along the way. A few seconds later, I'm on my back on the sofa. I guess he was too impatient to walk the extra few feet back to his room, and that's fine by me.

"I love you wearing my clothes." Nix positions himself between my legs and pulls the neck of my borrowed t-shirt down so he can kiss along my collarbone. "Love the thought of being close to you, even when I'm not around."

"They smell like you." I inhale sharply as his soft lips move down to my stomach. "And I love that."

Nix stops his kisses, peering up at me through his lashes. "Oh really?"

"Yes." I tilt my head with a smile. "I love everything about you."

Nix's mouth pulls up on one side—a sexy grin with eyes that reveal all of the wicked plans he has in store. Before I can even try to wrap my head around the intensity of his stare, he crashes his mouth against mine.

CHAPTER TWENTY-SEVEN

These past couple of weeks with Nix have been my own personal paradise.

We've spent almost every free moment we have together, and Nix has even started helping David a little in the kitchen, so I get to see him at work from time to time. It's bliss—heavenly, heavenly bliss and I have no idea how I've lived my life without him up until now. And the best part? I'm still me. As a matter of fact, I'm a better me.

Even though we spend so much time together, Nix constantly encourages my individuality. He forces me to make decisions, when I'd usually defer the responsibility because I'd be more concerned about other peoples' preferences over my own. Nix always presses the issue, making me choose the movie to watch, the food to eat, the trail to hike or the music to listen to, but he's no pushover. He humors me by trying new things but makes it perfectly clear when he dislikes one of my preferences. Thankfully it's not that often, but I do enjoy the innocent little tiffs we have over who likes what and why. I've learned to hold my ground because Nix is incredibly stubborn and if he can't win verbally, he usually takes it out on my body. In which case, I still win.

Of course there will always be that part of me waiting for the other shoe to drop, but the more time we spend together, the more confident I become that Nix and I are strong enough to make it through just about anything. My one nagging concern is that he's still holding back in a lot of ways, and I often worry that I'm being selfish. Perhaps I'm asking too much from a man like Nix. Even his mom mentioned that he's always been a private person, so why should I be the one he bares his soul to? I'm certainly not in the market to change anyone, not that I would want to but even if I did, I've been through enough to know that's just not possible.

I guess what concerns me most is feeling like he's hiding something from me, and my poor track record with men makes that particular character trait hard to accept. I trust Nix. I do. And we all have our demons, but my guess is Nix has something close to an arsenal of them built up inside. I'm worried that his tendencies to keep things bottled up will eventually end in disaster, and I've become too attached to lose him now.

Since I've been staying the night with him, I've learned his nightmares happen fairly often. At first, he wasn't too keen on me witnessing that kind of vulnerability. But when he saw that I could be there to comfort him without asking any questions, he seemed more open to my company.

Some nightmares seem worse than others, but I'm only judging by his reaction because he's pretty closed lipped about them. I assume they're about his time overseas, and I can understand him not wanting to drudge up those memories, but maybe if he got things off his chest, it would help him find some peace.

Some nights he wakes up and leaves the room. I find him on the back patio or down near the creek, and I usually sit with him until I can persuade him to come back to bed. Other times, I wake to a scream and the next thing I know, his lips are on mine, begging for a connection I'm all too willing to give.

The worst ones are where I have to help pull him out of it, shaking his shoulders and calling out his name as he screams and writhes in agony. I've only been witness to two of those so far, and both times my eyes were wet with tears before I could bring him back to me. When he finally came around, he started apologizing so profusely it was alarming, but I pushed my own fear aside and took care of him the only way I could. I ran my fingers through his damp hair and kissed his face, assuring him it was okay and that it wasn't his fault, that he didn't do anything wrong. It took a while, but eventually he relaxed under my touch and, no matter the gravity of the situation, he always asks me to sing to him. So I do. Because when he hurts, so do I. And some nights, holding him close and singing him to sleep helps to soothe us both.

Even still, Nix's unfortunate dreams aside, these past few weeks with him have been some of the best days of my life. I had no idea I could feel this way. I had no idea I could feel so empowered, so resilient. Nix and I enjoy the things we have in common, but we also celebrate our differences. I love who I am when I'm around him. And he loves me.

Blessed does not even begin to cover it.

"There you are."

I turn to find Nix walking toward me through the grass. I've been standing out here, admiring his handy work on the new deck at *Geoffrey's* while he's been inside installing a new water heater in the basement.

Nix opens his arms to me and I gratefully dive in. "Are you guys done?" I ask as I stare up at my favorite brown eyes.

"Yep, and David told me to tell you that he'll be back soon. He's gone to the hardware store to return a part we didn't use, and I'm about to pack up the tools and head back to the cabin for a much needed shower."

Nix leans down for a kiss and I grab his face, keeping him there for a while.

"I like you hot and sweaty."

"There will be plenty of time for that later," he assures me. "Most likely followed by another shower, and I will make sure you enjoy every second. Immensely."

"I'm looking forward to it."

Nix quiets my giggling with a kiss and I sigh against his lips.

"I guess I'd better go in and starting prepping," I pout, reluctant to let him go.

"I'll probably be leaving in a few minutes, but I'll come say goodbye before I go."

"I miss you already."

I kiss him deeply this time, giving him a taste of what's to come later this evening. I learned this trick from him, but he's still better at it.

"Damn, Rose. How am I supposed to let you go after that?"

I smile up at him. Maybe I'm not so bad after all.

"I wanted to make sure I stayed on your mind until I see you later."

"As if that wasn't a given?" Nix gives me one more chaste kiss on the lips before grabbing my hand and leading me back toward the restaurant.

We part ways once inside, and when I get to the kitchen, I see that David has already finished the meatloaves, so I decide to start on the veggies. I toss some potatoes into the sink and turn to grab the peeler from the drawer, but then I feel my heartbeat falter in my chest when I see who's standing in the kitchen doorway.

"Hello, Rose."

Oh no. Not today.

"How did you...why...?" I blink a couple of times, praying this is a figment on my imagination that will soon disappear.

Vick Delacroix takes a few steps in my direction with a cocky smile on his pretty face, probably thinking I'm flustered by his good looks, when what I'm really worried about is the fact that Nix is still somewhere in the restaurant.

I wipe my hands on my apron and shake off the nerves. "What are you doing here?" I ask Vick as he continues to move closer to me. "How did you even get in?"

"The front door was unlocked."

"Really?"

David must have left the front door unlocked when he left, which is very unlike him. Of all days...*Dammit!*

"And I came to see you, of course." Vick smiles his perfect smile, and I immediately notice it doesn't have the same effect on me it once did. That's a relief.

I cross my arms over my chest, hoping he takes the gesture as a request to keep his distance.

"Well, I appreciate you stopping by, but I haven't spoken to you in months," I remind him. "Why now?"

"I've missed you." Vick sighs deeply. "And I wanted to apologize for how I treated you, Rose. The truth is I kind of freaked out."

"Freaked out? About what?"

"You. Us."

"*Us?*"

Vick's staring at me as if I should know what he's talking about, but I'm clueless. There never really was an "us". He made sure of that.

"You've always meant so much to me, Rose. You know that."

"As a matter of fact, I don't."

"Come on, Rose." Obviously irritated, Vick runs his hand roughly through his shiny black hair. "You know how I feel about you."

I stare at him in disbelief. All this time, I thought he had gotten bored with me. I thought after a few dates, he realized I wasn't as great as he'd expected. I guess I was wrong.

Feeling almost sorry for him now, I uncross my arms with a sigh. "Look, Vick..."

I'm about to tell him it doesn't matter, that I'm in love with someone else. I'm about to suggest we remain friends, but before I can speak, Vick takes full advantage of my pity by capturing my face in his hands and pressing his lips against mine.

I think the surprise of it all is what has me kissing him back. Or maybe I subconsciously wanted some kind of goodbye, some sort of closure, so that's why I'm prolonging a kiss that is nothing but a poor imitation of what I'm used to from Nix. Thankfully, it's only a matter of seconds before I come to my senses and start pushing him away.

But it's too late.

My lips are still locked with Vick's when I open my eyes and see Nix standing in the kitchen doorway. His fists are clenched at his sides and his face is red with anger or humiliation–probably both. I push Vick away with two hands on his shoulders, but Nix is gone before I can even say his name. Still, I run after him.

"Nix!" I call, after he finally comes back into sight. "Nix, please wait!"

But he doesn't wait. I follow him out the door, and regardless of my tearful pleas, he gets in his Jeep and peels out of the driveway without looking back.

Oh my God. How am I going to fix this?

Because I have to fix this.

Losing him is not an option.

I wipe the tears from my eyes as I run back into the house, and Vick catches me on my way to the kitchen.

"Rose, I'm sorry," he says, but I push him out of the way.

"Not now, Vick. I have somewhere I need to be."

Vick follows me to the kitchen and I can feel him watching me as I grab my purse from David's desk drawer.

"Rose, please. I really am sorry."

I couldn't care less how sorry he is right now.

"Please do me a favor and tell David I'll be back soon," I request, as I search frantically for my keys. "I have to go."

Vick grabs my arm when I go to walk past him. "Do you love him?" he asks me, and when I look up at him, I'm shocked by the sadness in his eyes. "Am I too late, Rose?"

"Yes," I say without hesitation. "I'm in love with him."

"And you would choose him over me? Over our friendship?"

"I will *always* choose him."

Vick releases my arm and bows his head in defeat. "I never should have let you go."

"But you did," I snap, and then realize I'm not really angry with Vick.

I doubt he even knew I was seeing someone, and either way, Vick is famous for making impulsive decisions. Our two minute relationship can attest to that.

"You don't have to let me go." With a sigh, I reach out and take one of his hands in mine. "We can still be friends."

"Friends?" he scoffs, looking down at my hand holding his. "You're putting me in the friend zone?"

"It's better than nothing, right?"

"Friends it is," Vick laughs. "But if this guy ever screws up, you know where to find me."

I nod and reach up on my toes to kiss his cheek. "Thanks, Vick, but I don't think there will ever be anyone else for me. Nix is…well, he's everything."

A tear slips out of my eye as I remember that right now he hates me, and I have to get to him before I lose him forever.

"Then go get your everything, sweet Rose. You deserve it."

Vick kisses my hand before releasing it, and I run toward the front door as fast as my feet will take me. I feel awful for leaving David like this, but nothing feels as important to me right now as getting to Nix.

Completely lost in thought the entire ride, I'm pulling into the driveway of the cabin before I know it. Seeing Nix's Jeep in the driveway is a huge relief, but then I realize I still have no idea what I'm going to say to him. I just know I have to make him understand. I have to make him see how much I love him, how he means everything to me.

I hop out of my car in a rush, nearly falling face first in his driveway as I trip over my own feet, but I manage to stay upright all the way to the front door. I knock a few times, but when no one comes to the door, I quickly make my way to the back. I'm rounding the side of the house, praying the back door is unlocked, when I see him standing at the edge of the creek. I walk in his direction, afraid to speak until I get closer. He's still in the dirtied up white t-shirt and shorts he was working in earlier at *Geoffrey's* but he seems to have lost his shoes. I watch as he paces along the water's edge, his hands alternating nervously between his hips and the top of his head.

"Nix?"

His shoulders stiffen at the sound of my voice, and a shudder ripples through me. Oh God, he hates me. He already hates me.

I continue walking in his direction, even though he doesn't turn to face me. Honestly, I hope he never does. As weak as it sounds, it would be easier if I didn't have to look into those unfathomable eyes right now.

When I'm only a few feet away, I try again. "Nix, you have to let me explain."

Nix turns so quickly then, it startles me. "I don't *have* to do a damn thing."

"Please..." Tears immediately start down my cheeks. "It was a misunderstanding."

Nix is visibly shaking as he closes his eyes, and I stay quiet and still, letting him have his time. But when he opens his eyes, I can see that no matter what I say, I've done irreversible damage. I pull a hand over my mouth so he won't be witness to my silent screams.

"All or nothing." His voice is quiet but firm. "I told you that I wouldn't have this any other way, and you promised me. You fucking promised me, Rose."

Instinctively, I take a step toward him, but he immediately backs away. "Please," I beg again. "He's a friend and that's all he'll ever be."

"All or *nothing*!"

Between the look on his face and the pain in his voice, he may as well have slapped me. He turns away and it hurts like nothing I've ever felt before, but something inside keeps pushing me forward. I have to fight. I can't give up on him, on us. He's the only thing that matters.

Nix starts pacing again, but I catch his arm to stop him. He whips his head in my direction and pulls his arm out of my reach. "Don't touch me right now, Rose. Please don't."

"Nix, I love you." I try to palm his cheek, but he pulls his face away before I can make contact. "I love you. You have to know that."

"It's not enough," he whispers, and when he takes a step back, I take a step forward, landing us both in the shallow water. "Loving me isn't enough because now I can't trust you, Rose. I can't even look at you."

Tears form in his eyes before he turns from me again, but I refuse to let him get away. The black flats I wear for work sink into the mud at the bottom of the creek, so I step out of them. I have more important things to worry about right now.

"Nix, you can't possibly think he means anything to me." I stare at the back of his head, willing him to understand. "You know me. You know me better than I know myself. Do you honestly think I could love anyone the way I love you? You *know* me, Nix. I would never do anything to hurt you. Never."

"Too late." He won't turn to face me, but at least he's stopped trying to get away. "You've already hurt me. Seeing you with him...." Nix reaches up and pulls at his hair with both hands. "Just go. Please just go."

"No." I stand firm, still keeping my distance, but refusing to leave him like this. He has to listen. *Please listen, Nix. Oh God, please.*

Nix looks to the sky and shakes his head, then finally turns to face me. I cover my mouth to hide my shock when I see tears on his flushed cheeks. His eyes are red-rimmed, but fierce, and I immediately know what I'm about to hear is going to break me.

"What do you want from me, Rose?" Nix takes a step toward me and I stagger back onto dry land, shocked by his intensity. "You want me to open up to you? Is that it?"

"No...I just...well, yes, but---"

"You say you want me to share this...this shit inside my head with you," he interrupts, "but I can promise you, you don't want to hear about it."

Nix starts pacing again and my hands are trembling at my sides as I realize he's lost control. My strong, well-ordered soldier has officially gone AWOL. And it's all my fault. I've broken him, and now I'm not sure if I even deserve him back.

"What you don't understand," he continues, "Is that this ugliness inside of me—this evil left over from ten years and seven tours to some of the most miserable places on earth...sometimes I feel like it's eating me alive, Rose. The memories, the nightmares, they're with me always, and some days, I swear I'm only a breath away from letting them devour me. It would be so damn easy."

Tears are pouring from my eyes and I have no idea what to say or what to do to make this better. I feel so selfish. I feel so greedy now for wanting more when he was giving me all he was capable of giving and then some. Vick or no Vick, I fear I would have eventually ruined this. I would have eventually lost him, just as I'm losing him now.

"Ten years, Rose." He continues his pacing in front of me. "Seven tours in ten years taught me that just when you think you're on top of the world, everything comes crashing down beneath you. I learned to never let my guard down. I lived my life with one eye open for ten fucking years, so you would think I'd be smarter than this. And then all of that shit with Maggie..." Nix stops pacing but keeps his back to me. "God, I was so pissed at myself for trusting her when she wasn't worth it. She wasn't even fucking worth it, but you..."

I can't imagine what I look like right now, but when Nix turns back to me, his eyes widen as if he's surprised by what he sees. I remain unmoving, frozen in my misery until he takes my tear-soaked cheeks in his hands. The second his skin touches mine, I'm flooded with relief, even though I know that's not what's he offering.

"Nix..." I pull his hands from my cheeks and hold them in mine. "I don't know the first thing about what you've gone through over the last ten years, but maybe if you'd just talk to me, or talk to anyone, maybe it would help. Maybe it would stop some of the worry, stop the nightmares."

Nix looks down at my hands holding his. "The nightmares aren't always..."

He shakes his head and I narrow my eyes in confusion. I release one of his hands to lift his chin so he'll look at me. "Please don't stop," I beg him. "Please talk to me."

Nix closes his eyes briefly and with a resigned breath he tells me, "Sometimes the nightmares are about you...about losing you."

I cover my mouth as a sob rips from my chest. *Me*? I'm causing him that kind of pain? The thought is abhorrent. I shake my head and slowly back away from him, but he moves quickly toward me and pushes my hands from my face, replacing them with his own.

"I know you love me, Rose. And even after seeing what I saw this afternoon, I love you too. I probably always will." Nix inhales slowly as he smoothes a thumb over my cheek. "But all I see when I look at you right now, is your lips–the same soft lips that I've kissed a hundred times, that I've studied and worshipped over the last few months like a man obsessed–I see those lips attached to someone else's, and it makes me physically ache."

My breath feels trapped in my lungs. This can't be the end of us. This is not happening. I love him. He loves me. We can move past our fears. We can work this out.

Before I can try once more to plead my case, Nix releases me and takes a step back. "I can't do this. I don't have it in me to share you, Rose. I told you all or nothing and I meant it."

"You don't have to share me." I try to move closer, but he keeps pulling away until we're both nearly back in the water. "Everything happened so fast. Vick and I were talking, then the next thing I know, he's kissing me and I pushed him away. I pushed him away and ran after you to explain. Please believe me. He means nothing to me. You mean *everything*."

For a brief moment, I can see he understands. He hears me. His eyes meet mine and all of that familiar love and longing that I look forward to seeing every day, it's there again and shining. My heart melts at the sight, but then it all disappears, morphing into some unfamiliar mask of suspicion and doubt. How could he doubt the way I feel about him?

I stumble backwards in shock. "You don't believe me," I whisper, praying he'll deny it, praying he'll tell me I'm crazy, that of course he believes me, but he remains silent, his expression wary.

"I thought I could do this, but with you…it's so different with you." Nix crosses his arms over his chest, distancing himself further. "The fear, the nightmares…I'm not right in the head, Rose. This is too hard. It shouldn't be this hard."

"You're scared, Nix, and that's perfectly normal. Nothing worth having comes easily."

Don't give up. Please say you'll fight for us.

"I just don't think I have it in me right now. I'm tired, Rose. I'm so fucking tired and I don't want to fight anymore."

And there we have it. How can I stay and fight for him, fight for us, if he doesn't believe we're worth it?

Nix shifts his eyes around, doing that move where he looks at everything but me, and I feel the air leave my lungs as if I've been punched in the stomach.

"The oddest thing is…you *are* a fighter, Nix." Tears continue streaming down my face as I plead with him. "You're a soldier. You fought for your country, and I can't imagine the horrors you've seen, but you survived. And that strength, that kind of bravery…it's admirable. But here I am asking you to love me, asking you to trust me when I've never given you a reason not to, and you can't do it.

275

Where's all of that bravery now?" I try to catch his eyes, but he refuses to look at me. I don't care. I want him to hear this. "You have your heart broken one time and you throw in the towel? My heart's been broken more times than I can count, but you put the pieces back together and do it all over again because when you find someone worth fighting for, it's worth the risk is it not?"

Nix finally looks in my direction, or maybe he doesn't. I can't see a thing through the tears.

"I would've fought." I continue to pull away, and each step hurts a little worse, as if I'm separating from some part of myself, leaving a piece of me behind. "I would do anything for you, Nix. Anything. Because I think you're worth it. You're worth fighting for."

Nix makes a small move in my direction, but I turn and run away as fast as my bare feet will take me. I'm grateful to find the keys in the ignition when I reach my car. I crank it and peel out of his driveway with no clue as to where I'm going. I just know I have to get away from here, and what feels like centuries later, I'm pulling into the driveway of *Geoffrey's*. I'm not sure how I got back or why I even came here. I could barely see through the tears as I drove, and they're still pouring down my cheeks as I get out of the car and walk toward the front porch.

"Rose? Are you okay, my angel?" I look up to find David coming through the front door in a rush. "Vick told me what happened. I've been worried sick."

I plow into his open arms and sob like a baby. "I'm so sorry for leaving like that, but I can't...I don't know how...Oh, David. What have I done?"

David holds me tight, running a hand down my hair. "It's okay. Whatever's happened, we'll get through this. We'll fix it. Don't you worry."

I shake my head against his shoulder, but I'm crying so hard now I can't speak. David and I stand on the porch and I let him sway with me in his arms until I can finally catch my breath.

"Breathe, Rose." David reminds me. "Deep breaths. You'll be fine. I promise."

It's a little while before my breathing evens out and I manage to lift my head. "I'm sorry," I immediately say to David for acting so insane. "I didn't mean to worry you."

David gives me a sad laugh. "Rose, you're like the daughter I never had, so naturally, I worry. That's what parents do."

I nod and try to smile, but smiling appears to be lost on me at the moment. "David..." and the tears are back. "I've lost him. He didn't trust...Oh God, I've lost him."

David pulls me back into his arms. "That can't be true. Just give him time."

"It's over," I sob, my tears soaking his already drenched shirt. "He doesn't want to fight. I'm not worth it. We're not worth it."

David forces me to look into his soft brown eyes. "Now you listen to me, there will be no more of that talk. You are more than worth it, and Nix knows it. He's scared, but that's *his* issue. Don't make that about you."

"How can I not?" My voice is too high, too loud even for my own ears. "He'll fight for everyone else, everything else, but he won't fight for me! He thinks I don't understand, David. He thinks I don't understand heartache. *Me*! I'm a twenty-eight year old divorcee, living at home with her recently-divorced mother whose bitterness and passive aggressive bullshit threatens my sanity on a daily basis. I understand heartache. Trust me."

I've officially lost my cool, and if I couldn't recognize that myself, David's cautious expression would convince me.

"Did you ever tell Nix any of this?"

Pain lances through my chest as David reveals my truth. No, I haven't told Nix about my divorce, and now all I can do is hang my head in shame. All of that time, silently pleading with him, begging him to let me in, to talk to me, and I was the one not being fully honest with him or with myself.

"No," I shake my head as tears continue to fly out of my eyes. "I never told him about Danny. I was scared he would think less of me, like I was defective or broken somehow because I couldn't make my marriage work."

"Rose, Rose, Rose..." David shakes his head with a sigh. "Do you believe that about yourself?"

"No."

"And do you honestly think Nix could ever feel that way about you?"

"No," I admit. "I wanted to tell him, but the more time that passed, the graver things became in my head. He's too important to me. I was so afraid to risk what we had, and now..."

I can't even bare to say the words. *Now, we have nothing.* Oh God, what have I done?

"You should give Nix more credit than that," David scolds. "We all have our weaknesses, but you said so yourself Nix is a fighter. He may be afraid of risking his heart, but so what? He shouldn't be mocked for that. For some of us, getting out there again is the scariest thing imaginable."

My eyes search David's, surprised he's putting himself in that category.

"*Us?*"

David looks at me, his expression grave. "I thought Nadine took my heart with her when she passed away. For many years, I let myself believe that I would never again have what we shared. Then I opened myself up to the possibility. I let love in again, and although it's nothing like what I had with my Nadine, it's wonderful all the same."

"Lila," I whisper, and David nods.

"Just give him time. He'll come around. I promise."

"How can you know that?" I question. "How can you be so sure?"

"Hope." David smiles down at me and kisses my cheek. "Sometimes, that's all we have left."

I wrap my arms around his waist once more, silently thanking the heavens for bringing this man into my life. "I'm so happy about you and Lila," I whisper against his chest. "I had hope for the two of you, so maybe you're right. Maybe that's all we need."

"Thank you, angel." David kisses the top of my head. "And trust me. Hope and love. That's all you need."

CHAPTER TWENTY-EIGHT

I pull into my driveway and check my phone. Still nothing from Nix, but I can't say I'm surprised. I know him well enough now to know that he needs time to himself to think things through. Of course I'm worried, but I know that no matter what he decides, I won't give up. I'll hang on, kicking and screaming if I have to. My love for him won't go down without a fight.

I walk into the house, more tired than I've ever felt, to find my mom crocheting on the sofa. She looks up at me with a huge smile that quickly turns into a frown over what I'm sure is my ghastly appearance –muddy, creek stained pants, bare feet and a tear-streaked face.

"Good heavens." She pops off the sofa to make her way toward me. "What's happened to you?"

"Long day," I sigh. "Let me take a shower and I'll tell you all about it."

"Okay, sweetie." Mom looks worried, but she lets me pass with only a gentle pat on my arm. "I hope this doesn't have anything to do with Vick being back in town."

I immediately stop to turn and face her. "How did you know Vick was in town?"

"He came by here looking for you," she informs me, her voice excited. "We had a lovely chat. He's such a nice man."

I can't believe it. I can't believe she'd do this to me. After everything I've done for her. How could she purposefully hurt me like this?

"He stopped by to see me at *Geoffrey's*." I can barely get the words out, I'm so angry. "I assume you told him I'd be there?"

"Of course, I did. Why wouldn't I?" Mom takes a seat on the sofa and resumes her crocheting as if she can't see I'm fuming.

In a bold move, I stomp over and rip the yarn out of her hands. "Rosaline Parker!" my mom scolds. "What do you think you're doing?"

"What are *you* doing?!" I shout back at her. "Funny thing, Mom....if you and Vick had such a lovely chat, why wasn't he aware that I was seeing anyone?"

"He didn't ask," she says to me with a raised brow. It's a challenge, and it's been accepted.

"And when he asked where I was or where he could find me, you didn't think it was important to tell him I was at work with *my boyfriend*?"

"Rosie..." Mom stands and puts her hands on my shoulders, but I shake them off. "Rosie, I'm just trying to do what's best for you."

"Seriously? You're going to pull some 'mommy knows best' card with me right now? Have you seen your love life, Mom?"

She recoils as if I've punched her, and I don't blame her. I'm a horrible person. How could I say those things to her? What's gotten into me?

"I'm sorry," I whisper as she falls back into the sofa, tears already streaming out of her eyes. "Mom, I'm so sorry."

I sit down next to her and pull her into my arms. She doesn't resist, but she doesn't hug me back either.

"I shouldn't have said that to you," I ruefully admit. "You've been doing so well. You're so strong. I'm so sorry, Mom. Please forgive me."

After what feels like an eternity, she finally wraps her arms around my waist and we cry together, soothing each other as only a mother and daughter can.

"It's okay," Mom eventually speaks up. "It was harsh, but it's true. I have no business giving anyone relationship advice."

I pull away and take her hands in mine. "I've been through it too, Mom. Sometimes I think you forget that. I'm divorced too. And I don't think that means we're forever broken."

"I know," she sniffs. "It hurts a little less every day, but it's still hard."

I have to smile as I realize this is the most my mom and I have talked about what she's been through since I've moved back in.

"Will it always hurt, Rosie?" she asks me. "Will it always feel like a piece of me is missing? Like there's some part of me that's just out of reach and I know I'll never get it back, but I just can't seem to let it go?"

I have to stop and think about this because the one big difference in my mom's divorce and mine is that I didn't love Danny like Mom loved my dad. So to give her an honest answer, I think about Nix. I think about what happened today and I think about what I would do if he never came back to me, if it really is over forever.

"Yes." I breathe through the pain in my chest. "It will always hurt. The pain will never go away."

My mom looks down, defeated, but I lift her chin so she'll look at me.

"But we can learn to live with it," I assure her. "We are strong, Southern women. And we have each other. We can get through this, Mom. I know we can."

My mom smiles before leaning in and kissing my cheek. "I'm sorry, my Rosie. I'm sorry for what I did today. I just want what's best for you."

"I understand. As much as I want to hate you for it, I understand."

"Vick is kind and successful and very nice looking," she goes on. "You have to understand why I would put those things before love these days."

"I do," I laugh at her. "But Nix happens to be all of those things as well."

"Really?"

"If you would ever let me tell you about him, you would know this," I remind her. "But trust me. Nix is the better catch. And he gave me his heart. He trusted me with the most important part of himself and I ruined everything."

Mom sits up straighter and wipes at her cheeks. "Oh no, sweetie. That can't be true. You have the kindest, most gentle soul I've ever known. You couldn't hurt a fly."

"He saw me kissing Vick," I blurt and Mom covers her mouth in shock.

"This is all my fault," she whispers in horror. "Oh Rose. I'm so sorry. What can I do?"

"Nothing." I shake my head. "And it's not your fault because the biggest problem is that Nix wouldn't believe me when I told him the truth. I tried telling him kissing Vick was a mistake, and it was. I was surprised and shocked and it took me a few seconds to figure out what was happening. I tried explaining all of this to Nix, but it didn't work. He wouldn't listen. He didn't *want* to listen, as if I'm not worth the trouble."

"That's enough." Mom's face is fierce and resolute. "You, my daughter, are worth fighting for and you will not ever let anyone make you feel otherwise. Not as long as I can help it."

My head snaps back in shock as my mom hops up from the sofa, straightens her outfit then goes searching for her purse.

"What are you doing?" I question as I watch her dig for her keys. She hasn't driven a car in months.

"I'm taking you to talk to him," she tells me. "And if he won't listen to you, then he'll listen to me."

"Mom, stop."

But she doesn't. She finds her keys and walks back over to me. "Let's go. I won't sit back and watch your heart be broken again, especially knowing I may have had some part in it."

"It's not your fault," I say again and pull her back down on the sofa with me. "And Nix needs time to figure this out on his own. I've said my piece. He knows how I feel."

"But if you love him like you say you do, you can't just give up."

"I'm not. I promise."

Mom studies me a moment, then concedes. "Fine. But if you haven't heard from him in the next twenty-four hours, I'm going to have a little chat with him whether you like it or not."

"Thanks, Mom." I pull her into me with a laugh and hug her tight. "I love you."

"I love you too, sweetheart. I know I haven't been myself for a long time, but it's coming back to me. Slowly, but surely. And I couldn't have gotten here without you."

"Without me?" I question. "I don't feel as if I've helped at all, especially lately."

Mom smiles and looks away as if recalling a fond memory. "It was the day your dad called to say he was getting married. A couple of important things happened that day. First was when you told me you wouldn't go to the wedding, and second…" She takes a deep breath then looks back in my direction. "It was the first time I participated in a therapy session."

My eyes go wide with shock. "Mom, are you telling me you went to therapy for a year without….?"

"I never spoke a word," she admits with a sad smile. "The therapist would ask me questions and I would refuse to answer. Sixty minutes of awkward silence. Those were my sessions before that day."

I can't believe my ears. She told me she hated therapy. She told me she thought it was useless and it would never help her, but I had no idea she spent nearly a year of that poor doctor's time sitting on a couch not saying a word.

I take a few seconds to try and fathom her confession, before I turn my face back to hers. "So, me telling you I wasn't going to the wedding…that's what sparked the change?"

Mom's smile is warm and familiar as her eyes cloud with tears. "I knew it all along. I knew that I wasn't alone, but that day…that day was the first time I let myself believe it." She reaches over and takes one of my hands in hers. "I realized that day the one thing your father didn't take from me was *you*. I know he'll always be your father and I know you'll always love him, but you still love me too, more than I probably deserve." Mom and I laugh as tears stream down both of our faces once again. "I want you to know that I love you too, sweetheart, and I'm sorry it took a year for me to remember just how much."

Mom hugs me close as we both get out a year's worth of apologies in tears. If I didn't have all of this mess with Nix in the back of my mind, this moment would be pretty close to perfect. Either way, I'm thrilled to see my mom moving back into the light, and it's forward progress for her from now on. I can feel it.

Eventually, I'm able to talk her into letting me go so I can head toward the shower.

"I'm going to make us some tomato soup and grilled cheeses," she tells me. "What do you say?"

"Will there be ice cream for dessert?"

My mom gives me an understanding smile. "I can make that happen."

"Then count me in."

I take my shower—a very long, very hot shower—then eat dinner with Mom. I try not to check my phone every five seconds, but it's not easy. Mom and I watch a movie—"Dirty Dancing", her favorite—and she heads off to bed around eleven, leaving me all alone with my worry.

I move to my bedroom and try to get some sleep, but of course it's a wasted effort. So I pick up my phone, remembering some of the awful things I said to Nix before I left. I consider texting him to say I'm sorry and that I love him, that I will always love him, but then I decide against it. My words may have been harsh, but they were honest. Now he knows how I feel. He knows I'm willing to fight for us. The rest is up to him.

   I put my phone down and stare at the ceiling. The tears start falling on my pillow sometime around two in the morning, and that's the last time I look at the clock before eventually falling into a dreamless, albeit tear-soaked sleep.

CHAPTER TWENTY-NINE

"He's gone back to California."

Fearing my legs may give out, I take a seat on the top step of the porch at *Geoffrey's*. "When did he leave?"

"Early this morning," David says, as he takes a seat beside me. "Sent me a text message in the middle of the night, knowing I wouldn't get it until this morning, so I wouldn't be able to talk some sense into him. You know me and texting. I'm too old for that mess."

I nod and fake a smile, but I can't keep the tears from sliding down my cheeks. "Is he...is he gone for good?"

"I don't know, angel. His message to me said he was leaving this morning for California and that he was grateful for all my help while he was here."

I look away from David and close my eyes. That sounds pretty final to me.

"He's finished with the deck," I whisper. "He's finished with me. I guess it was time to go."

David grabs me up in his arms just as the first sob breaks free. "He'll be back. He's just hurting right now, but I know that boy better than anyone. He'll be back. Don't worry."

I let David try to soothe me. I let him brush at my hair. I let him rock me back and forth, telling me over and over everything will be fine, but I know better. I've been through this before. It may hurt much worse this time around, but I'm no stranger to heartbreak.

Nix is gone. He's not coming back. It's over.

I cry on David's shoulder until I have no tears left, and then I head inside to help him open the restaurant for the night. David tried to protest, but the last thing I want is to be alone with my thoughts right now. Working will be a welcome distraction.

I go through the motions throughout the evening, and for the few customers that know me well, it's obvious my smiles are forced. They can tell my courtesy is an unconscious effort, but no one says a thing. No one asks any questions, and I'm incredibly grateful.

Lila stops by to help finish up the preparations for Sydney's shower next weekend, and even she doesn't say a word. David most likely had something to do with that one, and I'm once again grateful. I know I couldn't talk about Nix right now without breaking down, and I'd prefer to save that for my bed tonight and what I assume will be several nights to follow.

My only saving grace right now is that my best friends will be in town in a few days. I'm sure they'll help take my mind off things, if only temporarily.

"Be careful going home tonight." David kisses me on the forehead as we say goodbye on the porch. "Get some rest and I'll call you if I hear anything."

I nod and fake another smile before walking to my car. Out of habit, when I pull to the end of the driveway, I look to my right, expecting a black Jeep to be there, waiting to follow me home. Of course, it's not there. Not tonight and probably never again.

The tears immediately start to fall, but I decide that this will be the last time I cry, at least for a while. I miss him. So very much. But the tears won't bring him back, and I'm not ready to give up hope. Not yet. So I allow myself a good cry as I drive home, and when I pull into the driveway of my mom's house, I wipe my face and head inside.

I follow my normal after work routine–drop my keys in the dish on the table by the front door, walk to my bedroom and place my phone on the nightstand and my purse on the dresser. Then I grab a towel and head to the shower.

A creature of habit, I check my phone when I get back to my room and bite back the disappointment. *It's not over*, I chant silently to myself, trying to hold on to the little hope I have left as I put my phone back on my nightstand and finish getting ready for bed. By the time I'm under the covers, it's after midnight, and I think once again about texting Nix. No matter what he thinks of me now, I want him to know I'm thinking of him. I want him to know I still care.

I pick up my phone and jump as it buzzes in my hand. My heart leaps in my chest, but it's not from Nix. It's from Sam.

Packing and getting more excited by the minute! Can't wait to see you!

I smile as I text her back, despite my disappointment.

Excited to see you too! Counting down the days!

I won't burden her with the news about Nix until she gets here next week. Between her, Sydney and Liz, I'm bound to feel a little better about the situation before the weekend is over.

But before I put my phone back on the nightstand, I type one more text.

I will always love you. Sweet dreams.

I don't try to fight the tear that rolls down my cheek as I hit send. I'm also not surprised when I wake up and find no reply from Nix. But what does surprise me is a text from an unknown number.

Rose, this is Lennon. Call me ASAP.

I close my eyes and shake my head. This can't be good.

****

I went for a morning run in the park before calling Lennon. I told myself it was to clear my head before I spoke with her, but it was avoidance, pure and simple.

Now I'm sitting on my bed, phone in hand, staring at the wall across from me. I've been sitting here for a half hour or more, since I got back from my run, still avoiding the inevitable.

I have no idea what Lennon wants to say to me, but I'm certain it's going to be an earful. She wouldn't be contacting me if she didn't know what happened, and as much as I know I'm not one hundred percent to blame in this situation, I still hate the thought of Lennon being upset with me.

When I finally muster up the courage to give her a ring, I realize it's still early in California. Hopefully, she'll be sleeping and I can just leave a message.

"Hello?"

No such luck.

"Hey, Lennon. It's Rose."

There's shuffling on the other end then I hear her say, "I'm going to take this outside. It's Davy."

There's a smile in her voice, and I have no idea who she's talking to, but after a minute or two of more shuffling around, she finally says something to me.

"Hi there, Rose."

I flinch at the way she says my name, similar to the tone she used when telling me about Nix's ex, Maggie. Lennon is definitely not happy with me right now, and I guess I can't blame her.

"Hi, Lennon. Am I interrupting something?"

"Nix is here," she tells me. "And I don't want him to know I'm talking to you."

"Oh, okay." Just hearing her say his name makes my heart ache. "So you and Davy are still talking? That's so great, Lennon."

"Nice try," she scoffs. "But we're focusing on you and my brother right now, and you have some explaining to do."

I wasn't trying to change the subject. I really am happy for Lennon and Davy. They're a great couple. But it seems Lennon isn't having any distractions this morning.

I take a deep breath and settle into my bed before I tell Lennon my side of the story. I explain my relationship with Vick and what happened between us all of those months ago. I explain to her what that kiss meant to me, which is absolutely nothing, and I also explain to her how Nix's immediate reaction was to run, to give up on us instead of staying and working things out.

"The kiss was a mistake, a huge misunderstanding," I tell her. "Lennon, you have to know how much I love your brother. I would never intentionally do anything to hurt him."

"I know you wouldn't," Lennon sighs. "That's why I wanted to talk to you. Nix isn't thinking clearly right now. He's too upset."

"He has every right to be upset with me for what I did," I admit. "I know how it must have looked, but when I tried to explain, he wouldn't listen to reason. I know he's scared, and so am I. What Nix and I have…it's different from anything I've ever experienced before, but none of that was enough to convince him to stay. I don't want to give up on him, Lennon, but if he's not willing to fight for us, then I'm not sure what else I can do."

Lennon is quiet for a long time on the other end—too long. I'm about to question whether or not she's still there when she finally speaks up.

"Don't give up on him, Rose."

"Okay?" The question in my voice is me hoping she'll tell me she knows something I don't.

"He is scared. There's no denying that," she tells me. "But I knew all of this had to be some kind of misunderstanding. You're the best thing that's ever happened to him, Rose. You're exactly what he needs, and I promise you, he knows that."

I sigh at her vague yet encouraging remarks. "Lennon, do me a favor?"

"Sure."

"It's important to me that if he's going to forgive me, it has to be on his terms. He loves you and would do anything for you. I'm afraid if you push him on this, he might come back to me, but it may be for the wrong reasons."

"I understand, and I won't push," Lennon agrees. "But it will be tough to resist beating some sense into him. His stubbornness is mindboggling."

I laugh, glad that Lennon forgives me, even if her brother won't. "Could I ask one more question?"

"Should I be afraid?"

"No," I smile. "I just want to know how he's doing. Is he okay? How does he look?"

"He looks like a dumbass."

"Lennon."

"Fine," she sighs. "He looks awful, Rose. He's really hurting, and as much as I hate seeing him like this, I'm glad you and I talked. Now I know now he has a choice. That makes a big difference."

I wish I were more confident about Nix's decision making.

"I'm so sorry for all of this mess." I try to choke back the tears I promised myself I wouldn't shed. "I never wanted to hurt him. God, I'm so sorry."

"It's going to be okay, Rose," Lennon tries to reassure me. "No matter what happens, I promise you, it's going to be okay."

"You're right," I tell her, but I'm not sure I agree. I know that if Nix doesn't come back to me, I'll never be the same. Living without him may get easier over time, but I'll never stop loving him. Never.

"Of course I'm right. I'm crazy smart," Lennon teases. "And I'm still holding you to your promise of coming to visit me, with or without my idiot brother."

"I'll do it. I promise. And thanks for hearing me out, Lennon. I know you must have been really upset with me when you found out what happened."

"I absolutely was," she confirms. "But as I said before...deep down I knew there was more to it than what Nix was telling me. I saw the two of you together and I know a good thing when I see it. Crazy smart, remember?"

"I do hope you're right," I admit. "And thanks again for being so understanding."

"You're welcome, Rose, and keep your chin up. I'm confident this will all work out for the best."

Before Lennon can hang up, I have an idea. "Hey Lennon? Could I ask for one more thing?"

"Sure."

"Would you mind sending me your address? I'd like to send Nix a letter."

"A letter?" Lennon questions. "Rose, this is the twenty-first century. Send him an email like a normal person."

"No," I manage a laugh. "I want to send him a letter. Please? It's important."

"Okay fine," Lennon concedes. "I'll text you my address."

"Thank you."

"You're welcome, Rose. Hope to see you again soon."

We say our goodbyes and I hang up feeling a little more hopeful. I'm glad Nix is with Lennon. I'm happy he has someone to talk to about this, and even though I asked her to stay out of it, part of me hopes she's somehow able to help him understand that he and I are worth fighting for. Maybe my letter will help.

CHAPTER THIRTY

As promised, Lennon texts me her address right after we hang up, and I immediately search my room for paper and pen so I can start writing.

After an hour, I have six pages, front and back, so I decide to break them up and send him a letter a day, hoping it will bring him back to me. I may not have been there to write to him when he was in the Army, but while he's away from me now, I want him to know how much I miss him.

I write about how sorry I am for what happened but remind him it was innocent. I tell him that I understand why it's so hard for him to trust, but I urge him to not let the past dictate his future. He said so himself, I'm different. I encourage him to believe in that, to believe in us.

And as cowardly as it is to do on paper rather than in person, I tell him about my divorce. I give him all the gory details, including how it affected me emotionally, how I realized I had allowed myself to become everything I thought Danny wanted, which was nothing that I wanted to be. But then I go on to tell him how I'm the opposite with him. I tell him how much I love that he forces my individuality and how much I love him for helping me find myself again, helping me recognize that I'm perfectly fine just as I am.

I remind him how we were together, how it felt when he made love to me. I remind him of the times we would both reach for each other during the night at exactly the same time, as if we sensed each other's needs as easily as we did our own. I remind him of the night he told me the story about what he would miss most about me if he knew me while he was overseas. I tell him how much that story meant to me and how much I would love to sing to him right now. I tell him that I would sing to him every minute of every day for the rest of our lives if I thought it would bring him back to me.

And I dedicate an entire letter to telling him how sorry I am—not about Vick, but about how I pushed him to open up to me, not realizing that what he was giving me was already more than enough. I apologize for not being satisfied with what I had, but I also explain why it was hard for me. I explain that what I needed most from him was his trust, and how I hate that now, after it may be too late, I finally see that I had it all along.

Throughout all of the letters, I make sure to tell him how wonderful he is, how wonderful he was to me—always opening doors, following me home, cooking for me, keeping me safe, loving me. I tell him that if he decides to never to come back to me, I want him to know that what I will miss most about him is his love. I tell him how his love, his beautiful, unconditional love for me has changed me forever. And I will always be grateful.

I spend hours writing and when I'm done, I have seven letters, all multiple pages and all tear-stained and filled with every ounce of love I have for him. Some may think it's silly, but I'm glad I wrote them. It was a satisfying, cathartic process getting my thoughts on paper like that. But now that I'm done, I'm not sure if I want to send them. I put them all in envelopes and address them anyway. I won't allow things to end between us without him knowing exactly how I feel, but I'm still holding on to hope. Maybe I won't have to send the letters. Maybe he'll come back to me without my having to pour my heart out to him. He should already know, shouldn't he? How could he not know how much I love him?

But after the next few days pass without a word from Nix, my hopes for any sort of reconciliation slowly start to fade. And when my friends finally arrive the Thursday before Sydney's shower, I'm afraid I'm not the best company.

"Who is this girl and what have you done with our Rose?"

I give Sam a sad smile and notice the rest of the girls are looking at me the same way. We've been occupying the living room of Sam's mom's house for the past couple of hours, eating Ben and Jerry's and catching up. But I'll be the first to admit I haven't been myself. It's not a shock that my best friends notice the change.

"I'm sorry, you guys." I feel like I've spent the past few days doing nothing but fighting back tears. "I think I'm just tired. I've been working at *Geoffrey's* all week to prepare for the shower."

"You know you didn't have to go through that much trouble for me," Sydney declares. "Simon and I would have been happy with pizza and breadsticks."

"Yes, we all know Sydney's more excited about the presents than anything else," Liz teases, and even though Sydney smacks her on the arm for the remark, she doesn't deny it.

We keep up the small talk for a few more minutes before Sydney reaches her breaking point.

"Okay, if no one else has the femballs to ask, then I'll do it." She turns an interrogating glare in my direction. "Rose, what's going on with you and your new man? Sam told us you met someone, but you've yet to bring him up and ever since we've arrived, you've been walking around like someone stole your beloved Ryan Atwood poster. So spill it."

I glance over at Sam and at least she has the decency to look remorseful. "Sorry," she shrugs. "I was excited for you. I had to share."

"It's okay," I sigh. "I was excited for me too."

"So talk to us, Rose," Sydney's voice is gentle and kind, and I'm so proud of how much she's grown over these past few months. "We love you and we want to help. And if he's done something to hurt you, I'll have his balls in a vice by morning."

Okay, so maybe the old Sydney's still in there somewhere.

We all laugh at our sweet friend, but eventually all eyes are back on me, waiting for an explanation. So once again, I relive mine and Nix's story. Some parts are harder to talk about than others, but I make it through without crying until I get to the fact that even after my call with Lennon, he still hasn't contacted me.

"Did you write him a letter?" Liz asks and I nod.

"Seven, to be exact."

Sydney's eyes are wide with disbelief. "And he still hasn't called you?"

"I never sent them," I confess and Sydney quickly threatens to find them and put them in the mail.

"Rose, he has to know how you feel," she says, "and if he won't talk to you, then you have to send those letters."

"I'll send them eventually," I say just to calm Sydney down. I glance over at Sam and she's eyeing me skeptically. "I will," I assure them all again. "It's just that I was kind of hoping I wouldn't have to. I was hoping to see him again, maybe tell him everything in person."

"I can understand that," Liz acknowledges. "But if he's really as jaded as you say he is, then he may need the extra encouragement."

"Maybe," I nod. "But I'm not sure those letters would make a difference either way. I think it may be over." I wipe at my cheeks, as Sam pulls me into her side. "I thought he loved me. I've never been more certain of anything in my life. But I guess love just wasn't enough."

"I'm so sorry, Rose." Sam kisses the top of my head and pulls me closer. "But you can't give up on him yet. It sounds to me like heartbreak is in his top five list of fears, so maybe he just needs some time to see the truth."

"Agreed," Liz interjects. "We count on you to be the hopeful one for all of us, and now it's our turn to return the favor."

"You never know," Sydney adds, and I have to smile.

"You never know," I repeat, wishing I still had these women in my life on a daily basis. Life is so much easier when they're here.

I give Sam a kiss on the temple before sitting up and wiping my face of tears completely. "So enough about me. Someone please tell me some good news."

"Oooo, I know!" Sydney immediately raises her hand and waves it like an excited school girl.

"Do share," Liz encourages.

"I finally found the perfect lingerie to wear under my wedding dress," Sydney gushes, as we all smile and shake our heads. "What? I've been searching for ages. I want everything to be perfect."

"We're so happy for you," Sam teases. "I'm sure Simon will be very grateful."

"Hell yes he will," Sydney smirks. "So who's next? Liz?"

I look over at Liz and I catch a strange look cross her face. It was brief, and I'm not sure if anyone else noticed, but I'm wondering if something is bothering her. It's hard to tell because Liz has a poker face to rival a Vegas pro, but something has seemed off about her since she's been here.

"Nothing too exciting to report on my end." Liz tells us. "Sam? How about you?"

"Don't even try it," Sydney shakes her head at Sam. "Nothing's topping my new lingerie."

Sam smiles at her. "I'm pregnant."

Gasps, followed by screams, echo around the room before we're all giggling and scooping Sam up into a group hug.

"I think Sam wins," Liz says to Sydney as tears start to slide down all of our cheeks.

"Overachiever," Sydney teases Sam, officially sending all our worries into the clouds with a chorus of joyous laughter.

CHAPTER THIRTY-ONE

It's Friday morning, the day before Sydney's shower, and I'm surprised I'm not more nervous as I get ready to head to *Geoffrey's* to help put the final touches on everything. I guess it's because I've had more help that I thought I would in pulling things together.

Lila has been a huge help from the start managing the details, finding the decorations, hiring the DJ. Sydney left most everything to me, and Lila's help has been a godsend. She's done an incredible job bringing the vision to life.

As for the food, Nix obviously hasn't been here as promised to help with the menu, but last night we found out that one of Simon's bandmates, Rob, happens to be quite the chef. He agreed to come today and help us prepare the food that we had planned.

Sam's husband, Ethan, and the groom-to-be agreed to be around later to help move some furniture around inside the restaurant, in case the weather turns on us and we need to bring the party inside. And the girls and I will spend some time either tonight or tomorrow morning finishing up the decorations.

Everything is coming together perfectly. But despite the joy I feel over having my best friends in town to celebrate what I know will be a happily ever after for two incredible people, I can't ignore the hollow feeling deep inside that Nix left behind.

I haven't done a very good job sticking to my "no crying" rule. As a matter of fact, I've failed miserably. It's been six days—six excruciatingly long days since he left, and I haven't heard a word from him. Not one word.

I woke up this morning, promising myself—as I have every day since he's been gone—that I wouldn't ask David about him, but I don't think I can keep that promise any longer. I even hold my phone in my hand every night before I go to bed, trying to convince myself not to text Lennon to see if he's still there, see if he's okay. I want to know if he's hurting like me, or if he's trying to move on. Is it really over between us? The unknown is killing me, and as much as I'd hate to hear that it's over, I'm starting to think knowing would be better than all of this unbearable silence.

"Good morning, sunshine."

I turn to find Sam standing in my bedroom door. "What are you doing here? I thought we were meeting later for decorations."

"Pregnancy," Sam shrugs. "I feel exhausted all day, every day, but I can't sleep."

I go over and hug her with a smile. "You have no idea how excited I am about this baby."

"I know. Me too." Sam smiles. "But with my insomnia and the boys' highly anticipated fishing trip this morning, I was up at the crack of dawn so I decided to come and pay you a visit."

"Oh I forgot about the fishing trip," I admit, not surprised that yet another thing has slipped my foggy brain these days. "I know Jake must be ready to jump out of his skin. God, Sam, he's getting so big."

"Twelve years old. Can you believe it?" Sam shakes her head with a laugh. "But he'll always be my baby, and he's so happy to be home. We all are."

"I'm happy you're here too," I assure her. "It's kind of miserable here without you guys."

"Yeah, that's kind of the reason I came to chat with you."

"You're moving back?" I don't even try and hide my excitement, but Sam shakes her head.

"Not that I'm aware of."

"Oh," I shake my head. "Well then what are we talking about?"

"You," she says. "You're miserable, and I don't like it."

"Oh that." I plop down on my bed with a sigh. "I'll be okay. You don't need to worry about me."

Sam rolls her eyes and sits next to me. "Rose, you're my best friend and I love you, but ever since I've known you, you've always put everyone and everything above yourself. You've told me over the last few weeks how Nix has started to change that and I've seen it. I've heard it in your voice over the phone, and I can still see it now. It's a faded glow in the back of those pretty brown eyes, but it's there. And I love it. I've wanted you to find your voice for years, but no matter how hard I tried, I just couldn't make you see it. I couldn't convince you how wonderful you are, but somehow he did. Nix gave that to you, and you're just going to let him slip away?"

I look down at my feet with tears in my eyes. Sam's right. I keep saying I'm going to fight for us, but what am I doing? I wrote letters I'll probably never send. I type a dozen texts a day then delete them. I've dialed Lennon's number too many times to count, but I never press send. I may not have given up on us, but how will Nix know that if I don't tell him, if I don't show him?

"Oh my God, you're right," I confess. "I'm sitting here doing the same thing I would always do. I'm allowing myself to not fight for him because I think it's what he wants."

"But is that what *you* want?"

My eyes snap back to Sam's in a panic. "No. That's not what I want."

Sam reaches to pull something out of her back pocket. She hands it to me and when I see what she's given me...

"A plane ticket?"

"Go get him, Rose."

I look over at my friend then back down at the ticket. "But the wedding shower..." I mumble, as I try to decide what to do. "I can't just leave you guys here. I never get to see you and---"

"We're not going anywhere," Sam interrupts. She puts a hand on my knee and leans in to catch my eyes. "You love him, Rose. And from what I hear, he loves you too. I think he just needs a reminder."

"You want me to go to California?" Sam nods and I look down at the ticket again. I scan over the details and something hits me. "Wait, how did you know he was in Los Angeles?"

I know I told Sam he was from California, but I told her he grew up near Sacramento.

"Oh, well you told us that he was in Los Angeles."

"I did?" I continue to study the ticket, trying to remember. "I told you he was visiting his sister?"

"Yeah, the other night at Mom's house."

I look up at Sam and shrug. Yet another thing that must have slipped my mind.

"I don't feel right leaving," I admit. "Maybe I can go on Sunday, after the shower."

"No," Sam quickly interjects. "It has to be today and everyone is fine with this. I've already talked to the girls."

"Sydney was okay with me missing her shower?" I question and Sam nods with a smile.

"She was the one that bought the plane ticket."

Tears stream down my face as I'm reminded how lucky I am in the friend department. "Okay. I'll go."

Sam squeals as she wraps me up in her arms. "You're flight leaves in a couple of hours, so pack a few things and the girls and I are going to drive you to the airport."

I hold onto her a little longer than intended. "I love you, bestie."

"Love you too," she tells me, then stands and pulls me up next to her. "Now let's get your stuff together, and we need to hurry. The girls will be here in twenty minutes."

I nod excitedly and start moving. I grab some clothes and throw them into a duffle bag, then basically scoop the contents of my bathroom counter on top. I toss in a few more essentials, then go to change out of my work clothes and into something more comfortable. I opt for jeans, a tank-top and sandals, then I grab a sweater in case it's cold on the plane. Thinking I have most everything I'll need, I turn back to Sam to let her know I'm ready, but my phone rings right before I can speak the words.

I pull it from my purse and see that it's David, probably wondering where I am, since I told him I'd be there early this morning to help in the kitchen.

"David, I'm so sorry—"

"Rose, is everything okay?" he interrupts, his voice laced with concern.

"Yes, I'm fine. I'm glad you called, actually. You see, Sam came by this morning and convinced me to go see Nix in California, and I'm going to go. "

"Oh my goodness. Have you already left?"

"I'm about to be on my way to the airport in a few minutes. David, I'm so sorry to do this to you, but you should have plenty of---"

"Rose, I need you to come here before you go," David interrupts again, which is odd behavior for him. "This old refrigerator is acting up again and I need your help."

My brow furrows in confusion. "David, you and I both know that refrigerator never acted up in the first place, so please tell me what's going on. You're worrying me."

David sighs on the other line. "I guess I am kind of crying wolf here, but I really do need your help this time. Could you just make a quick stop by here before you go? I won't keep you long."

I want to say no, but I have a hard time saying no to David. Plus, the panic in his voice is leaving a dreadful feeling in my stomach. David wouldn't deliberately keep me from going to see Nix if it wasn't important.

"I'll be there shortly," I tell him. "Just promise me you're okay."

"I'm perfectly fine," he says, and even more reassuring is the smile in his voice. "See you soon, angel."

I hang up with David and turn to tell Sam what's going on. She's not happy about it, but she agrees that I should probably check on David if I'm worried. I decide to go alone since the girls aren't here yet. I tell Sam to make herself at home and assure her that I'll be back as soon as I can, then I leave my bag at the door and make my way to *Geoffrey's*.

****

When I pull into the driveway, I'm surprised that David's car isn't there. Panic immediately sets in as I wonder over what could have possibly happened in the few minutes since I got off the phone with him. Maybe the fridge really did break this time and he went to the store for a part? Maybe it's something else entirely. Maybe something's happened between him and Lila. Oh God. I hope he's okay.

I get out of my car and head quickly toward the front porch, but when I knock on the door there's no answer. I pull my phone from my back pocket and decide to call him, but then I hear…

I tilt my head, wondering if the faint music playing in the background is real or just my imagination. I turn to my right and move slowly toward that side of the house, realizing the sound is coming from somewhere in that direction. Maybe Lila decided to come early and finish up the decorations on the deck? I asked her not to. I had planned to do that with the girls, but it would be so like Lila to disobey my requests.

Confused, and still a little panicked, I turn the corner but stop when something squishes under my shoe. I lift my foot to see that I've apparently stepped on…a piece of *cake*? I squat down to inspect things further, and that's when I notice them—a line of perfectly spaced donut holes.

Blueberry, to be exact.

My heart starts racing, begging my feet to follow, so we can find out what's at the end of this happy little trail, but I force myself to stay put. I refuse to move. I refuse to even look up. Instead, I stay crouched beside the remains of the one I stepped on, trying to convince myself that this is real. But I hardly have time to catch my breath before my heart decides to pull rank, forcing me to my feet. I still refuse to look up, holding my ground, as I slowly follow the trail laid before me. Then I finally recognize the song playing in the background, and my heart delivers the knockout blow.

Oh my God.

Tears pool in my eyes as I raise my head, and there he is–standing on the deck in a white t-shirt and jeans, looking like an angel from heaven. I vaguely notice he's holding a bouquet of something in his hands that I can't quite make out from this distance, but I hardly care. My legs start to move involuntarily toward my every desire, and by the time I reach him, tears are silently streaming down my cheeks.

Nix reaches over and turns down the music before giving me what he's holding in his hands. I reluctantly pull my eyes from him and look down to find a bouquet of blueberry Munchkin' kabobs.

"My favorites," I whisper at the delicious looking bouquet, but Nix remains silent, as the tension reaches epic proportions between us.

I try to focus on something, anything other than what I really want to do right now which is to launch myself into his arms and never let go.

"This song..." Yes, the music. I can talk about the music. "How did you know?"

The song he has playing on repeat is my favorite one to sing to him, but I've only ever sung the words while he's sleeping. At least I thought he was sleeping. It's the song I sang the first night he asked me to sing to him. It was the night before we left for California to attend his grandfather's funeral, the trip that changed my life forever.

"I find it funny that the title of the song is 'Asleep at Last'," Nix finally speaks. "Because all of those times you sang it to me, I was never asleep. I never wanted to miss a second of that beautiful voice in my ear."

I close my eyes and take a deep a breath. *Please let this be real. Oh God, please.* And as if my prayers have been answered, a warm hand palms my wet cheek and a relieved sigh stutters from my lips.

"I'm so sorry." I open my eyes to find Nix's face only inches from mine. "I'm so fucking sorry, Rose. I was just so damn scared."

I cover his hand with mine and hold it to my face, enjoying that simple touch so much it brings a fresh set of tears rolling down my cheeks.

"I knew the minute I left it was a mistake," he admits, "but then I convinced myself that you'd never take me back for being such a coward."

"I don't think you're a—"

"I am a coward," Nix interrupts, then pulls his hand from my cheek and takes a step back. "I've been so scared, Rose, and I hated myself for it. I blamed you for it. That's why I'm a coward. I didn't realize until it was too late that what I was feeling was perfectly normal. I should have listened. I should have talked to you. I should have let you in, but I wasn't sure you would understand. Then I read your letters."

My eyes pop open in shock. "My letters? How did you...?"

You Think You Know

Nix pulls something from his back pocket and hands it to me. It's my letters–all seven of them, with a note on top that I take a minute to read.

Nix, these letters are from Rose. She was hesitant to send them to you, not because she didn't want you to read them, but because she has an awful habit of thinking of everyone's happiness but her own. I believe you've started to change that about her, as the old Rose probably wouldn't have even written these letters in the first place, and that alone makes you okay in my book. So even though I may get an earful from my sweet friend for sending these on her behalf, I know it will be worth it because I don't get the feeling you've given up on her any more than she's given up on you. All I ask is that you treat her heart with the same love and care that you would treat your own. I can promise you she's worth it.

Best of luck, Sam (the best friend)

"Sam..." I whisper her name as my tears fall onto her hand written note. "I should have known she'd do something like this."

"Rose, I want you to know I was already packed with a plane ticket purchased when I got those letters." I look up at Nix, stunned silent as I try and wrap my head around everything that's happening. "But I have to say that when I read these on the plane this morning they gave me hope. And I'm not sure I deserve it, but I'm begging for a second chance." Nix takes a cautious step forward. "Even if you tell me it's too late, I want you to know that I'm here to fight for you. I'm going to fight for us, harder than I've ever fought on any battlefield. You are everything to me, and I'm so sorry for doubting that. I can promise you it will never happen again."

Without a second thought, I drop the letters and my donut bouquet, wrap my arms around my love and kiss him like I've wanted to every minute I've had to be without him. And I'm relieved and thrilled to find I get every bit of my passion in return.

"Please don't leave me like that again." I whisper against his lips. "I thought it was over. I thought I was going to have to learn to live without you."

Tears come rolling down my cheeks again with the thought, and Nix pulls me closer, his hands trembling as he rubs them up and down my back.

"Stop it, baby. Please stop crying. I'm here now," he says softly before burying his face in my hair. "I'm just so happy to hold you again. I don't know what I would've done..."

I still in his arms, shocked to feel his warm tears on my neck, but I don't say a word. I put my hand on the back of his head and hold him close, listening to his uneven breathing, feeling like I'm falling in love with him all over again.

Nix's eyes are dry by the time he pulls away, and for the first time in a long time, so are mine.

"Thank you for coming back to me," I smile up at him and he smiles back.

"Thank you for giving me a second chance."

"Thanks for fighting for me."

"Always," Nix whispers, his face serious. "I'll always fight for you, and I'll never be able to apologize enough for making you question that."

I reach up on my tiptoes to kiss him once more. "No more apologizing." I run my fingers through the sides of his soft, dark hair. "You had me at blueberry Munchkins."

Nix smiles as he holds me close. "I brought coffee too."

"Why Mr. Taylor, are you trying to seduce me?"

"Most definitely," he chuckles. "But first I believe we have some food to prepare for your friend's party tomorrow, and honestly, I'm just happy to be near you again, to touch you, to kiss those pouty lips of yours. I've missed you so much, Rose. So, so much."

I shake my head, wondering if I'll ever know what I did to deserve this incredible man in my life. I decide for now I'm just going to accept it and move on. Maybe I deserve a little happiness for a change. Maybe we both do.

I reach up and put my mouth to his ear. "Dance with me," I whisper, and Nix immediately starts swaying with me to the music.

"Sing to me," he whispers back, and I do as requested, easily and without reservation as I hold my forever close to my heart.

EPILOUGUE—NIX

I'm a lucky man.

I survived seven tours in the Army, a few times by a pretty narrow margin. Now I'm back in the states and happy to say I have a roof over my head, food to eat and my grandfather left me more than enough money to live comfortably for the rest of my days. And as much as my little sister likes to push my damn buttons every chance she gets, I realize now more than ever the importance of family. Whether I've deserved it or not, their support and encouragement through the years have always come unsolicited and unconditionally. They're the ones who taught me how to love, and I'm grateful for that, especially today.

Because seven tours and a nice home to live in and food to eat and money to spend hardly make me feel as privileged as the gorgeous redhead I'm staring at right now through the window. Even if I didn't know her, I would think she was the most beautiful woman I've ever seen. But as my good fortune would have it, I do know her. Very well. And I can safely say that for me, she seems like nothing short of a miracle.

I opted to help out in the kitchen today so Rose could spend time with her friends. She wasn't very happy with that decision. She wanted to be involved, to make sure everything went perfectly, but I was finally able to persuade her with a lengthy make-out session before we left the cabin this morning, promising her more if she relaxed today and let me take care of things. She immediately agreed, saying she had a hard time denying me anything when I kissed her like that. If only she knew she was the one in control. Not me. Just a few commanding words in that slow, Southern drawl, and I'd be on my knees.

"How's it going in here?"

I reluctantly pull my eyes from Rose to look over at David. "It's good," I tell him, as I resume slicing the dough for the next dish. "I just put a new batch of stuffed mushrooms in the oven, and I'm about to start on the pastries. Would you mind handing me the pears and blue cheese from the fridge?"

David smiles as he grabs the ingredients and brings them over to me. "So, the party seems to be going well."

"It does," I nod in agreement. "Rose and Lila did a great job pulling everything together. Looks like everyone's having a good time."

"Did you get to talk to many of Rose's friends?"

"Yeah, she paraded me around earlier," I laugh, remembering how excited she seemed to introduce me to everyone. "They all seem like good people."

"I agree," David smiles. "Especially Ethan and Sam. Delightful couple."

I nod my head and smile, agreeing that Rose's best friend and her husband are definitely at the top of my list. But everyone seems to love Rose, even the people who haven't known her much longer than me. I can't say I'm surprised. The woman had me at first sight. But it was nice to see all of her friends care about her almost as much as I do. I even got the "you break her heart, I'll break your face" conversation from that Ollie guy and Rose's friend, Sydney. I have to admit it's hard to feel threatened by a guy like Ollie, but Sydney? Even though I'm probably three times her size, I'll be keeping an eye on that one.

"So, have you told her yet?" David asks, and I quit slicing to meet his eyes.

"No. I was waiting for the right time. You don't think she'll be upset, do you?"

"Are you kidding? She's going to be thrilled," David assures me. "And I couldn't be happier for you both, or more grateful."

I quickly look away and get back to my preparations. "After everything you've done for me," I start, finding it hard to speak now with a throat suddenly clogged with emotion, "this is the least I can do for you. You deserve this and so much more."

With some of the inheritance I received from my grandfather's death, I decided to purchase *Geoffrey's* for Rose. I know she'll argue that it's too much, but I had the money to spare and as far as I'm concerned, what's mine is hers. Plus, she's always talking about repaying David for everything he's done for her and I owe him as well, so what better way to thank him than keeping his and Geoffrey's legacy alive. I made sure to have the house appraised and forced David to sell it to me for what it's worth plus a little extra. Now, David has enough money to buy two or three restaurants if he decides retirement doesn't suit him, but I have a feeling Lila won't let that happen.

"You think Rose will hire me?" I tease, and David laughs.

"She'd be a fool not to with the way everyone raves about your cooking."

David tugs at my shoulder, silently asking that I face him. I put my knife down and do as requested, but I can't look at him. David may be several inches shorter than me, and probably close to a hundred pounds lighter, but to me, he's always seemed larger than life. There's no way I can see him breaking down without doing so myself, so I cross my arms over my chest and stare at my shoes.

"Have I ever told you how proud I am of you?"

"Only every day of my life," I laugh and David laughs too.

"And I'll continue to do so every day for the rest of mine." David pulls my chin up, and I immediately shift my eyes to the side. "It's going to be hard to let this place go, but it couldn't be in better hands. You're a good man, Nix Taylor, and being a part of your life has been an honor. Love you, son."

A damn tear slips down my cheek before I can stop it, but thankfully David doesn't say a word. He pulls me into his arms and hugs me like a father to his child, and it feels just as right as when my dad does the same thing. The embrace is heartfelt but quick, which I'm also thankful for. I scrub my face with my hands, wiping away the few tears that I allowed to fall, and when I finally catch his eyes, he's smiling—like the proud, second father that he is.

"You'll have to let me know what she says," he tells me before moving over to the other counter to wash some more mushrooms. "I would say you're spoiling her, but my angel deserves it."

"She certainly does," I agree as I find her again through the kitchen window. "She's more than worth it."

And giving her *Geoffrey's* isn't the only surprise I have in store.

While I was away from her over the past week, I did a lot of thinking, and I decided that no matter what happened between us, her happiness would always be important to me. Even when I thought I had lost her forever, there was no denying she would always have a permanent place in my heart.

So the first thing I did was make a call to Mr. Lowell and convince him to sell me the cabin. At the time, I thought I may never even see that cabin again, but owning it was my own messed up way to preserve our memory. I just couldn't stand the thought of anyone else living there, and I'm grateful now that I don't have to worry about that. Instead, I can look forward to making even more memories in that cabin for as long as Rose will have me.

And my last surprise involves one of my least favorite people, but I managed to find some unexpected retribution, thanks to my lovely sister.

When I was out visiting Lennon, she had an ex-boyfriend of hers over for dinner one night. I refused to join them, too busy nursing my broken heart, but I did overhear part of their conversation. Turns out Lennon's ex is some big Hollywood producer, and he was telling her about a new show they were about to start shooting in Atlanta. But what really cut like a knife was when he said he was thinking of hiring Vick Delacroix in one of the lead roles.

When the guy left, Lennon immediately sat me down so we could have a talk. With a sly grin I'm all too familiar with, Lennon suggested she talk to her ex and see what she could do to convince him Vick wasn't right for the part. I know I shouldn't have allowed Lennon to interfere. I should have said no, but I couldn't make myself do it. Honestly, I loved my sister so much in that moment, I could have kissed her.

So to help ease my guilty conscience, I asked Lennon to see if she could find out if the show had already hired a director. I thought maybe she could recommend Rose's best friend's husband for the job. I knew how happy it would make Rose to have her best friend back home, and Rose doesn't know it yet, but everything worked out as planned.

Like most men Lennon dates, that producer is still madly in love with my sister and eagerly agreed to all of her suggestions. Vick wasn't chosen for the part, and Ethan was made first choice for director. No one has any clue Lennon or I were involved, and hopefully, they never will. Ethan should get the call in a couple of weeks, and I highly doubt he'll turn it down. I know his wife, Sam, would like to be back in Georgia as well, and after seeing him with her, I get the impression there's nothing he wouldn't do for her happiness.

And I'm well acquainted with that feeling.

With a victorious smile on my face, I once again drag my eyes away from my girl so I can concentrate on getting fresh food out to the guests. I'm kind of surprised how much I'm enjoying this. If she'll have me, I'd love to help Rose out in the kitchen. I think together we can help make *Geoffrey's* what it once was, and I certainly wouldn't complain about getting to spend some extra time with her.

Speaking of the beautiful boss lady...

I feel her nearby before she even walks into the room. I look over in time to catch her smiling at me from the doorway and my heart immediately starts pumping triple time in my chest.

"I came to give my compliments to the chefs," she says to both David and me, but her eyes never leave mine.

"Well, my boy's the one in charge tonight." David puts a basket of cleaned mushrooms next to me on the counter. "I'm merely a servant, and I'm enjoying every minute of it."

Rose comes closer and gives David a kiss on the cheek. "That's not true and you know it."

"Oh, yes ma'am, it is." David confirms. "Nix is the head chef this evening, and that's why I'm allowed to go out and enjoy the party without a care. That is, unless you need me for anything further, boss man."

I roll my eyes at David with a smile. "You are relieved from your duties, minion."

David grabs the finished batch of mushrooms from the oven and quickly plates them before heading out the door. Rose watches David leave then her eyes are back on me.

"Thank you so much for your help today," she says as she walks slowly toward me. "How will I ever repay you?"

I wipe my hands on a nearby towel and take her in my arms. I kiss that sexy grin off her face, leaving her needy and breathless in my arms—just the way I like her.

"That was payment enough," I tell her, but Rose lifts an eyebrow, knowing damn well I'd never be satisfied with only one kiss.

With a resigned sigh and a guilty smile, I keep her eyes on mine as I walk backward, pulling her toward the back of the kitchen. The minute I have us away from prying eyes, I take her in my arms again and kiss her like a madman. I can't help it. I can't keep my hands off of her. And she's wearing pink. I love it when she wears pink.

But I also know that as much as I crave her mouth on mine it's not nearly as much as I crave her closeness. All of the time. Every second. And being somewhat of a loner my entire life, I never expected to feel this way about another person. I never thought I would need someone's company like I do hers. I feel complete when she's around.

Her soft lips and wandering hands are just an added bonus.

"We'd better get back," she breathes, but then her kisses move to my neck and her hands to my ass, giving me zero inclination she's ready to go anywhere.

Of course, neither am I.

"Well then let's go," I tease her as I grab a handful of her breast. Her moan vibrates against my neck, and I know I could take her right here in this dark corner, if I wanted to.

And good God, I want to.

But with all of her friends and family outside, this is one of those times I should probably be a gentleman, no matter how difficult she makes it for me.

So I bury my face in her neck and pull her close with both arms. Her frustrated sigh tells me she wants me just as much as I want her, but she knows as well as I do that we can't do this now. And besides, anticipation can be fun.

"I'm sorry for dragging you back here," I apologize when I'm not really sorry at all, and she knows that. "I just needed you close."

I squeeze my eyes closed, glad my face is buried in her long, red hair at the moment. Admissions like that slip from my mouth a lot these days and I'm still adjusting. I have no idea how to do this with her, but so far, she's making it pretty easy.

"I'll never be too far away," she soothes, running her long fingers through the back of my hair. "And I love being close to you, so anytime you have the urge to pull me into a dark corner, do feel free."

And just like that, she steals another piece of my soul, binding it permanently with hers. There is never any judgement from Rose, just love—unreserved, rock-steady love. I've never been more grateful for anything in my life.

"I love you," I tell her for what is probably the twentieth time today, but I don't care. And neither does she because she always says it back, without hesitation.

"I love you, sweetheart."

She stretches up on her toes and tightens her arms around my neck, holding me close. I take the opportunity to breathe her in, and the fresh smell of orange trees and vanilla is like a soothing balm to my war-torn nerves. If I can't hear that sweet, Southern voice in my ear, her scent is the next best thing.

Rose is the first to pull away, as usual. I'm sorry, but it seems criminal to me to let this woman go in any capacity.

"The only reason I'm okay with going back out there is because I get to have you all to myself later," she tells me, and I smile because she basically pulled the words right out of my mouth. She has a tendency to do that, and it used to freak me out a little, but I can't find it in me to be scared anymore. Like I told her a long time ago, from the moment I met her she became necessary to my survival. I didn't understand it then, but I do now. The thought of losing her feels like a death sentence.

"You can have me every night for the rest of my life, if you want," I vow, once again surprised by how easily these types of declarations roll off my tongue nowadays, but I can't imagine ever feeling like this with someone other than Rose. She's all I'll ever need.

"Promise?" she questions, and my smile quickly fades with the uncertainty I see in her eyes.

I did that. I put that doubt there because I was a fucking punk bastard and couldn't man up, even when I had perfection staring me in the face. I would do anything to erase the last week and half, to change the way I acted when she came to explain what happened between her and that piece of shit that dared put his hands on what's mine. But I can't change any of it. All I can do is spend the rest of my days apologizing and convincing her that I won't run again.

"Listen to me, pretty girl." I take her face in my hands and force her eyes to meet mine. "The only thing that's strong enough to keep me from you at this point is death, and I'll fight for my last breath if it means I get one more second of holding your hand or kissing those soft lips or hearing that beautiful voice. You understand?"

"Promise," she says again, but it's not a question this time. It's a demand. And I'm instantly turned on.

"Baby, I'd marry you today if you'd have me."

Rose's eyes widen. "You wanna marry me?"

"Hell yes, I want to marry you." I shake my head at how much work I have in front of me. "But you know I like surprises. I'll hold onto my proposal for when you least expect it."

Rose's eyes remain dazed and unblinking as I smile down at her, and suddenly, I'm nervous. Maybe I took it a step too far this time. My eyebrows automatically pull down as I catch a single tear with my finger as it rolls down her cheek.

"Does me wanting to marry you make you sad?" I hate I had to ask her that, but even after the last damn near perfect twenty-four hours, I still find it hard to believe this incredible woman chose me.

"No." She shakes her head and reaches up to kiss me softly. "I'm not sad."

"Then why are you crying?"

"Haven't you ever heard of happy tears?" She smiles at me, and I smile back. "You better get used to them."

"No self-respecting man enjoys seeing a woman cry," I inform her. "Happy tears or not, it just doesn't seem right."

"Always the gentleman." Rose runs her fingers through the side of my hair and I close my eyes, honing in on that electric touch of hers. "My knight in shining armor," she whispers and I open my eyes just in time to see her mouth headed toward mine. I take charge this time, kissing her deeply, making her forget all about that "perfect gentleman" she somehow sees in me.

She whimpers when I pull away, and I know that one more kiss like that will have me carrying her out of here like a caveman so I can take her home and have my way with her.

"We'd better get back to the party," I suggest and she nods.

"Okay, just a minute."

After a few deep breaths, we both have ourselves together enough to head out back. Right before I open the doors leading to the backyard, Rose puts a hand on mine, stopping me from pressing down on the handle. I look at her, waiting for an explanation, but instead Rose lifts up on her toes and wraps her arms around my neck. She gives me this sweet, lingering kiss that has my pulse pumping loud and steady in my ears, and the way she looks at me afterward...it's like I'm the grand prize or some coveted honor. She looks at me like this all the time. It's another one of those things that used to put me on edge, but not anymore. I need that look more than I need air to breathe or food to eat, and I plan to devote the rest of my life to making sure I deserve it, making sure I deserve *her*.

"What was that for?" I ask, licking my lips as I watch her eyes slide down to my mouth.

"Because I love you." She looks up at me with this adorable grin on her face, and I could fall to my knees at her feet.

"I love you more."

"Forever?"

I shake my head. "Forever with you isn't long enough."

I watch as her eyes quickly fill with tears and I try not to grimace. *Happy tears*. That will take some getting used to, but the smile that lights up her face as she stares at me makes me feel a little better. And when she tightens her arms around my neck, forcing me to pull her close, I take comfort in the feel of her heart beating against my own, filling me with her goodness and warmth. She calls me her protector, her soldier, her "perfect gentleman", and I suppose I am all of those things. But the only thing I really want to be from now on is *hers*. And by some miracle, she seems to feel the same way about me.

Like I said, I'm the luckiest man in the world.

THE END

Melinda Harris

ACKNOWLEDGEMENTS

I can't believe I'm publishing my fourth book. My FOURTH book! How did that even happen?!

Okay, okay. I know how it happened, and let me just tell you...it takes an army. There's no way I could do this alone, so I'm grateful for the chance to thank all the incredible people that help me bring my dreams to life.

And number one on the list? The readers! How do I even begin to thank you for taking a chance on me? I'm a voracious reader myself, so I know how many talented authors there are out there. The fact that you chose me out of that mix is humbling beyond words, and I'll never be able to thank you enough. Just know that you are my everything, and I look forward to sharing my stories with you for as long as you'll let me.

To my sweet husband: Oh, my sweet, sweet husband. The guy rarely gets a warm meal and hardly ever has clean underwear or socks, yet he continues to love and support me unconditionally. Sometimes I have to wonder why, but then I realize I probably shouldn't question it and simply count my blessings instead. H, thank you for being the man of my dreams. I couldn't possibly love you more.

To all of my dear friends and family: You are the backbone of this silly little fantasy of mine. It's not easy to pursue something when the odds of succeeding are slim to none. But every time I think of quitting, you're there to remind me that writing makes me happy, and that being happy is what's most important. I really, really, really, really love you for that.

To my soul sister, Kristi: Hey Soul Sister! Wait, am I your soul sister? No, I'm the freak. Man, I've missed you. Where have you been? The next time I hug you, you better bring it in nice and tight. And if you stop coming to see me at conventions, I'll be really sad. To be continued...*wink, wink.*

To the brilliant, Kara at Kara's Kreative: I'm grateful beyond words that I've had you in my corner, making me look pretty these past couple of years. But what matters most is that I have you in my life. Period. I love you, my kindred spirit, and I always will.

To Maria at Necessary Design: I wanted to thank you for stepping in and helping with this cover design. I realize you had very little wiggle room, which is a form of torture to us creative types, but I couldn't be the happier with the outcome. You da bomb!

To the real life David: I knew from the moment I met you that you would be a part of one of my stories. Your personality is simply too big not to share with the world. I only pray I did you justice. Thank you for being you.

To my lovely cover models, Lance and Carolina: This book was at a complete standstill until I found you. I will never be able to thank you enough for the inspiration and for helping to bring my vision to life. I wish you both nothing but the best in all you do. You deserve it.

To my photographer, Michael Meadows: I am yet to work with anyone in this business with your brand of consideration or kindness, good sir. Your passion for what you do is remarkable, and I will be singing your praises for all eternity. You can count on it.

To my boss lady, Dawn: I'm proud to say we've been friends since the beginning of time, and I want to thank you for always being there. Honestly, I could write an entire book on our many adventures…or…ummm…yeah, maybe not. How about I just allow you to boss me around for another few decades and we'll laugh until we shoot wine out of our noses. Sound good?

To my Pimp, THE Ashley Hampton: Please know how much your support and advice mean to me. I just adore you. And the next time I see you, I'll try to have your official t-shirt in hand. Along with a really decorative cup. And a cane maybe. A fur coat. Some stylish glasses. You get the idea.

To the best Beta Readers and Editors on the planet: Writing the book is the easy part. Putting it out there for the world to see? That's when Melinda starts losing sleep. But I know it would be so much worse if I didn't have you ladies by my side. I try and thank you as often as I can, but it never feels like enough. So until I can afford to buy each of you your own villa in the French Riviera, I do hope my Lennon-style hugs will suffice.

To my blogging friends: A special thanks to Catherine at A Reader Lives 1000 Lives, Danielle at Short and Sassy Book Blurbs, Tabitha and Gia at Amazeballs Book Addicts, Neilliza at Four Chicks Flipping Pages, Ali at Ali's Books, Tabby at Shattered Hearts Reviews and Yamara at Panty Dropping Book Blog. This is certainly not a complete list of every blogger I've had the pleasure of working with, but these women have gone above and beyond. Ladies, I want you to know how much I appreciate all you do. Your support is priceless and will never be taken for granted.

To all the lovelies over at Boston Babes Go South: I know we're still getting to know each other, but I feel incredibly honored that you've accepted me into your realm. Thank you for all of your hard work and dedication and I will strive to always be an author you're proud to represent. And Alisa and Melanie? I worship at your alters of fabulousness, just so you know.

To my beautiful hearts in The Fangirl Bookclub: You ladies are the ones that make me want to be a better writer. You push me in the best possible way, and your enthusiasm is positively contagious. I am so blessed to call each of you my friend. Please don't ever leave me.

And of course, I saved the best for last…to all of my fangirl soul sisters out there: It's not often in life that you find someone who truly accepts you for who you are. As for me, I found more than *one* someone. I found a tribe. And whether we're blood relatives, lifelong friends or recent acquaintances, I love you all the same. Because you accept me for who I am, "mom face" and all. Thank you for everything.

ABOUT THE AUTHOR

Melinda Harris is a part-time author and a fulltime fangirl. She currently resides in the great state of Georgia with her family, and when she's not writing, she likes to spend rainy nights with her nose in a good book and sunny days on a playground chasing her son. And most anytime–rain or shine–she can be found engaging in her favorite pastime, which of course is eating ice cream...lots and lots of ice cream.

To learn more, please visit Melinda's website:
www.melindaharrisauthor.com

Or, you can find her on the following social media sites:
www.goodreads.com/MelHarris
www.facebook.com/melindaharrisauthor
www.twitter.com/MelHarrisAuthor

Made in the USA
San Bernardino, CA
29 September 2015